FLY AWAY

The Metamorphosis of Dina Savage

Books by Ray Dan Parker

The Tom Williams Saga
Unfinished Business: Retribution and Reconciliation
Fly Away: The Metamorphosis of Dina Savage

Coming Soon!
The Tom Williams Saga
Pronounced Ponce: The Midtown Murders
Last Gleaming: Love and Death in the Age of Pandemic

For more information
visit: www.SpeakingVolumes.us

FLY AWAY

The Metamorphosis of Dina Savage

Ray Dan Parker

SPEAKING VOLUMES, LLC
NAPLES, FLORIDA
2023

Fly Away

ISBN 978-1-64540-993-9

I dedicate this work to my wife, sons and daughter-in-law,
who continue to amaze and inspire me.

You've heard it said, "You mustn't murder anyone. Anyone who commits murder will be judged." But I tell you, don't be angry with anyone. If you're angry with others, you will be judged.
—Matthew 5:21

You've heard it said, "You mustn't commit adultery." But I tell you that if a man looks at a woman and wants to sin sexually with her, he has already committed adultery in his mind.
—Matthew 5:28

Acknowledgments

I want to thank Jerry Weiner, Will Ottinger, Judy Aust, Mel Coe and William Brust for all their story-telling advice and Bob Babcock, who saw something in this novel so long ago.

Foreword

The idea for this novel began, years back, when I received a summons for what turned out to be a date rape trial. The circumstances, not to mention the outcome, were quite different, and the people involved were not artists or computer hackers. They were ordinary people like you and me. After carefully listening and taking notes, I found myself, like Jeff Sax, not knowing who was telling the truth, the accuser, the accused, neither . . . or both.

From that humble beginning, this tale has grown in the telling to become an exploration of the many ways we objectify and exploit each other and their unimagined consequences.

Prologue

Tunica, Mississippi
Saturday, June 22

Dawn Sawyer stepped into the air-conditioned embrace of the Shamrock Casino, relieved, at last, to escape the mascara-melting summer heat of the Delta morning. The sliding doors closed behind her with a cool hiss. She stopped to check her hair and makeup in the mirror beside the fountain . . . perfect despite the three-hour Greyhound trip from Clewiston, thanks to the help of Cissy Johnson, Dawn's best . . . make that her only . . . friend.

Colored lights flashed. Bells and whistles echoed from dozens of slots. At first, the noise and confusion overwhelmed her. Dawn had been out of Clewiston only once, an interminable bus ride to Greenville with her single mom, Sheila Mitchell, for the funeral of an elderly aunt. Dawn closed her eyes and breathed deeply, relaxing the knot in her stomach.

She'd awakened that morning, relieved that Sheila had, for once, come home from work alone. The men she brought into her bed these days were such creeps.

Before leaving, Dawn had laid a note on the worn Formica-topped table in the trailer's meager kitchenette. Scrawled on a piece of blue-lined notebook paper, it said Cissy had invited her to spend the weekend, not that Sheila cared. It would be two in the afternoon before the woman awoke from her drunken stupor.

Dawn and her mom had fought the day before over what started out as Sheila's casual comment about the way Dawn dressed. Before it ended, Dawn had called her mother a whore and received a backhand that sent her sprawling across a cheap coffee table, splintering it under her slender frame and enraging Sheila even more.

Cissy did an artistic job covering the bruise and added ten years to Dawn's apparent age. Now, Dawn could easily pass for twenty-six, the age on the fake driver's license she carried in her new pocketbook. The four-inch spiked heels she "borrowed" from Cissy's mom only enhanced the illusion.

The cost of the makeup, pocketbook, new dress and bus fare came from tip money Dawn pilfered from Sheila in small amounts over the past three months, money Sheila would otherwise have spent on booze and pills. *The woman's killing herself,* Dawn thought, *but not fast enough.* She cringed in disgust, recalling the feel and smell of the wet bills collected from drunken patrons at the Happy Tails Exotic Dance Club on Highway 6.

As she gazed about, Dawn noticed the absence of windows and clocks. A customer, caught up in the fever of gambling, could easily lose track of time. The establishment, as noted on its entrance, stayed open twenty-four hours a day.

Cocktail waitresses plied the clientele with alcohol and cheap hors d'oeuvres, for which Dawn had no appetite. Meanwhile, the casino raked in the life savings of elderly gamblers, many in wheelchairs or breathing from oxygen tanks. Dawn watched them feed quarters into the machines. Occasionally they'd win small amounts, sometimes large, but their comatose expressions never changed. They might as well have been denizens of an opium den. For all its garish décor, the Shamrock didn't come close to the images on its glamorous Vegas-style web site.

Avoiding the slots, craps and roulette, where she had no competitive advantage, Dawn worked her way toward the poker and blackjack tables. Over the next three hours, she cruised among them, careful not to win too much in one place, lest she attract the attention of pit bosses.

Everybody, Dawn thought, *has some God-given talent. Sheila Mitchell's little girl can count cards.*

From time to time, she cashed in her chips and dropped the winnings into a hidden compartment in her purse. At each table, she studied the cards as they came up and determined the odds of winning, not as a conscious calculation; more a feeling that came over her.

As a child she learned how to gamble from Shorty, the six-foot-seven bouncer at Happy Tails. That was before she stopped meeting her mother at the club after school. Now she played with such concentration that everyone else seemed to fade into the colorful cacophony. She failed to notice, for example, the man who'd followed her for the better part of an hour.

At three-thirty Dawn called it quits. She converted the last of her chips and was on her way to the exit when a voice called out behind her.

"Hey little darling, you can't leave now, the way your luck's been running. Why don't you stay here and party a while with old Eddie? See if some that luck can *rub off on me*."

Dawn rolled her eyes but made no reply. She quickened her pace without so much as a glance in his direction. Then she felt him grip her arm. With one move, she turned halfway toward him and smiled. She brought her left foot up and planted a stiletto heel in the top of his brown, tasseled loafer, watching in satisfaction as pain registered and the leer left his face. His grip loosened, and in a moment, she'd reached the door.

The heavily muscled security guard materialized from nowhere. "Stop right there, ma'am." He gazed at her through wraparound sunglasses rendered black by overhead fluorescents.

As Dawn tried to move past him, he raised his hand to stop her. In his reflective lenses she watched two attendants escorting the now crippled "Eddie" from the premises and fought to suppress her fear.

The guard's face remained impassive, his voice low and calm. He had the look of an interior lineman for the Saints. "We've been watching you, ma'am. You need to take your winnings, leave and don't come back." With that he stepped aside and let her pass.

Later, in her room at the Howard Johnson, Dawn counted more than twenty thousand dollars, mostly in large bills . . . not bad for a day's work. Tomorrow she'd hit another casino before catching the Greyhound back to Clewiston. Her next problem would be where to hide the money from her mother.

As a third grader, Dawn discovered she could remember things she'd seen only once and realized that that made her different from other kids, what Cissy called a *photographic memory*.

Dawn sat on the edge of her bed watching WWA on the small television. As a child, her favorite wrestler had been Randy "Macho Man" Savage. She would watch him pin his opponent and pound his face. What she admired most about him was that he didn't take shit off anybody.

In time Dawn would become a smarter, female version of the Macho Man, and one day she'd have the wealth, power and influence to make others do as she wished. She'd become a well-known celebrity, and her face would grace the covers of magazines like *People* and *Us*.

When the match ended, Dawn turned off the TV and stripped out of her clothes. She frowned at her reflection in the full-length mirror. Disgusted by her thin, flat chested body and acne scars, she pondered the many things she'd do with her newfound lucre. But first, she would get the hell out of Clewiston, Mississippi.

Dawn did well in school, and earned grades and test scores that would get her into the most prestigious colleges in the nation. With her gambling money and her new career, she'd have her teeth straightened, get a boob job, change her name, lose her accent and start a new life.

The only people in Clewiston she'd miss were Cissy and Shorty. She'd write and let them know she was okay. Maybe she'd send them money to come visit her . . . maybe not.

Of all the people in her life, only Cissy knew about Dennis Ramsey. Ramsey came home one night with Sheila. While Sheila snored in the next room, he crept into Dawn's bed, clamped his hand over her mouth, and raped her.

Since then, she'd slept with a stolen steak knife under her pillow. She'd learned long ago not to count on *anyone* to protect her, and she promised herself that *no man* would lay hands on her again without her consent. Dawn would return to Clewiston someday, for one purpose— to settle matters with Ramsey.

For now, though, she banished that idea and entertained more pleasant thoughts. She took a deep breath, picturing herself strolling across a college campus, meeting good looking boys and taking them back to her room. She'd study martial arts and marksmanship. Most of all, *she'd learn to fly.*

Dawn Sawyer pondered all this as she closed her eyes and wrapped her naked body in the crisp sheet like a cocoon.

* * *

Six years passed.

In the wee hours of a crisp October morning, Stanley Russell sat Buddha-like in a thicket, his back propped against a tall pine. The incipient dawn, little more than a white glow above the treetops, cast shadows as dark as the middle of night. He focused on a young doe as she stepped into a glade about twenty yards away.

Covered from head to toe in Mossy Oak camouflage, he knew she couldn't see him. Standing upwind, she wouldn't catch his scent, either.

Gracefully, she lowered her head to the salt lick. A dapple of sunlight played over her russet pelt. Russell took a deep breath, slowly let it out and raised his Winchester .243, sighting her through the scope. The gun had been a birthday gift from his wife, and this would be the first time he used it.

The doe must have caught his movement from the corner of her eye. She bolted as he squeezed the trigger. The bullet grazed her neck, how badly Russell couldn't tell. She staggered for a moment and bounded into the woods. By the look of things, she wouldn't get far.

"Shit!" he exclaimed.

He followed her with a flashlight, coming upon an open trail, popular with off-roaders, judging by the tire tracks. Red drops led him to a point where she appeared to have stepped into a thicket.

Pulling back an overhanging limb, he stepped over a fallen tree and spotted something, perhaps the doe. Then he saw clothing and panicked, thinking he'd accidentally shot another hunter . . . and then the wind shifted . . . and he gagged.

The torn blue jeans and tattered, brown-stained shirt bore what appeared to be multiple knife wounds, yet, from the label, they'd been expensive when new. The purple face, swollen beyond recognition, reminded Russell of a burst pomegranate teeming with maggots.

He pulled out his phone and dialed 911, but nothing happened. He walked all the way back to where he'd parked his truck before he finally got a signal. This had not shaped up as the hunting trip he'd planned.

Twenty minutes later, Leflore County Sheriff David Hodge pulled up in a four-by-four, and Russell directed him to the spot where he'd found the body. Animals had made a mess of the corpse; coyotes, judging by their tracks in the loose sand. Hodge pulled a wallet and driver's license from the torn pants pocket and identified the remains as missing Clewiston resident Dennis Ramsey. Ramsey's car had turned up two months earlier in the parking lot of a nearby motel. Hodge called in Clewiston Police Chief Gene Tilley, who arrived with a young officer named Don Parquet.

Given the overpowering stench, investigators could only speculate as to how it had gone so long undetected by the countless ATVs passing only yards away.

Book One

Chapter One

Liam Sanstrom

Atlanta, Georgia
Saturday, September 10

Liam Sanstrom leaned back in his chair, stretched his long legs, and set his Nikon on the table before him. His white dress shirt, its sleeves rolled up past his elbows, gaped at the top revealing a crop of bright red chest hair. He took a deep breath of early fall, held it and released it slowly.

Liam's love of outdoor amphitheaters began with his mother's London Symphony Orchestra performance at Brighton's Royal Pavilion. Eight-year-old Liam and his father took the train down from Victoria Station. Afterward, the family strolled the Palace Pier and rode the carousel as summer dusk lingered until midnight.

Startling him out of his reverie, Liam's fetching blonde date leaned over and placed her tongue in his ear. Beneath the table she ran her fingers lightly along the inside of his thigh. Her hair tickled his cheek, and her starched sleeveless blouse parted momentarily, revealing one ample and quite naked breast.

Twenty feet away, a sound technician tested a microphone as roadies manhandled amplifiers, unrolled cords and set instruments in place. The overhead intercom played the Rolling Stones classic *Paint It Black*.

Beyond the hill behind the venue glowed an auburn and gold sunset. A faint breeze stirred the treetops behind the stage, the previous night's rainstorm having cleansed the air. Liam took it all in as he closed his eyes, reconstructing the scene as he might have painted it, laid out in fine, painstaking strokes. His fingertips caressed the table-cloth as if it were a blank canvas.

He raised his camera in time for a quick shot of a teenage girl in stacked heels tentatively descending the stone steps. He caught the an-ticipation in her face as she peered down, extending her open-toed san-dal, like a wood nymph testing the water of some sylvan pool.

His gaze shifted as he sighted a slender woman with a thick shock of white hair wending her way toward him holding the hand of a younger woman, perhaps college aged.

Liam waved. The woman smiled and waved back.

"Bonnie," he said, as he stood and gave her a peck on each cheek, "I'd like for you to meet my date, Dina Savage. Dina, this is Bonnie Baron, my agent."

"Pleased to meet you," said Dina, extending her hand. "I understand we have you to thank for these wonderful seats. How kind of you to invite us."

"My pleasure . . ." Bonnie turned to her companion. "And this is Heather Lindsey. Heather interned for me this summer. She's an art major at SCAD."

The girl lowered her head, light brown curls falling across her eyes, and managed a shy "Hello."

"We're still waiting for Tom and Colleen Williams," said Bonnie. Her eyes scanned the crowd, and a broad smile lit her face. "There's Tom now," she said. "He's the writer I told you about."

A tall, slender, gray-haired man approached, followed by a pleas-ant-looking blonde. Liam put them somewhere in their mid-seventies.

"Tom," squealed Bonnie as he rounded the nearest table. Throwing her arms around him, she kissed him and introduced the newcomers to her other guests. "Tom's a freelance writer. Colleen's a partner in a prestigious law firm."

"Tom Williams! I've read your magazine articles," said Liam, bowing slightly as he spoke.

Turning to Dina, Bonnie asked, "So, tell me how you and Liam met."

"We have a mutual acquaintance."

"Sally Meister," interjected Liam.

"Sally's a dear friend," said Bonnie, giving Dina a curious look. How do you know her?"

"I'm a regular customer."

"What sort of work do you do?" Tom asked.

"She's a spy," said Liam.

Dina gave him a disapproving smirk. "I do market research for the firm of Moore and Frye."

"Like I said, she's a spy."

Colleen's eyes narrowed. "You look familiar. I could swear we've met before, but I don't recall the name Moore and Frye."

Before Dina could respond, Bonnie broke in. "Where are you from originally? I can't quite place the accent."

"All over," said Dina. "I moved here from Boston."

"Really!" said Colleen. "I'm from there myself. What part of town?"

"Actually, I just went to school there."

"Dina has a Harvard MBA and a bachelor's in computer science from Case Western," said Liam, running a lock of her hair between his fingers.

Colleen settled her gaze on a butterfly tattoo on Dina's left arm just below the shoulder, brilliant in hues of lavender, gold, silver and turquoise. "That's really quite lovely," she said. "Where'd you get it?"

Dina smiled. "I got it while living in Cleveland. It means quite a lot to me."

"What do you do besides market research?" asked Tom.

"I recently took up flying. I have my license now, and I'm leasing a small Cessna at Peachtree DeKalb."

Liam gave her a surprised look. "My, but you *are* a woman of many talents."

She turned and gazed into his eyes. "Maybe I'll take you for a spin one of these weekends."

"I'd like that."

Liam reached into the cooler beside him and selected a Meiomi Pinot Noir 2012, one of three unopened bottles. From a large picnic basket Colleen produced a box of water table crackers and an assortment of lobster and goose liver pates.

"Liam," Bonnie asked, "why don't you get pictures of everyone?"

As the others leaned together and smiled, Liam leaned back and took a series of shots.

"Nice camera," said Tom.

Liam gazed at it as if it were his child. "Thank you. I use it to capture subjects I can use for my paintings."

"Do you sell any of your photographic work?"

"No. I'd rather paint. I keep my photos and sketches for myself."

"I've been trying to get him to let me show them for as long as I've known him," said Bonnie. "They're quite good."

"You seem to know a few things about cameras, Mr. Williams," said Liam.

"I have an old Nikon F I bought at a pawn shop in Da Nang in 1966."

"You were in Vietnam?" asked Dina.

"Briefly."

"Maybe I should be showing *your* work," teased Bonnie.

"I haven't done professional photography in years. I use it mostly as Liam does, to capture ideas for stories."

"Would you mind taking a picture of Dina and me?" asked Liam.

"Not at all."

Liam handed the camera to Tom and leaned back as Dina kissed his cheek and ran her fingers under the hem of his shorts.

Moments later a roar echoed through the amphitheater as the piped music died and the house lights dimmed. Speakers above the stage bellowed, "Ladies and gentlemen, the Delta Classic Chastain Summer Concert Series is proud to present, for your evening's entertainment, Mr. Harry Connick, Jr."

Over the next three hours wine bottles emptied and tongues loosened. Midway through the concert, Dina rose and made her way up the long stone steps to the women's restroom as Liam studied her unsteady progress.

"She an interesting person," mused Bonnie.

"She certainly is," Liam smiled. "I see a part of myself in her."

"I just bet you do," said Colleen between sips of wine.

* * *

When the concert ended, Liam and Dina made their way to Parking Lot B, where, in a distant corner, he'd parked his red Porsche convertible. As he held the passenger door, she slid into the leather-upholstered seat, her miniskirt riding up to reveal a translucent white thong trimmed in lace. She gave him a coy smile and licked her lips.

It took them a good thirty minutes to edge through traffic onto Powers Ferry Road and down to Mount Vernon. They'd just crossed the bridge to Cobb County when Dina reached across the console and stroked Liam's crotch.

Without a word, he pulled into an empty shopping center and parked behind a deserted restaurant. Opening the roof, he eased his seat back and stared up at the stars as Dina leaned over the gear shifter, worked open his fly, and put her face in his lap. A faint aroma of honeysuckle rode on the breeze, and Orion stood tall in the clear night sky. Liam's eyes closed in a beatific smile. *This*, he thought, *is the perfect ending to a beautiful evening.*

Chapter Two

Dina Savage

Liam lived in an unpretentious brick tri-level at the end of a long cul-de-sac overlooking the Chattahoochee River. He led Dina through the kitchen and into the den as they shed their clothes. Straddling on top of him on his leather couch, Dina leaned back and rocked her hips, admiring her reflection in his sliding glass doors. When they'd finished, he offered her a pinstriped dress shirt from his closet and poured her a snifter of cognac. He told her to make herself at home, that he'd be right back with a special treat.

Exploring the den, Dina took in the immaculate décor. Pencil and ink sketches of nude women covered every wall, among them photos of Liam at exotic locations, Liam with a young brunette on a balcony overlooking the Mediterranean, Liam on skis atop a snow-covered slope. Devoid of pictures from his childhood, the house could have been a model in any of Atlanta's new upscale neighborhoods. The place even smelled new.

Atop a shelf filled with books on art and architecture stood a small portrait in a gilt frame, a middle-aged couple, presumably his parents. The woman, a redhead, resembled Liam. The man, tall and thick through the shoulders, had more of Liam's personality about his eyes and mouth.

Thinking she might enjoy some fresh air, Dina slid back the glass door and stepped out onto the deck. Leaning against the wooden railing, she sipped the cognac, its golden warmth coursing through her body. The mild September afternoon had given way to a deliciously cool evening. A faint fetid scent rose from the marshy riverbank below, resonating with a chorus of bullfrogs. There came a crackling in the brush and a muted splash. Traffic from the nearby interstate murmured soft and low.

Dina reflected on how far she'd come in the past seven years. She'd long ago given up the casinos, most of which, by now, had her photograph and would ban her from their tables. Now she had a promising career and a sizable bankroll. Cosmetic surgery had transformed her into a beautiful woman, and she'd learned that most men were little more than boys, easily manipulated, once you knew how. Liam would prove no different.

The one thing that still eluded her, that she'd dreamed of as a little girl, was the lifestyle of a celebrity. She smiled to think of the countless hours she'd spent in front of the small television in her mother's trailer gazing at blurred images of the rich and famous. Now it lay within reach. She would become the mysterious girlfriend of a brilliant young painter fleeing the paparazzi, only her profile visible to their cameras. Then someday, somewhere, another lonely, abandoned little girl would gaze at a television screen and dream of becoming Dina Savage.

Liam's humble abode would become little more than a refuge for their occasional return from tours of New York and European art galleries, the beaches of Monte Carlo, the Caribbean and the South Pacific. Liam's wealthy patrons would provide ample opportunities for Dina's *other* activities. The secrets people disclosed once they had a few drinks in them never ceased to amaze her.

The glow of Atlanta's skyline silhouetted the treetops. To Dina it represented everything she'd spent a lifetime seeking. She stretched out her fingers, as though to grasp it in her palm.

Behind her the door opened, and from inside floated the soft, warm notes of Nora Jones singing *Come Away with Me*.

As Dina turned, Liam took her in his arms, kissing her long and gently on the lips.

"I love this place," she said. "How long have you lived here?"

"I bought it three years ago. Before that I had a condo in Midtown."

"How long have you been in the States?"

"About fifteen years . . . I came here to study at the College of Charleston."

"What brought you to Atlanta?"

He glanced away. "I met an older woman in Charleston. We moved here. That lasted for about a year." He paused, and his expression brightened. "Come back inside. I have a treat for you."

On the coffee table lay an old-fashioned mirror, its ivory handle inlaid with silver. Across its surface stretched four neatly manicured lines of white powder, beside them a plastic red-and-white striped soda straw and a single-edged razor blade.

Dina slid onto the couch beside him, grasped the straw, snorted the drug and felt its radiance surge through her body. Liam took the remainder, licking the glass clean. For a time, Dina went away, oblivious to time and place.

Liam rose, carried the empty mirror to the kitchen and carefully washed it. Returning, he lifted her from the couch as though she were a child, carried her up a short flight of steps and down a long hallway to a bedroom. There they made love again between the cream-colored satin sheets of a king-sized waterbed, this time with Liam on top.

As he rolled off and caught his breath, Dina placed her cheek against his chest and twirled his chest hairs between her fingers. Above them a ceiling fan gave a low hum as it swung lazily, its soothing breeze caressing their naked bodies.

"I've told you everything about me," Liam said. "Now tell me about yourself."

17

She stiffened momentarily. "Well, I graduated from Case Western and completed my graduate business studies at Harvard."

"I know all that. Tell me about your childhood." He stroked her back with his fingernails, sending a thrill down her spine. "What were you like as a little girl?" he asked in a mockingly lecherous tone.

She laughed, struggling to collect her thoughts, wondering exactly what to tell him. "I had a boring childhood. I grew up in a small town, raised by a single mom. I had good grades and test scores. I left at the first opportunity and never looked back."

To change the subject, she asked, "What are your plans for the rest of the weekend?"

"Unfortunately, I'm preparing for a show in New York next week."

"New York!" she gasped, propping up on an elbow to face him. "Can I come? We can take in a show, go to a museum . . ." She stopped short, caught by his sudden change of expression.

Staring at the ceiling in the faint light from the hallway, his face had the look of a porcelain mask, his voice cold, the Scandinavian accent more pronounced. "I'm afraid it won't work out this time. I'll be very busy." He paused, his voice softening. "But I'm going back in a few weeks. Maybe we can go then."

"Surely you won't be working the whole time you're there."

"Well…" He paused again as though searching for words. "There's someone I'm seeing there."

Something in the back of Dina's mind clicked, something she could barely sense through the drug-induced fog. She pulled away and struggled to the edge of the bed. "And when were you going to tell me this?" She closed her eyes against the whirling colors.

He reached out, touching her back, but she shied away.

"It's not what you think," he said. "This isn't a serious relationship at all. We…just…see each other whenever I'm in town."

"And how often is that?" She tried to feign a more casual interest.

"Two or three times a year."

"And she waits for you all that time?"

"Actually, she's married to a prominent investment banker and is active in various art societies. She has quite a lot to keep her occupied."

"Does her husband know about your arrangement?"

Liam laughed. "Yes, he does. You see they have an *arrangement*. He cares nothing about her boyfriends, and she cares nothing about his."

Dina took a moment to process and then shuddered. "So how many people would you say are involved in this extended ménage?"

"I wouldn't worry about that. He hasn't touched her in years."

Despite his assurances, Dina suddenly felt dirty, like a used Kleenex. Her change of mood cut through the fog as she reconsidered their nascent relationship.

Staggering to her feet, she pulled the satin sheet from the bed, wrapping it tight around her. Despite her growing anger, she felt immense pleasure in the way the fabric caressed her skin. "Listen," she slurred, "it's getting late, and I need to go."

"Don't be silly. It's three in the morning, and we've had a good deal to drink. Why don't you stay here and spend the night with me?"

"No!" she practically shouted.

He gave her a look of shock and hurt. "Okay. You can sleep in another room if you like. But neither of us is in any shape to drive. I can take you home in the morning when we wake up."

Dina considered for a moment, then shook her head. "No." Wrapping the sheet tighter, she began searching for her clothes. Blinded by tears, she located all but the thong and dressed quickly in the den.

Hanging in the foyer, an oil of a young girl, perhaps twelve, caught her eye. With short bangs and straight brown locks down to her shoulders, she sat at a dressing table, legs drawn up. She wore a thin cotton top with spaghetti straps and pink shorts that folded into her body. Caught in the act of painting her toenails a deep crimson, she chewed her lower lip, her face a mask of intense concentration.

Draped across a nearby chair lay a lavender sun dress, its design far more appropriate on a grown woman. Reflected in a dressing table mirror a window opened onto a cloudless sky and a white oleander in full bloom. For some reason, the scene struck a familiar chord. Dina closed her eyes, taking in the warmth of the sunlight and the scent of the blossoms.

Somewhere beyond that window, she knew, stood a swing set beside an inflatable pool, perhaps an old dollhouse lovingly constructed from scraps of plywood and pasteboard. From the deep recesses of her mind came the briefest glimpse of a memory, something she'd lost in forgetting an entire childhood, a treasured toy accidentally thrown out with the garbage. This could never have been Dina's childhood. *Had it been someone else's, something she'd dreamt of?*

Shaking off the thought, she opened her eyes.

"So, what do you think?" The voice made her jump. He'd come up behind her unnoticed.

"It's powerful," she whispered, wiping a tear.

As he stepped closer, still naked, redolent of sex and after-shave, she let him take her into his arms.

"I'm sorry things got off to a bad start tonight," he said. "I hope we can see more of each other. I like being with you and we could have so much fun together. I wish you'd reconsider and stay tonight." He turned her to him, gazing into her eyes. "You haven't lived until you've had one of my omelets."

She felt herself weaken, under the rush of drugs and alcohol. But mustering what little remained of her resolve, she said, "No. I really do need to get home and sleep this off. I'll call you when I wake up. Maybe we can see about getting back together."

"Okay." He stepped back, palms outstretched in a gesture of submission. "I'll go get dressed and we can look for my car keys . . . But first, let me show you my studio."

She started to say "no," again, but relented. *What harm could there be?* As she followed him down the basement stairs, she studied his every contour, his taught muscles and graceful moves . . . like those of a cheetah advancing on its prey.

Chapter Three

Henry Massing

Vinings, Georgia
Sunday, September 11

At precisely five a.m. a kitchen light came on at the house on the corner of Overton Road and Morning Glory Circle. Seventy-two-year-old Henry Massing fed his aging Cocker Spaniel, Molly, put on a pot of coffee and took down the leash for their morning walk.

In the living room, the low chime of a mantle clock marked the hour while the rest of the house remained dark and quiet. Its only other inhabitant, Henry's wife, Martha, lay snoring upstairs.

Molly let out a yip and ran to the foyer. Massing paused, thinking he might have heard something, perhaps a light rap at the door. He couldn't imagine who it would be at this hour. When it came again, this time a bit louder, he went to the peephole, stared out and removed the chain.

At first he thought the beautiful young woman had had an automobile accident, another late night carouser missing a turn on the winding street and ending up in a ditch, or worse. Out of breath, her hair disheveled, she must have run some distance in her spiked heels, but she bore no sign of injury, as far as Massing could tell. Her red-rimmed eyes brimmed with tears. "Can you help me?" she whimpered. "I need to call the police."

"My word!" he said. "What happened?"

Her eyes scanned the hallway, as though unsure what refuge it offered. Struggling to regain her composure, she croaked, "I've been raped."

"Who is it, Henry?" Martha called from upstairs.

"Please get dressed, darling, and come down here. I need your help."

He offered the young woman a cup of coffee, which she declined. Sitting on the carpeted staircase, she put her face in her hands, and began to sob.

Massing reached for the nearest phone and dialed 911, glancing at the purpling marks on the woman's wrists. Dazed and disoriented, she sat knees apart, oblivious to the fact that she wore nothing beneath her short skirt. Henry turned discreetly toward the door as he spoke to the dispatcher.

Martha, in pink housecoat, hair curlers, and fuzzy slippers, sat beside the young stranger, placed an arm around her, and let her sob into the soft fabric of her cotton robe.

* * *

Consumed in grief, anger, and frustration, Dina Savage pressed her fingertips against her temples, running the same questions through her mind. *What happened? How could I let someone do this to me again after all these years? How could I get taken in by such a smooth and deceitful sociopath?*

The haze of drugs and alcohol cleared, replaced by an old, familiar feeling, a deep-seated obsession for vengeance. This time, however, she'd take a different tack. She had far too much to lose. *She would trust the police.*

* * *

The first officers on the scene were Cobb County Police Sergeant Dave Landrum and Officer Kimberly Kelly. Kelly sat with Dina and took her statement while Landrum questioned Massing. Moments later an ambulance arrived and took Dina to Kennestone Hospital, while Landrum called for backup.

Standing beneath a corner streetlamp, twenty-three-year-old Kelly fidgeted, her eyes following the moths waltzing above her. She flinched and caught her breath as a bat swooped into view, snatching at one of them before disappearing into the darkness.

Landrum grinned at her. "This your first takedown?"

"How'd you guess?"

"Don't worry. You'll be fine."

"How long you been doing this?" she asked, trying to pass the time while waiting.

"Fifteen years in November."

"What made you choose police work?"

"I liked the idea of busting bad guys. How about you?"

"Me too, I guess. My dad was a cop. I suppose I wanted to be like him."

"You know, that was great the way you handled that girl back there. What was her name?"

"Dina something . . ." She thought for a moment. "Dina Savage."

Detective Mark Samuels arrived in an unmarked car. Parking sideways across the entrance to the cul-de-sac, he motioned to Landrum and Kelly as he strode toward Liam Sanstrom's front door. Kelly and Landrum took the rear of the house to prevent escape.

The ground in back declined sharply toward the river. The officers fought to keep from slipping on the thick carpet of wet leaves as they navigated in leather-soled shoes.

Wooden steps led to a deck off the upper level, beneath which sliding glass doors gave access to the basement. Landrum padded up the stairs, while Kelly waited below.

The skyline had brightened, yet the trees still cast impenetrable shadows. Kelly scanned the underside of the deck. As she stepped beneath it, her flashlight beam caught a large web. She stopped just in time to avoid taking it full in the face. A brown wolf spider perched three inches in front of her left eye.

Carefully she maneuvered around it and stood close to the sliders, waiting for a signal from Samuels. Flattening against the side of the house, she took a deep breath, gave the basement a furtive peek and moved in for a closer look.

An overhead fixture in an interior stairwell provided the only light inside. A partially completed painting stood on an easel near a window while other canvases leaned against the far wall. In a darkened corner lay the outline of a bed.

A doorbell rang and Samuels shouted for Sanstrom to open up. When he didn't, a crash shook the house, echoing to the sounds of splintering wood. On the deck above, Kelly heard Landrum rip open the French doors with a pry bar taken from his cruiser.

The two officers called for Sanstrom as they cleared the upstairs rooms. From a distant corner of the house a muffled voice shouted, "Cobb County Police . . . Keep your hands where I can see them!"

Kelly pulled a nail file from her pocket and picked the basement door lock, releasing turpentine and linseed oil fumes. Glancing about, gun drawn, she inspected the bed in the corner and froze.

Taking the stairs two at a time, she sprinted down the upstairs hallway, following Samuels' voice. She found him with Landrum, towering over a tall, slender, red-haired man lying handcuffed and naked on the floor. She stared at him for several beats, then averted her gaze.

"Detective," she said, "there's something downstairs I think you should see."

Landrum allowed Sanstrom to dress, while Samuels followed Kelly. Angled into a corner stood an unmade single bed with two mattresses and a set of box springs. A bedspread and top sheet lay folded neatly on the floor, but the fitted sheet remained on the mattress. Samuels pulled a small camera from his pocket and took pictures from various angles.

The bed, otherwise normal in appearance, had an added feature. On either side a pair of silk scarves, knotted together, extended from between the bottom mattress, a loop at the end of each about the size of a woman's wrist. Kelly recognized the scene from Savage's description.

Landrum took Sanstrom into custody, while Kelly spent six wearisome hours on the street shooing away curious neighbors, and Samuels combed the house taking more photos.

* * *

Golden, afternoon sunlight filtered through a canopy of ancient oaks as Tom Williams raked leaves in his backyard, some already garbed in brilliant autumn splendor. He stuffed them into large paper bags marked "Lawn Waste" and placed them in a rolling container beside his house. The weather, mild and dry, carried the first hint of fall. Colleen considered yard work a chore. For Tom it was therapy.

As he resumed his task, his three-year-old pointer, Bogart, bounded toward him, ears flapping, and dove into a fresh pile of leaves. Tom knelt to let the dog lick his face. The yard lay in deep shade, but for a small, sunny area where Tom had planted a garden, surrounded by a wire fence to keep Bogie out.

The tomatoes and butternut squash had died off long ago, and the peppers would soon follow. In a couple of weeks Tom would remove the dead stalks, turn over the soil, and plant his fall vegetables; beets, collards and kale.

In a darkened corner stood the playhouse Tom built years earlier for his daughters, Kathy and Marie. A blanket of green moss now covered its roof. He would spend the next few days cleaning it off for his granddaughters to enjoy.

A porcelain doll sat in the tiny window, anticipating the young girls' return. A sun-faded Band-Aid on one knee bore testimony to the loving care she'd received long ago from a little girl who'd grown up to become a pediatric oncologist.

As Tom reached his back door his phone buzzed in his pocket. He considered shutting it off then noticed the caller ID, Mitch Danner, a long-time friend and fellow *Atlanta Journal-Constitution* reporter. Danner, a member of the Cherokee Country Club, had invited Tom for eighteen holes the previous day. Thinking he wanted another round, Tom answered.

"Hey, man. What's up?"

Tom watched Bogie chase a neighbors' cat, who'd wandered into the yard. Eluding the dog, it leaped atop the wooden fence, preening and feigning indifference.

"Hey," said Danner, "didn't you tell me yesterday you and Colleen were going to that Harry Connick concert at Chastain?"

"Yep."

"You mentioned something about meeting a friend, an art agent, and her client."

"Yes."

"Was that artist, by chance, Liam Sanstrom?"

"Yes."

"Well, Cobb Police arrested him this morning on date rape charges."

"You are shitting me."

"Nope. According to sources, the date's accusing him of tying her up in his basement and raping her repeatedly."

"Oh my God! We sat at the same table with them last night. She was all over him, yet he seemed aloof."

"Well, he must have gotten over his *aloofness*. Apparently some weird shit went down at his place, drugs, bondage, you name it. I just got back from there. I couldn't get in, of course, but I got some great shots of the basement from outside. Looked like something out of an old Roger Corman movie with Vincent Price and Boris Karloff."

Tom took a deep breath, recovering from shock as his reporter instincts kicked in. "Did this source mention when Sanstrom's up for arraignment?"

"Nope, but the word is he'll make bail tomorrow morning. I'm on my way to Marietta now to see if I can pick up anything else."

"Bail? On rape charges?"

"Yep. Seems his dad's a Swedish diplomat. The old man pulled some strings. Junior will have to post a hefty bond and surrender his passport, but he'll be a free man awaiting trial."

"Couldn't he claim diplomatic immunity?"

"Nope. He's not a diplomat or the child of one. He's an adult and a U.S. citizen."

From the back door Colleen yelled, "Hey, are you through out there?"

"I'll be right in." Tom put the phone back to his ear. "I gotta go, Mitch. I'll call you later."

Tom pictured the scene at Chastain the night before, realizing how little he knew about Sanstrom, even less about Savage. He recalled how affectionate she'd been, given they'd known each other such a short time. They'd met, according to Dina, through a mutual friend. *What did Liam say her name was?* He could ask Bonnie.

* * *

Colleen had been inside all afternoon cleaning and cooking. She and Tom often entertained on Sunday evenings. Tonight's guests were Father John O'Malley, a retired priest, and his elderly, unmarried sister. The Williamses had also invited their daughter Kathleen, her husband Sean, and granddaughters Lauren and Mary Frances.

As Tom spread the tablecloth, set the dining room table, and lit candles, voices echoed along the front walkway. Everyone took their seats as Colleen brought glasses, a pitcher of water and two bottles of wine. Over excited conversation, Tom caught the sound of television news from the adjacent living room. He stepped into the doorway to watch the broadcast.

An attractive young woman stood at a podium behind a bank of microphones wearing her straight auburn hair pulled back in an old-fashioned bun. The text beneath her read "Sara Radford – Attorney for Liam Sanstrom."

"There is *no* foundation for these allegations," Radford said. "Liam's an accomplished artist and upstanding member of this community who has never been charged with a crime in his life. We will defend him vigorously, should this come to trial, but it's our expectation that the grand jury will recognize this for what it is, an attempt at vengeance by a spurned and vindictive woman . . ."

In the dining room Tom's guests prattled on as Colleen called out, "Darling, would you please turn off the television and come join us."

"Baby, you need to see this."

In the upper right corner of the screen appeared a still shot of a young woman, hair matted, mascara streaked, eyes red and swollen. She wore what appeared to be a hospital gown and stared straight into the camera, hands outstretched, purple bruises encircling both her wrists. Tom wouldn't have recognized her but for the caption beneath the photo.

Next up, a State Department spokesman said his agency had no intention of intervening in a local criminal case. A final shot showed the Swedish consul declining comment as he climbed into a black limousine and sped away.

As the camera returned to the news anchor, mug shots of Liam Sanstrom appeared behind her, his expression one of utter bewilderment.

"Oh, my God!" said Colleen. "Isn't that . . ."

"Yes, my dear. It seems we spent an enjoyable evening in the company of a rapist."

Colleen's eyes never strayed from the television. "*Alleged* rapist."

Over supper, Tom explained to their guests that they'd sat at the same table the night before with a young painter and his date and that Cobb police later arrested the painter on charges of drugging and molesting her. Neither Colleen nor Tom professed an opinion as to Liam's guilt or innocence. Father John's eyes narrowed as he followed the narrative. He'd investigated similar cases many times, as a former Chicago police officer, never knowing whom to believe.

Tom, raised Southern Baptist, hadn't been to a Protestant service since his grandmother's funeral. Over the past forty-four years he'd attended occasional masses with his family, mostly Christmas and Easter, but had never considered converting. If he stopped to think about it, he couldn't decide what denomination he was.

He believed in God, and had vague notions of Christianity, as far as that went. But for him, the closest thing to a religious experience was working his vegetable garden or spending a weekend at the lake with his family. Still, he admired this simple, unassuming ex-cop who had taken to the cloth late in life following the death of his wife. He could easily see why Colleen and their daughters adored the man.

"The priest shook his head, "This is what comes of looking upon others as objects for our pleasure. In this case either the man has preyed on an innocent woman . . . or he has suffered the worst sort of character assassination . . . and for what?" He held up his hands as though expecting an answer from on high. "We forget that we're all children of God, as responsible for each other as we are for ourselves."

"The crazy thing," said Colleen, "is that you don't know who to believe. It's not like there were witnesses. We met Liam. I couldn't imagine him as a *rapist*. He seemed so . . . innocent . . . in his own little world."

Silence ensued, followed by a change of topic. Later, when their guests had departed, Tom called Bonnie, who answered on the first ring.

"Oh my God, Tom! Can you believe this?"

"Wow! You never know. What do you suppose happened?"

"It was a setup," she said. "I'm going to see Liam tomorrow. I called the Cobb County Sheriff's office. They said I couldn't visit him tonight." She paused and Tom heard her take a drag from her cigarette. "I can't believe this. This lawyer of his better be good. That's all I have to say. I just hope he hasn't said anything stupid . . ."

Or done anything stupid, Tom thought. "What do you know about this . . ." He stopped to recall her name . . . "Dina Savage?"

"Nothing, but I intend to find out. I'm calling Sally Meister first thing in the morning."

"I understand Liam gets out on bail tomorrow. Do you know where I can get in touch with him?"

"I hope you're not thinking of interviewing him. Because if you are . . ."

"I thought it might be helpful to get his side of the story."

"Yeah. Right. That's what reporters always say. Just wait until he talks to his lawyer first. I don't want you asking him anything that'll come back on him later."

"Okay. I understand. I've gotta go. I'll call you in the morning."

Book Two

Chapter Four

Colleen Williams

Vinings, Georgia
Friday, March 1

Colleen removed her glasses and laid them on her desk. She straightened a stack of papers, returned them to their manila folder and placed them in a tray for her secretary to file. Her firm had long ago converted to electronic documents, but Colleen still preferred the feel of paper and manila folders to scanners and screen images.

I'm getting too old for this, she thought.

Leaning back in her swivel chair, she turned to the window of her nineteenth-floor corner office with its commanding view of Vinings and the Atlanta skyline. The late morning sky had cleared but for a few white clouds sliding northward toward Smyrna.

Basking in the afterglow of a major acquittal, Colleen tried, in vain, to remember at what point such triumphs had become a substitute for sex. With nothing on her calendar for the next week, she'd promised Tom a romantic getaway at their cabin on North Georgia's Lake Rabun.

A loud ring from her phone startled her. The caller identified herself as Sara Radford with the nearby firm of Statham and Riley.

"Ms. Williams, I'm not sure if you remember me. We met a few years ago at a bar association function in Buckhead."

Colleen couldn't place the name.

"I'm defending Liam Sanstrom," Radford said, "on allegations of rape. I understand you and your husband were at the Harry Connick concert and sat at the same table with Liam and his date."

Suddenly Colleen recalled Radford's televised statement the night of Liam's arrest. "We did."

"I was hoping I could meet with you and Mr. Williams to see what you might recall from that evening."

Colleen thought for a moment. "I don't see why not, but I have to tell you up front that, but for a brief introduction, we really didn't have much conversation with Mr. Sanstrom *or* his date. We were there at the invitation of a mutual friend. Besides, it was . . ." she thought for a moment. "Oh my God! *Eighteen months ago?*" As soon as she said this, Colleen recalled something about Liam's date. *Should I tell her about it?*

"At this point," said Radford, "I'm just gathering background and would appreciate any insights you might have. As a fellow defense attorney, I'm sure you understand." The woman spoke with the syrupy drawl of a Southern debutante. *Affected perhaps?*

"Sure. Just a second . . ." Colleen paused to create the impression of consulting her calendar.

"The only opening I have at the moment is late this afternoon. I'm not sure about my husband. I'll need to check with him. Where did you have in mind?"

"There's an Italian restaurant on Paces Ferry, called Paulo's, in the small shopping center across from your office."

"I know the place."

"If we can, I'd like to get there before the supper crowd arrives. We could get a booth in the back where we'll have some privacy. This shouldn't take long."

"Sure. Give me your cell number. I'll call my husband and get back to you right away."

As Colleen returned the phone to its cradle, she again contemplated how much she should tell Radford. It had taken her most of the concert to recall why Savage looked so familiar. One of Colleen's partners represented a young man in a wrongful discharge suit against Dina's former employer, Silas-Burke. The suit resulted from Savage's false allegations of sexual harassment, and the young man's subsequent termination.

In the end Silas-Burke reinstated him, and Savage issued a written apology. Within months Savage left Silas-Burke, calling it a *hostile work environment*. Were these rape charges another false accusation, or perhaps something else?

Colleen recalled the news story the night after the concert. Sanstrom's street address had sounded familiar. She rolled her chair closer to the window, gazed at the river valley below, and imagined herself looking down into his front yard. She shivered to think she'd sat but a few feet from him only hours before the alleged rape, chatting and drinking wine.

She remembered something else about Savage; Sanstrom's calling her a *corporate spy*. What work did Savage do for Silas-Burke and her subsequent employer, Moore and Frye? Colleen would make discreet inquiries, if for no reason than to satisfy her own curiosity.

She reached into a drawer, removed a cigarette pack, and took the service elevator down to the loading dock. She'd promised Tom and the girls she'd quit. This was the one smoke she allowed herself each day.

* * *

Colleen and Tom kept their appointment with Sara Radford. Radford, a freckled, fresh-faced UGA Law School grad when they previously met, now wore her auburn hair shorter and dressed more professionally. She still spoke like a sorority girl interviewing for an internship, but Colleen sensed she'd grown more confident, not easily overawed by older attorneys.

Radford, as promised, kept the meeting brief. Tom and Colleen reiterated that they'd never met Liam before the concert and knew nothing about the case besides what they read in the newspaper. Radford inquired about Sanstrom and Savage's behavior at the concert and finished by asking Colleen and Tom if they'd mind testifying on Sanstrom's behalf.

"Normally I'd have no problems with that," said Colleen, "but there *is* something I need to tell you. Before the concert, neither of us had met Ms. Savage either, but a couple of years ago my firm represented a gentleman in a defamation and wrongful discharge suit against Savage's former employer, Silas-Burke. Ms. Savage accused him of unwanted sexual advances. Burke settled the suit, and Ms. Savage apologized as a condition of her continued employment. Naturally, I can't go into further details without permission from our client, and I'd rather not testify about this."

"The employer kept her on after settling a defamation suit?" Radford asked, looking shocked.

"I've often wondered about that. Obviously, I can't speculate. Ms. Savage, however, left Silas-Burke a few months later, apparently for another position."

"Do you think the parties to the lawsuit would be willing to testify?"

"I'll need to confer with my partner and his former client. Obviously, I can't speak on behalf of Silas-Burke."

Radford gave Colleen a thoughtful look. "You know," she mused, "I haven't had any luck finding out exactly what Ms. Savage does for Moore and Frye. All they'll give me are vague references to *market research*. When I press them they fall back on *client confidentiality*. I doubt I'll get much further with Silas-Burke, especially if what she does is . . . questionable. I wonder if your former client might be more forth-coming."

"I have no idea," shrugged Colleen.

* * *

Driving home Tom asked Colleen if consensual sex prior to an al-leged rape might sway a jury in favor of the defendant.

"You never know, but a woman always has the right to say *no*. I don't care how many times she's fucked him, or even if they're mar-ried."

"Does a man have the right to tell his wife no?"

"Not if he wants to get any later."

"I see . . . Maybe when we get home we could explore that subject some more, put on some Bad Company and . . ."

"Yeah . . . and fall asleep like we always do."

"What was that about Silas-Burke not firing Dina after they'd set-tled a lawsuit because of her? Might it have anything to do with Liam's calling her a *spy*?"

Colleen shrugged. "Not sure. And, by the way . . . I know you've been trying to interview Liam."

"Yeah. I called his home a few times, even drove by there. Then Bonnie told me he'd moved out temporarily on advice of Ms. Radford. He's gone to ground somewhere to avoid the press. That's all she knows."

* * *

On the following Monday Colleen overslept. Worse yet, a thunder-storm settled in, snarling traffic throughout the city. Running late for work, she saw a strange man step onto the front porch, shaking water from his yellow slicker. He seemed familiar and carried a sheaf of legal paper in a blue binding.

Opening the door, Colleen recalled his name. "Frank Willoughby, what brings you down to Midtown in this weather? Is that for me, by chance?"

"Good morning, Ms. Williams. Actually, I need to speak to your husband."

"Just a moment."

Tom appeared in his standard work attire, cutoff jeans, sandals and a faded Peachtree Road Race tee shirt.

"Mr. Williams," the process server said as he extended the document, "I believe this is for you."

No sooner had the paper left his hand than he thanked them, turned and left.

"What's this?" asked Tom.

"It's a subpoena. Let me see it." Colleen opened it and scanned. "It's from Cobb Superior Court. You've been asked to testify in Liam's defense."

"Oh great," he moaned. "Just what I need."

"Don't give me that crap. You're excited about this, and you know it. To you it's another interesting adventure, perhaps material for a story."

Ignoring her, Tom asked, "Why would she want *me* to testify? It's like I told her. I met the guy once and barely spoke to him. I know nothing about what happened afterward."

"You were at the concert and saw Liam with that Savage woman. She was all over him. If I were representing him, I'd say they had consensual sex, something pissed her off and now she's claiming rape."

"You were there too. And you're a lawyer. Why didn't she subpoena you?"

"Precisely *because* I'm a lawyer. Don't worry, you'll have a good time. You might even get a byline out of it."

"What am I going to do?"

"You're going to show up on the appointed date, smile for the cameras and stick to the facts. Don't hold back anything and don't answer any unasked questions. Hell, she might not even call on you. Lawyers do this all the time. They subpoena people they have no intention of questioning. It's their way of fucking with the opposition."

Halfway out the door Colleen turned back. "Oh. By the way . . . you can stop trying to interview Liam, Dina, or anyone else. Now that you're a witness you can't do anything seen as prejudicing your testimony."

"Okay."

"Promise?"

"Promise." *She said nothing about me visiting a close friend. I haven't seen Bonnie in months.*

Chapter Five

Jeff Sax sipped his coffee and gazed out on an early morning as devoid of color as a Polaroid resurrected from the bottom drawer of an antique bureau. Through budding trees, he could just make out a tiny creek trickling down a narrow gorge beneath a blanket of decaying leaves.

Reflected in the glass, his face looked drawn and tired. The gray streaks in his black curls had become more evident in recent months. His daughter, Misty, said they made him look sexy. To Sax, they made him look old.

He'd worked most of the weekend reviewing information requests from private equity firm Simonton Duval, prospective buyers of his software business, DataScape Solutions. For the first time since college, Sax would become someone else's employee, at least until his one-year contract ran out. Not sure yet how he felt about this, Sax simply wanted it to end.

Cheryl Patterson tapped on his glass door, early as usual for their eight a.m. executive meeting, quite fetching in her conservative charcoal skirt, white starched blouse and pearl necklace. Her stacked heels created the illusion she stood three inches taller than Sax, something that didn't bother him in the least.

The Emory MBA and John Marshall Law School graduate had been Sax's chief financial officer since the company's inception. She took a seat in a black leather swivel chair at the conference table.

Moments later, HR Director Derek Schmidt and Chief Operating Officer Goldwyn Shah joined them. Goldwyn sat patiently waiting for Lance Barclay, VP of Sales and Marketing.

Sax took his customary seat, pushed back for a moment and rubbed his eyes. "First off, I need to tell you that Derek and I met yesterday afternoon with Lance at Bahama Breeze. We had a brief discussion, the upshot of which is that Lance no longer works here."

The others sat in stunned silence, but for Schmidt, who scratched notes on a legal pad.

Sax cleared his throat. "I know this comes at an inopportune time, but we had to move as quickly as possible. As officers I needn't remind you that what I'm about to say is in absolute confidence. Last week Derek brought to my attention a complaint lodged by a junior member of our marketing department. She claims that over the past several months, Lance has made continuous unwanted sexual advances despite her refusals. She provided names of two other employees who've corroborated her story. Derek put together a report. Everyone signed it, and we conferred with counsel prior to meeting with Lance."

"What did he say?" asked Cheryl.

"First, he denied it. When we confronted him with the evidence, he tried to brush it off as a trivial misunderstanding. He couldn't seem to grasp the seriousness of the matter. I told him that, in accordance with our zero-tolerance policy, we no longer required his services but that his confidentiality and non-compete agreements remain in force. He refused to sign a resignation letter and said something about suing for wrongful discharge. Can you believe the prick wanted to know if this affected his bonus and stock options?

"Derek and I escorted him back to the office so he could clean out his desk. Goldwyn, I hope you won't mind, but I took the liberty of inactivating his domain account and collecting his key fob, laptop, and company mobile."

"You did what you had to do," Cheryl said. "Have you spoken with our buyers?"

"I haven't had the opportunity yet. Before I do, I'd like to propose an interim successor, pending board approval. The person I have in mind is Megan Finn." The team agreed, and Sax reached for his desk phone.

Director of Channel Sales, Finn had been with DataScape more than five years. She arrived looking like a pupil called unexpectedly to the principal's office. Sax asked her to take a seat before informing her of her promotion. When the officers had left, Sax called Simonton Duval and told them of Barclay's termination and replacement.

No sooner had he hung up than Goldwyn returned.

"Hey, Boss. You got a moment?"

"Sure."

"I was about to have one of my guys wipe Lance's hard drive but decided to check it out first. Guess what I found."

"What?"

He gave a look of disgust. "The SOB's been downloading porn . . . really sick stuff. I felt like I needed a shower after seeing it."

"But I thought our web controls prevented that."

"Only as long as he logged in here . . . He must have connected at home."

"Any chance he might have downloaded a virus or spyware?"

"We ran a scan. It appears clean, and the anti-virus is up to date."

"Tell you what. Don't wipe it yet. Lock it up instead. If Lance decides to sue us, we can use the porn as evidence."

"Sure, Boss. No problem."

* * *

For the first time in months, Sax left work early, returning to the two-bedroom condominium he rented from a fraternity brother. Located off Paper Mill Road in Cobb County, it commanded a spectacular view of the Chattahoochee River, but the surroundings had nothing to do with Sax's reasons for choosing it. Reasonably convenient to his Alpharetta office, it was also five minutes from the Indian Hills home of his wife, Barbara, and daughter, Misty.

From the garage he made his way through the empty interior and opened the front door to check his mailbox. Inside it he found a stack of envelopes, mostly junk, and a couple of bills. He tossed them on the kitchen counter and turned on the light.

Sax had lived here for the better part of six months following his *trial separation*, yet he still hadn't grown accustomed to living alone. Staring at the blank walls and sparse furnishings, a chill came over him. Though he ate, slept, and watched occasional television shows here, he would never consider it home.

As he leafed through the mail, his eyes fell on an envelope marked "Cobb Superior Court." He recognized the jury summons, and his heart sank. He'd received one three months earlier and managed to obtain a deferment. This time, he knew he wouldn't be so fortunate.

As he wondered what else could go wrong, his phone rang. The caller ID read "Jeffrey Sax." He took a deep breath before answering.

"Hey."

"Hey, what are you doing?" Barbara asked.

"I just got home."

"Wow! So early."

Ignoring her sarcasm, he asked, "What's going on with you?"

"Oh, I'm having a *lovely* day. Thank you for asking. I had a fight with your daughter. Now she's up in her room with her *music* turned up so loud the house is shaking."

Sax could hear it in the background. "Do you want me to talk to her?"

"No. I want you to appreciate what my life is like these days."

"Okay . . . So, what's the argument about this time?"

"She wants to go to the mall with a sixteen-year-old boy I've never met. I told her she couldn't, and now I'm the Wicked Bitch of the West."

"You did the right thing. She's fourteen years old. If she didn't get mad at you at least once a week, *then* I'd worry. You're a great mother and she'll thank you someday . . . maybe in about thirty years."

Barbara sighed, and Sax could almost hear her smile. "Thanks. Say, how's the buyout coming? Are we billionaires yet?"

"It's coming. Every time I turn around they want more information. On top of all that, one of my officers resigned yesterday."

"Who?"

"Lance Barclay . . . actually I fired him. The asshole couldn't keep his hands off the girls in the office. I should have canned him long ago."

"Yeah. The last thing you need at this point is a sexual harassment suit."

"I didn't fire him out of worry over a lawsuit. I did it because I can't afford to lose good employees by letting someone like him create a hostile work environment."

"Okay. So, what did the boys in New York have to say?"

"Nothing, really . . . I told them I'd promoted Megan Finn to the job. They've met her before and seem to like her."

"Good . . . she's an excellent choice."

They talked a while longer before Sax rang off. He pulled out a frozen dinner, popped it in the microwave and turned on the television, eating at the dining room table as he watched local news. Two important trials would soon begin in Cobb County. One involved a Pentecostal youth minister accused of molesting a teenaged boy, the other a date rape. Sax, realizing he needed sleep, hit the off switch.

As he dozed off his cell phone rang. At first all he heard between sobs was one word, *Daddy*. Awake in an instant, he replied. "Yes, Baby. I'm here. What is it?"

"Can you come get me? I'm at Towne Center Mall."

"What are you . . . What are you doing there? Are you alright?"

"I'm okay. I'm just inside the entrance to Macy's."

"Stay right there, where there's plenty of light. I'm on my way."

Hanging up, he threw on some clothes and ran over a trash can pulling out of the garage. He dialed Barbara with one hand as he drove. He could tell he'd awakened her.

"What?" she yelled. "Oh my God! She must have sneaked out. It's that boy. I know it."

"Calm down. Calm down. I'll be at the mall in twenty minutes. I'll call you when I get there."

She started to say something else as he hung up.

* * *

Misty settled into the passenger seat, eyes and nose red from crying, wiping snot with a ragged Kleenex.

"What happened? Are you okay?"

"I'll be alright," she said, drawing up her knees and staring out the window, her face shielded beneath her long red curls.

To Sax she seemed so much younger than her fourteen years. "Okay. What happened?" He asked quietly.

"I had a fight with Mom. I wanted to go out. I waited until I thought she was asleep and got a ride to the mall with someone. We weren't there long before we had an argument and he left."

Sax nearly ran off the road. "He left you at the mall? Who the hell is this?"

"Dad, Dad . . . it's not what you think. It was my fault . . . really."

"A boy drove you to the mall and left you there? Who is he?"

"A guy I know at school. It's not a big deal."

Recalling his promise, Sax speed-dialed Barbara. When she answered, he assured her their daughter would be okay and said they'd discuss it when he got to the house. He hung up before she could say anything else.

* * *

The two-story red brick traditional backed up to the Indian Hills Country Club, which Sax had joined fifteen years earlier for reasons he could no longer remember. He'd never played golf in his life. Barbara was the only one with any interest in tennis, and he could count on his fingers the number of times he'd been to the pool.

As he pulled into the driveway the garage door rose. Barbara stood there in house coat and pajamas, her face a mask of rage. She caught Misty's arm as the girl tried to brush past. Sax hesitated for a moment in his car.

"Get in here," Barbara shouted, "*both of you.*"

They gathered in the den, which had changed little in the months since Sax left. Barbara sat on the couch struggling to regain her composure. Misty sank into a chair opposite her, and Sax took a barstool at the kitchen counter.

"Okay. Start from the beginning," said Barbara, "and tell me everything."

Misty began to sob. "All I wanted to do was hang out for a while at the mall."

"We discussed that. I told you I didn't want you going out on a school night, especially with a boy two years older than you whom I haven't even met."

Sax said nothing, focusing instead on a red whelp on his daughter's right cheek. Before he could say anything, Barbara noticed it too.

"What happened to your face?" she asked.

"It was an accident. I swear."

Sax barely recognized his own voice, a cold monotone. "Did he hit you?"

"It was a misunderstanding."

"Who is he?"

With persistence Sax and Barbara managed to coax from Misty the name of Jordan Oliver. She wouldn't say what the argument had been about, but Sax could imagine.

Barbara went to the kitchen and pulled a copy of the Walton High School student directory from a drawer. She dialed the home number for Oliver and his parents, Scott and Millie. When a woman answered, Barbara said nothing. She hung up and dialed 911.

Twenty minutes later two Cobb Police officers arrived. The younger, an Officer Clark, had a slight build and a dark crew cut. The other, overweight with receding grey hair, was Officer Daniels. They took statements from Misty, from Sax and from Barbara.

"Mr. and Mrs. Sax, do you plan to press charges?"

"We certainly do," Barbara said.

Misty sat quietly on the couch with her head down.

Sax slowly nodded. Throughout the ordeal he'd spoken only when questioned.

Daniels studied him carefully. "Mr. Sax, I can understand how angry you are over this. I have two daughters myself. But it's very important that you hear what I have to say. *You cannot go anywhere near that boy.* If you do, you'll probably wind up in jail yourself. Do you understand me?"

"Yes."

The officers returned to Misty, asking again if she needed an emergency team to examine her. She said no.

Sax, meanwhile, excused himself and went to the kitchen to get Barbara and Misty some water. There on the counter lay the high school directory, open to the name of Jordan Oliver. Sax memorized the address, filled two glasses and returned to the den.

"Jordan Oliver is underage," Daniels explained as he and Clark left. "He'll come up before a juvenile judge. We'll get back in touch with you when we have a court date."

The Saxes thanked the policemen. When they'd left and Misty had gone to bed, Sax kissed his wife goodbye.

* * *

A week later, hearing that Jordan's family attorney had arranged a plea deal for six months' probation, an irate Barbara Sax called her husband at work. Sax did his best to placate her with vague statements about exploring legal options. As he hung up, he took out the notepad on which he'd written everything he'd discovered about Jordan Oliver. He contemplated it as he dialed an old friend.

Chapter Six

In celebration of warmer weather, Tom and Colleen Williams rose early and had breakfast on their patio. Tom cooked omelets while Colleen wiped pollen from the table and chairs. The planters Tom had built to either side of the back steps luxuriated in a riot of pansies and impatiens.

As they settled in, Tom commented, "according to the subpoena, the trial begins a week from Monday. When do you think Radford will call me?"

"There's no telling. First, they'll impanel the jury, then both sides will make opening statements, and then, around mid-morning on Monday, the prosecutor will begin presenting his case. The defense won't call its witnesses until the State rests. Depending on how long that takes, it could be one or two days, maybe more. Don't make any plans for next week."

"So, I'm supposed to sit around as much as a week waiting to hear from Radford?"

"She should know something by Friday. Hell, she might not even call you at all. The case could end up in a plea bargain." Colleen leaned across the table and gave him her best Cheshire Cat smile. "Why do you ask? Did you have something in mind?"

"Well . . . nothing. I'm between projects now."

"Exactly. Think of this as research for a *future* story."

As she left for work, Tom cleared and washed the dishes. When he'd finished, he called the office of Bonnie Baron.

* * *

The Baron Agency occupied a converted warehouse, south of downtown Decatur near the MARTA station.

By the time Tom arrived, morning traffic had cleared. A light south-easterly breeze stirred the trees. He found the last empty parking space across the street, and Bonnie met him at the door. She explained she'd been arranging a private showing for one of her clients and was happy for an excuse to take a break.

"Sorry. If I'd known you were busy . . ."

"No worries. We have everything we need. Heather's out running some last-minute errands."

Bonnie offered him a tour of her current exhibit. One of the smaller rooms in the back featured a collection of charcoal drawings that caught Tom's eye.

"Do you like them?" Bonnie asked.

"Yeah," he nodded, moving closer. "Simple, yet bold strokes. It's like they capture the essence of the subject with minimal work."

Bonnie beamed. "I thought so myself. I'll have to tell Heather. She'll appreciate that. I've been after her for two years to let me show her work. She only agreed yesterday."

Tom came around to the point of his visit. "I've been trying to reach Liam, but he doesn't seem to be at home. Tell me he hasn't skipped town." The look on Bonnie's face made him regret his poor choice of a joke.

"No . . . or at least I hope not. After he made bail, Liam called and asked me to go over and pick up his canvases and supplies for safe-keeping. I stored them out back . . . I haven't sold any of his works since . . . It's like they're toxic all of a sudden. He's guilty until proven innocent." She stopped, pulled a cigarette from her flannel shirt and lit it.

"I'm sorry to hear that," said Tom. "At least his case is coming to trial next week. We'll know soon, one way or the other." He paused, pretending to appraise a small sculpture. "Tell me,"He said, "when was the last time you and Liam spoke?"

"About a week ago . . . a brief conversation. He wanted to know how his pieces were moving. I had nothing to tell him."

"Did he sound optimistic about his case?"

She shook her head. "You never know with Liam. Sometimes I don't think he comprehends how much shit he's in. All he wanted to talk about were his next project and his new girlfriend. He says she's Jamaican, a real beauty. Calls her his *muse*. Liam's always had a way with women."

"I met his attorney," said Tom. "She's young, but she seems confident."

"I hope so. Liam's parents spared no expense. He says they're flying in from London today to attend the trial. You know I've never even met them?"

"This must be hard on them."

"Hard on his mom. From what I understand, his old man's a piece of work. He sent Liam to the U.S., as much as anything, to get him out of London where he might be an embarrassment."

"You make him sound pretty cold. At least he's showing up to support his son."

"Or to save himself a scandal . . . Anyway, he can afford the best defense in the world. I'm not sure why he'd hire someone young and inexperienced."

"Colleen says Radford's firm has one of the top criminal defense practices in the city, and she should know. I'm sure Radford has plenty of support. Did you find out anything from the woman who introduced Liam and Dina? What was her name?"

"Sally Meister . . . I saw her not long after the concert. She says she *did not* introduce them, that Dina met Liam at one of his showings and put a move on him."

"Hmmm . . . Were you able to find out anything about Dina?"

"Nope. It's like she fell from the sky the day before she met Liam. All he knows about her is what she says . . . she graduated from Case Western and got her masters from Harvard. For all I know, she's lying."

"Well, that ought to be easy to verify. Maybe I can find out something about this company she works for, Moore and Frye."

Bonnie took another drag, watching the smoke rise to the vaulted ceiling. "I just want Liam to get past this. I wish they'd never met."

"Bonnie, I appreciate your taking a break to meet with me. I'll let you get back to your preparations."

"Sure. Thanks for coming by. Give me a call later in the week. You and Colleen should get together with us. You could park here, we could have some wine and hors d'oeuvres, walk over to Eddie's Attic."

"Sounds like a great idea."

Back at his car, Tom had another thought. Pulling out his cell, he dialed Mitch Danner.

"Hey," Danner asked, "What're you up to?"

"I dropped by to visit an old friend. How about you?"

"Took the day off. I'm buying some grass."

"You're scoring some grass? Jamaican or Colombian?"

"Zoysia. I'm re-sodding my lawn."

"Oh my God! When did we get so old?"

"Tell me about it. I'm not putting it down myself, not with this back. I've hired a crew of Mexicans."

"Ah, life sounds *so* exciting out there in the burbs."

"Yeah. Sometimes it's more than I can take . . . So, what's up?"

"What do you know about Dina Savage?"

"Bupkus. The woman's a ghost."

"Have you asked any of your police sources?"

"Of course." Danner sounded insulted. "They don't know and don't care. She's the vic. All they care about's the perp, and, from what I hear, he's going away for a *long* time."

"Wow! I guess that depends on who you ask. His lawyer expects him to walk."

"That's what they always say. Trust me. The guy's cooked."

"Well, thanks anyway."

"No worries. Let's get together this weekend for some golf."

"Sounds like a plan."

As he shoved the phone back into his pocket, Tom pictured Dina. How could it be that no one knew, or cared, about her past? No doubt, Sara Radford had her investigators searching.

* * *

Kurt Olafsen scanned the travelers scurrying through Hartsfield Jackson's international arrivals hall, all in a hurry to get somewhere else.

He searched the faces of passengers disembarking from British Airways Flight BA0227. He had no need of a cardboard sign. He'd recognize the couple on sight.

Olafsen and his companion wore matching charcoal suits, stiff white shirts and high-gloss oxfords, but there the similarity stopped. The other man, medium height and ten years older than Olafsen, had the build of a wrestler yet seemed uncomfortable, as though his shirt collar might throttle him. His dark brown curls, thick moustache and broad, flat face reminded Olafsen of Joseph Stalin.

Trying not to look at him, Olafsen shifted his gaze. He'd met the man only an hour earlier, but already something seemed wrong about him; perhaps the exaggerated Swedish accent. He couldn't imagine what services such a person could provide for young Liam's defense, but they had to be illegal. Olafsen stifled a yawn, remembering the call that awakened him at five a.m.

Finally, he recognized a diminutive woman, red hair flecked with gray. She wore a broad-brimmed straw hat, dark glasses and the drawn and distracted look of someone who'd recently lost a loved one.

The older man looming behind her, also in dark glasses, wore a hand-made navy blue suit that could only have come from London's Savile Row. Tall and barrel-chested, his close-cropped, snow-white hair stood atop a high forehead like the bristles of a shoe brush. He gave Olafsen and his companion a curt nod and made his way over, his wife in tow.

"Gentlemen," he said in Swedish.

"Mr. Ambassador, it's good to see you," said Olafsen as they shook hands, "though I wish it were under happier circumstances." He turned to his companion. "I don't know if you've met Dirk Palme of Ross and Associates."

"I have not," said Bjorn Sanstrom, "but I've heard a great deal about you."

"I want to assure you," gushed Olafsen, "that the consulate is making every effort to find a solution to this unfortunate misunderstanding. We've employed one of the top defense firms in the area and an independent jury consultant. We've also hired . . ." He glanced sideways at Palme, "an investigative firm that should prove quite valuable."

Palme's expression gave away nothing as he spoke in a deep baritone. "Mr. Ambassador, we have already made significant progress. My colleagues are, even now, researching this Savage woman, and they've discovered matters that the courts of Cobb County may find quite interesting. They are also scouring social media and will assist us in . . . other capacities." As he spoke, he handed Bjorn a thick envelope.

The man's Swedish carried a flavor Olafsen couldn't place, perhaps Eastern European. He didn't know his real name, but it certainly wasn't Dirk Palme, and he didn't work for anyone named Ross and Associates. Bjorn had given the consulate the contact information in an encrypted message. By next week, Olafsen suspected, this man could be on another continent, in a different guise, with a different name and nationality.

"If you will follow me," said Olafsen, our limousine will meet us outside."

* * *

An Atlanta police officer blew his whistle at the stretch limo driver stopped at the curb and started to yell at him to move, then noticed the diplomatic tag. Instead, he turned and continued down the walkway, glancing over his shoulder at the Sanstroms and their companions.

Brigid took a front-facing seat, staring out as they drove north on the Connector. She wanted nothing to do with these strangers.

Though she'd never been to Atlanta, it looked to her like so many places she'd seen in her years as the wife of an ambassador, hot, crowded, filthy. The sun, setting low on the horizon, cast ominous shadows across the cityscape. What little she could see of the surrounding neighborhoods only depressed her more.

Her husband, seated beside her, spoke first to Olafsen. "I am not trusting the safety and freedom of my son to this little girl you have representing him. Nor am I trusting him to the American justice system. You need to understand that. The moment that woman charged Liam with rape, he became guilty in the eyes of the law. I will take matters into my own hands, as necessary. That is why I asked Mr. Palme to join us. Is that clear?"

Olafsen nodded but said nothing. He knew Bjorn by reputation only and knew better than to question the man. Before becoming ambassador to the Court of St. James, Sanstrom founded an international conglomerate, Svenska Global Holdings, and contributed to all the major political parties of Sweden, making frequent appearances with the prime minister.

Sanstrom turned to Palme, seated across from him. "The important thing for you to remember," he said, "is that this is a *limited* engagement. There are to be no . . . *extracurricular* activities." He spoke in low tones, but his precise diction left no doubt he meant every word.

"Understood," said Palme, his eyes expressionless.

"And tell me about this colleague of yours. Is he competent?"

"Yes. He will be *most* convincing. Already he has established an intimate relationship with our subject."

"Excellent. And your young female assistant?"

"I would trust her with my life . . . as I have on many occasions."

The foursome rode the rest of the way in silence. Brigid, grateful for the solitude, tried not to imagine her little boy spending the rest of his life among violent criminals, the same little boy who would burst into her practice room with a pastel of a butterfly or a dead animal he'd found on the grounds of their estate. She would marvel at the fine details and character in his tiny strokes. She also recalled the drawing he'd once made of a nude twelve-year-old girl, the granddaughter of their upstairs maid.

The meeting with Liam's attorneys would wait until morning. Brigid and Bjorn checked into a Buckhead hotel to make up, as much as possible, for sleep lost on the long international flight. Already she longed for the opportunity to bathe away the filth she felt in this Palme's presence.

* * *

Another limo picked them up the next morning. As the elevator opened onto the eleventh floor at the Cobb Galleria, a beaming Sara Radford greeted them. Towering above her in a navy-blue suit and maroon shirt stood Bjorn and Brigid's son, an enigmatic smile on his lips.

Brigid sprang upon him, burying her face in his chest. Bjorn nodded and extended his hand.

Radford escorted them to a conference room whose windows afforded a northern view of Kennesaw Mountain and the hills beyond. She stood in the doorway as they assumed their seats. "Can I offer you a Coke or some water?"

"I'll take sparkling water if you have it," said Brigid in her thick Irish brogue.

"Nothing for me, thank you," said the elder Sanstrom.

Liam simply shook his head.

When Radford had departed, they spoke in hushed tones as Liam assured his parents he was well. He'd spent only two nights in jail and another in a hotel under an alias, to avoid reporters. He now lived with a friend in town while awaiting trial. Brigid knew better than to inquire about his *friend*.

Liam explained that he'd brought his paints with him and had begun a new work, inspired by his recent experiences. On the table before him lay his ubiquitous Nikon.

Bjorn scrutinized him for a long time.

Finally, Liam said, "I know what you're both wondering. You want to know if I raped that girl."

The old man said nothing.

"I did not," said Liam. "I would never do anything like that."

Neither of his parents replied.

When Radford returned, she handed Brigid a glass filled with ice and a tall plastic bottle of seltzer. From a credenza she retrieved four fresh yellow legal pads and a set of pens bearing the firm's logo, distributing them around the table.

"First, let me say that, difficult as this type of case can be, I believe we have several advantages, not the least of which is the murky past of Ms. Savage, Liam's accuser. It seems she has a history of making false allegations. I have an appointment tomorrow morning with attorneys for one of her former employers. Apparently, Ms. Savage accused a coworker of sexual harassment. It turned out the young man was gay, and Ms. Savage had to make a written apology, a copy of which the firm can provide us."

Radford paused, making eye contact with each of them. "That said, I must caution you that there are no guarantees. Liam's fate will rest in the hands of twelve complete strangers. Their only knowledge of that night's events will be what they hear in the courtroom. Regardless of its outcome, this will *not* be a pleasant experience. The prosecutor will paint as gruesome a picture as possible, based on Ms. Savage's story. Every detail of Liam's past will be open to scrutiny. I need you to tell me everything that could possibly come out, no matter how trivial it may seem."

Brigid bit her lip and gazed out at a large military plane describing a wide arc across the sky.

"I've already discussed this with Liam," said Radford, "and I need to get your take on the matter. The prosecutor has no more assurance than I as to what will happen in the courtroom. He's offered to reduce charges to *Attempted Rape* in exchange for a guilty plea. The recommended sentence, which the judge would likely accept, is six years at the Alto minimum security facility, with the possibility of early parole. I must say that the alternative, in the event of a guilty verdict, would be life in prison."

At this Brigid closed her eyes, let out a low moan and began to sob. Liam showed no emotion, doodling on the yellow pad provided him.

At length, Bjorn cleared his throat. "Miss Radford, we will *never* agree to a guilty plea, no matter what this prosecutor offers. I am *as* confident, perhaps more confident than *you*, of an acquittal."

"Mr. Sanstrom, I admire your determination. It's just that I'm professionally bound to explain your alternatives."

"Duly noted. We can proceed with the trial."

"Very good."

Brigid averted her eyes, knowing the real reasons for her husband's recalcitrance, reasons that had far more to do with his reputation and career than any desire to protect Liam, whom he'd written off the moment the young man decided to become a painter.

* * *

While Tom collected supper dishes from the dining table, Colleen curled up on the couch with a glass of Pinot Noir and pressed the TV remote, bringing up Nancy Grace's lead story on the Sanstrom trial.

"Tonight, we're following a story out of Marietta, Georgia, where a young artist is about to stand trial on charges of raping his date eighteen months ago. Dina Savage, a marketing research specialist, alleges that Liam Sanstrom drugged her and sexually assaulted her *repeatedly* after they returned to his home following an outdoor concert. I have on the phone local newspaper reporter Mitch Danner, who has been on this story since it broke."

Tom came into the room, drying his hands. "That prick!" he laughed. "I spoke to him just this morning. Do you think he mentioned anything about being on Nancy Grace?"

"Uh, darling," asked Colleen, "do you remember me asking you to lay off this case until Radford calls you to testify?"

Tom gave her a sheepish look. "I called an old friend to see how he was doing."

"Right."

Grace proceeded. "It turns out that Sanstrom is the son of Bjorn Sanstrom, founder and former chairman of Svenska Global, who now serves as Swedish ambassador to England. What we have here is yet another instance of a rich, pampered young man who thinks he's above the law. From what Mr. Danner has seen, this young woman may be lucky to have escaped Sanstrom's home with her life."

"They can use words like 'alleged' all they want," said Colleen. "They've already tried and convicted him on Dina's word alone."

Chapter Seven

Scandinavians sometimes refer to late fall and the onset of winter as "going into the tunnel," that time of year when sunlight wanes and the days descend into perpetual darkness. For Liam Sanstrom, the tunnel had nothing to do with the calendar or seasons. It could as easily apply to spring or summer. For most of his life the tunnel had been a place of refuge, a sanctuary where he could shut out the noise and create his own world in the only way he knew, with brushes and paint.

Liam's latest hideout, the Southwest Atlanta loft apartment of thirty-year-old Martha Manley, had everything he needed. The Clark Atlanta University professor acquired it for its convenience to campus and to her favorite eatery, the Busy Bee Café. For Liam, its greatest feature was its northern light.

Liam found Martha easy going and, at the same time, highly intelligent. They'd met a few weeks before the Connick concert and Liam wrote her phone number on the inside of a matchbook, the first thing he searched for when he made bail.

The early morning glow illumined his latest canvas, perched on an easel where he'd left it overnight waiting for the ground coat to dry. He dabbed Cadmium Orange, Burnt Sienna, Titanium White, and Burnt Umber onto his palette and set to work.

From a far corner came the soft sounds of Martha's snoring. Soon she would smell the coffee brewing in the kitchen, rise from her futon, shower and dress for work. Liam would have the place to himself until three p.m. when she returned from school. The price for these accommodations, incessant late-night lovemaking, struck Liam as quite a bargain. He could become quite accustomed to it.

As he continued to paint, the meetings with his attorneys, acrimonious debates with his father and unanswered phone calls to Bonnie, became little more than muted voices from another room. Tacked to a cork board beside the easel hung rough sketches and photos from which he drew inspiration. An outline soon emerged, a woman standing semi-nude on a high-rise balcony overlooking a sun-drenched beach. For the next eight hours Liam worked, uninterrupted, his only food an occasional Power Bar washed down with a Diet Coke.

When he'd finished, he showered, threw on his suit, and once again trekked northward to the firm of Statham and Riley. He'd come to dread these meetings with his lawyers even more now that his parents had arrived.

* * *

Dina poured a black coffee and retreated to her office, where her state-of-the-art laptop, paid for by Moore and Fry, awaited. She smiled at a co-worker whose name she could never remember. *Is it Shelly? Suzy . . . perhaps Sandy? Whatever.*

Dina had plans for the evening and needed to finish by five. Like Liam, she could reduce the confusion around her to mere white noise. Though she would lose a week of work, she basked in the realization that her eighteen months of waiting would soon end. Trial would begin, and Liam would find himself in Reidsville, the favorite bitch of some biker twice his size. *Better stock up on tampons, Liam.*

Dina's latest project focused on Braxton-Milligan, a private equity firm negotiating the purchase of a small tech startup. Moore and Frye's largest client needed to know what competitive advantages Braxton-

Milligan would gain, which employees would likely depart and which customers would follow. Dina studied what little financial and sales and marketing data she could find on the company. She scanned its website and reviewed Dun and Bradstreet scores, all the while noting names and titles.

Then she connected anonymously to a site where she'd stored her latest spyware. This gave her access to the mail servers of the two businesses. She found their security measures laughable. Dina spent the next two hours poring over emails of top executives, finance officers, and HR directors. It made fascinating reading. She felt like a voyeur, peering through a neighbor's bedroom window.

She then logged onto Equifax, TRW, and several major banks and brokerage houses. Before long she'd compiled the mortgage balances and private holdings of every officer in both companies, their marital status, the life insurance they carried and their medical conditions. She created a cloud account under a false name, opened it and made a list of the company's clients and how long they'd been customers. Though technically illegal, these tactics only mattered if Dina got caught, which had never happened in the ten years she'd done this kind of work. No one at Moore and Frye questioned how she produced such uncanny predictions and insights so long as they experienced no blowback.

None of Dina's programs resided on her laptop. She'd hidden them on the networks of some of the most respected corporations and universities in the nation, in spaces so secret no one would discover them. As a safeguard, she periodically located new hosts and scrubbed her old sites. She collected and encrypted the data as she went, feeding it into high-speed external drives. Later, in the comfort of her condo, she would open them in clear text and embark on yet another of her prescient masterpieces. The technical writing courses she'd taken all those years ago at Case Western had paid off.

Throughout the day Dina's mind kept returning to the upcoming trial and the preparatory conversations she'd had with the prosecutor and her personal attorney. *What disgusting little men.*

When five o'clock arrived, she closed her laptop, removed the external drive and placed them in separate cases. The laptop went into the trunk of her car, while the hard drive fit neatly into a hidden pocket beneath the pistol she carried in her glove compartment.

Turning the ignition of her forest green Alfa, she felt the satisfying thrum of its engine surge through her body, looking forward to a weekend at Lake Lanier with her new boyfriend, handsome, recently divorced, and, quite by coincidence, a research analyst like herself. He held a significant stake, or so he said, in another company that would soon become a takeover target and would become a very wealthy man. Dina looked forward to spending all that money.

She put the top down, feeling the breeze in her hair and the warm sun on her face. The weekend promised beautiful weather. She would stop at Phipps Plaza on her way home and shop for a new bikini. While there she could grab a salad at a neighboring sandwich shop and still have time for target shooting at a nearby range, anxious to try out her new Glock.

Chapter Eight

Marietta, Georgia
Monday, March 18

Sax dug into his pockets, removed his keys, coins and phone and put them in a plastic dish on the conveyor belt. He stepped through the metal detector and waited patiently to collect them on the other side. A sheriff's deputy admonished him to turn off his cell before entering any of the courtrooms.

On the fourth floor,n Sax found a large room where he reported for jury duty and took his seat among others who had answered the summons. This could not have come at a worse time, and each second seemed to drag at an interminable pace. He opened his briefcase and began scanning documents from Simonton Duval. Startled at hearing his name called, he turned to see a short, middle-aged man standing in the doorway joined by a small gathering of people.

Entering the brightly lit courtroom, the prospective jurors took their seats in the gallery rather than the jury box. Windows along the wall provided light that, blended with overhead fluorescents, created a sickly glow permeating the room. A faint whiff of disinfectant struggled to overcome the bouquet of sweat and grime emanating from the seats.

The elevated oak-paneled bench stood empty, an American flag on one side and Georgia on the other. In front of it, on a lower platform, sat two women Sax guessed to be the clerk and the recorder. A thin wraith of a woman in red jacket and black slacks stood motionless to one side. Until she moved Sax couldn't tell if she were alive. A screen stood behind her and a projector hung from the ceiling in the center of the room.

A low rail separated the gallery from the trial area. At one table sat a man in a blue pinstriped suit, starched white shirt, red bow tie and suspenders. He wore an obvious toupee and what Sax's daughter, Misty, called a "pedophile moustache," neatly trimmed and waxed at each end. Sax pictured him standing on a playground on a sunny day wearing a raincoat.

Hunched over, he spoke in low tones to a thickly built police officer with a crew-cut a shade of blonde that must have come from a bottle. The prosecutor gesticulated with both hands as his eyes darted back and forth over the jurors.

At the opposing table a distinguished older gentleman in a three-piece tweed suit listened intently as two young women engaged in animated conversation. Between them sat Liam Sanford, whom Sax now recognized from his photo in the morning paper. With his thin face and spiky red hair, he reminded Sax of Vincent Van Gogh, only younger, handsomer and better dressed. Sax studied him, not knowing what to think.

A bailiff entered from beside the bench and bellowed "All rise. The Superior Court of Cobb County is now in session, Judge Eunice Gilmartin presiding."

Sax rose to a chorus of rustling clothes and squeaking pews. Behind the bailiff strode a middle-aged woman in a black gown, her brown hair piled in tight curls. She took her seat, donned her readers and examined a stack of papers before looking up. A desk lamp illumined her face. Though the day had only begun, she already wore the tired look of someone who'd just as soon go home and crawl back into bed.

"You may be seated," she said, scanning the prospective jurors. "Ladies and gentlemen, we'll begin this morning with what is known as a *voir dire*. It's Latin for 'Speak the truth.' We're going to ask you a few questions and that's all we expect you to do, *speak the truth*."

"We're about to try the case of Georgia versus Mr. Liam T. Sanstrom on charges of rape. As you know, these are serious allegations. At this moment Mr. Sanstrom is innocent . . . unless the prosecutor, Mr. Rainey . . . she nodded to the mustachioed man . . . can prove Mr. Sanstrom guilty. The object of our questions this morning is to determine whether you can, after listening to this case, fairly and impartially decide if Mr. Rainey has established guilt beyond a *reasonable* doubt."

The woman in red and black placed an easel and flip chart in front of the gallery, reading:

Name

Occupation

# of Children

Area of County

How long in County

"I'd like to start," said the judge, "by asking if any of you know Mr. Sanstrom or are related to him by blood or marriage." No one spoke.

She then asked if anyone knew her, Dina V. Savage, Horace Rainey, Ms. Sara Radford or any other parties involved in the case. She inquired if anyone lived near Overton Road or had recent occasion to drive by there. In each instance, the prospective jurors either remained silent or shook their heads.

Now, I'd like you to stand, when we call your name, and give us the information you see on the chart in front of you."

The jurors included a young Black man, an overweight computer programmer with a brown ponytail and Christine Posner, a bartender with a mural of tattoos down both arms. An elderly, pensive-looking

68

woman identified herself as Lucille Farmer. She cringed and kneaded a handkerchief between her fingers throughout the questioning.

Sax, when the judge came to him, described his occupation as *business owner*. This drew no apparent response from either counsel.

"Now," said the judge, "Mr. Rainey and Ms. Riley have some questions for each of you."

Rainey went first. Leaning against his table and clutching a sheet of paper before him, as though it might fly away, he seemed anxious to affect a casual style.

"First," he began in an effeminate drawl, "I'd like to thank you all for taking time out of your busy lives to serve on this jury. You've accepted a time-honored responsibility that is essential to the dispensation of justice and the protection of our community. Each of you received a questionnaire before you came here today, which you returned to the court. I've reviewed your responses and I promise you I'll keep my questions brief." Pausing, he added with a smile, "I also promise not to give out any of this information to telemarketers."

This elicited a chuckle from two members of the jury pool.

Rainey then apologized, in advance, if he mispronounced anyone's name. "Mr. Sax, I believe I'll start with you. You gave your occupation as *business owner*. Do you mind telling us what kind of business you own?"

"A software firm."

The computer programmer leaned forward for a better look at Sax.

"What kind of software?" Rainey asked.

Sax wondered how much of his answer the prosecutor would understand. "We provide a cloud-based ERP solution for service industries, including fleet tracking and maintenance."

Rainey raised his eyebrows and nodded his head as though he understood. "Mr. Sax, have you ever served on a jury?"

"No sir. I haven't."

"Have you ever been accused of a violent crime?"

"No sir."

"Mr. Sax, if a woman has consensual sex with a man and then tells him she does not wish to do so again, do you believe she has the right at that point to refuse?"

Sax shrugged. "Of course. 'No' means 'no'."

"If the prosecution's able to present what you consider a convincing case as to the defendant's guilt, do you see any reason why you could not support such a verdict?"

"No sir. I don't."

"Mr. Sax, do you own a gun?"

The question, apropos of nothing Sax could imagine, momentarily flustered him. He couldn't see what gun ownership had to do with a rape case. "Yes sir. I do."

"Are you married, Mr. Sax?"

He considered for a moment. "I'm married . . . but separated."

The female bartender with the tattoos gave him an appraising look.

"Would you describe yourself as a teetotaler, an occasional drinker, or a frequent one?"

Sax shifted uncomfortably. *Where's all this going?* he thought. "I guess I'm an occasional drinker."

"Have you ever been arrested on alcohol-related charges?"

"No sir. I have not."

"Just one more question, Mr. Sax . . . Do you believe that a man under the influence of alcohol or drugs is still responsible for his actions?"

"I certainly do."

Rainey asked similar questions of the other prospects. Sax studied their faces as they spoke. The elderly woman with the handkerchief,

Lucille Farmer, gave her occupation as *homemaker*. The Black man, Carlton Beasley, seemed even more annoyed than Sax at having to serve.

When the prosecutor had finished, he turned to the bench. "That's all the questions I have, Your Honor."

The defense attorney approached the railing, introducing herself again as Sara Radford. Her diminutive stature, soprano voice and Southern twang gave Sax the impression she lacked the experience and tenacity demanded of her profession.

Radford began with Lucille Farmer, who described her marital status as widowed and, after a moment's hesitation, said she had only one child, a son. Radford's inquisitive look drew further clarification that the woman had once had a daughter.

Turning to Sax, Radford went through several innocuous questions about his software business before asking, "Mr. Sax, in your response to the questionnaire you said you had one child . . . a boy or a girl?"

Sax stifled a smile. This, he thought, could be his ticket out. "Yes. I have a fourteen-year-old daughter."

"Would that, in any way, color your judgment or affect your ability to render an impartial verdict?"

Careful not to overplay his hand, he replied, "No . . . I . . . don't suppose it would."

"Mr. Sax, as a member of this jury you'll hear some graphic descriptions of what some might consider . . ." She paused as if seeking the right term, "rough sex. Might that influence your decision in any way?"

Sax found something ironic in the demure, elegantly dressed debutante's reference to *rough sex*. "I really don't care what people do in their own bedrooms." He paused and for emphasis added, ". . . *as long as it's consensual*."

"Thank you, Mr. Sax." Radford turned to the bench. "Those are all the questions I have, Your Honor."

She conferred briefly with Rainey. He rose, and they approached the bench, handing sheets of paper to the bailiff, who passed them to the judge.

The judge examined them and addressed the jury pool, "The following people will please rise, collect anything you brought with you and take a seat in the jury box. The rest can return to the assembly room down the hall to await further instructions."

Surprised when she called his name, Sax joined eleven others as they filed through the gate to the jury box.

* * *

In the rear of the courtroom, seemingly unnoticed, sat a small, ineffectual-looking man in a rumpled brown suit. Anyone who met Ron Dalrymple would have trouble later describing him. He may as well have been invisible, a valuable trait in his profession.

In his lap Dalrymple held a yellow legal pad bearing the names and personal information of every juror in print so small anyone peering over his shoulder would find it illegible. As the dismissed prospects filed out, Dalrymple, head down, slipped in among them.

Judge Gilmartin cleared her throat. "Before we begin, I need to establish some ground rules. For the duration of this trial, you can jot down everything you see, hear, or think. The bailiff will pass out notebooks for that purpose. But you are *not* to discuss this case with *anyone*, not your fellow jurors or anyone outside this courtroom. Under no circumstances will you have contact with the defendant, his attorney, the prosecutor, the press, or any witnesses. When we release you at the end of the day, you are not to go anywhere near Overton Road or attempt to gather pertinent information on your own. Do I make myself clear?"

Each of the jurors nodded.

"The trial will begin with opening statements by the prosecutor and defense attorney. These remarks are simply an explanation of what they hope to prove. It's important for you to understand that these statements, in and of themselves, do not constitute evidence. In the end, it'll be up to you to decide whether Mr. Rainey has proven beyond reasonable doubt that Mr. Sanstrom is guilty of rape. Remember, it's not up to the defendant to prove his innocence. He may or may not choose to testify in his defense. He's under no obligation to do so. If he chooses not to testify, that should not, in any way, influence your verdict."

Gilmartin studied her watch. "Before we start, I'm going to give you a ten-minute break. The bailiff will escort you to the jury room, where you can leave any personal belongings you won't need in the courtroom. No one will bother them there.

"You'll find restrooms and a water fountain outside near the elevator. You can use your cell phones in the lobby. *Just be sure to turn them off before you return.* If anyone's phone rings in this courtroom I will find you in contempt." Her expression left no doubt she meant every word. "Do not leave this floor without my permission. I expect all of you back *promptly* in ten minutes. Again, you are *not* to discuss any aspect of this matter with anyone."

Chapter Nine

Marietta, Georgia
Monday, March 18

Playing hooky from work, Colleen and her clerk, Melanie Starke-Ruiz sat in the gallery throughout the voir dire. During the break, they watched people passing through the lobby, the same kinds of people who haunt courthouses across America; lawyers, bail bondsmen, reporters, curiosity seekers.

The victims and accused, however, came from all walks of life, the good, the bad, the unfortunate, some seeking justice, others looking to avoid it. Colleen could see it in their faces, the care-worn, the grief-stricken, the defiant.

A middle-aged attorney in a dark suit and bad comb-over waited at one of the elevators. The door slid open, and out stepped a stylishly dressed blonde, seeming lost. It took Colleen a moment to recognize Dina. Her black knee-length skirt, crisp turquoise blouse and sensible shoes did little to hide her stunning beauty. Instinctively, Colleen looked away, hoping Dina hadn't noticed her.

Heads turned as the lawyer took Dina's arm and ushered her into a small conference room off the main corridor. A heavy-set older man in a white linen suit, with a florid face, red bow tie and matching suspenders studied her as she passed, his eyes flickering over her body like the tongue of a snake. Dina never so much as glanced at him.

* * *

Sax stepped into the corridor to call his office. Powering up his phone, he stood beside a window to get a better signal and escape the crowd noise. As he dialed Cheryl, his eyes followed the blonde and her attorney.

"Hey!" he said when Cheryl answered.

"Tell me you didn't get picked, Jeff. We need you here at the office."

"No such luck. I drew a rape case."

"Oh shit! Can you tell me about it?"

"Nope."

"Okay."

"Look, I have no idea how long this'll last. My understanding is they'll let us out each day about five. I can meet you at the office later, if you don't mind, and we can order in Chinese."

"Sure. But call me beforehand. It might not be necessary. I'm hoping to get all this paperwork completed before then."

Sax cut the conversation short and called Barbara to tell her that, between jury duty and working after hours, he'd be unable to drop by tonight as planned. As he hung up, Sax saw the other jurors returning to the courtroom. Stepping through the open doorway, he remembered his cell phone, reached inside his pocket and shut it off.

* * *

Horace Rainey rose and ambled to the rail, thrusting out his chin and smiling as he spoke, looking each juror in the eye. "Good morning, ladies and gentlemen. I want to thank you again on behalf of the people of Cobb County."

The smile faded. "I wish I could tell you that this will be a pleasant experience. I'm afraid it will not. This is the story of Dina Savage, a bright, ambitious young woman with her whole life ahead of her. Dina grew up in humble circumstances, raised by a single mother. Through hard work and determination, she managed to earn *two* college degrees before moving to Atlanta to embark on a promising career.

"Eighteen months ago, Dina met a handsome, talented young man, who seemed perfectly normal at the time. He invited her to an outdoor concert, and she agreed. As they enjoyed a relaxing evening with several of his friends, Dina had no idea that later that evening a much darker side of his personality would emerge."

Rainey paused and glared at the defense table, voice rising, "Dina couldn't have known that *this man* would lure her back to his home, ply her with drugs and alcohol and brutally rape her for his own pleasure." He punctuated the last sentence by repeatedly jabbing his finger in Sanstrom's direction.

"Time and again Dina begged him to stop, but he refused. When he'd finished, she gathered up what clothing she could find and slipped out of his house. At first, she hid in nearby woods, afraid he would come after her, drag her back and rape her again. Finally, she found a neighbor kind enough to call the police and sit with her until an ambulance arrived.

"Police officers knocked at Mr. Sanstrom's door and rang his doorbell repeatedly, yet he *refused* to answer. When they finally broke in, they found him *cowering* behind a locked bedroom door armed with an automatic pistol. They searched the rest of his house and his basement. There they found the bed to which he had tied Dina while assaulting her and threatening to kill her if she resisted or cried out for help."

Rainey raised an index finger for emphasis. "But resist she did. You will see pictures of bruises on her body and wrists where he tied her up. You'll hear graphic and disgusting testimony from those who treated her injuries. Dina's psychologist will describe how she spent months helping Dina recover from the trauma inflicted on her that night, trauma that brought back repressed memories of a similar brutalization she suffered at the tender age of thirteen. The defense will try to excuse this by saying Dina and the defendant were just *role* playing. This may have been a game for the defendant, but for Dina it was *not*. They'll bring up the fact that Dina and the defendant had consensual sex earlier in the evening. That is *completely* irrelevant. I assure you this last episode was anything but consensual, an outright case of *bondage and rape*."

"Nor is this," Rainey continued, "the first time this man has victimized an innocent young woman. You will hear testimony from another of his victims that he abused her as well."

Rainey stepped toward the jury box, lowering his tone, a look of concern clouding his countenance. "At times," he said, "I'm afraid you'll hear explicit descriptions of the defendant's depravities and perversions. For some of you it may seem too much to take. But make no mistake, ladies and gentlemen, this defendant is *not* on trial for having sex. Rape is *not* a crime of sex."

As he wheeled about, pointing at Sanstrom, again raising his voice, spit glistened at the corners of his mouth. "It is a *crime of violence*. Liam Sanstrom used his size and strength to take from Dina, against her will, what she would *not* give him voluntarily, his sole desire being to control and dominate her, to humiliate her in a way she'll never forget.

"Over time, this man's bestial nature has hardened to the point that he will *always* be a serious threat to society. He has *raped* before, and allowed to go free, will *rape* again. I am certain that by the end of this trial each of you will agree with me that we *must* separate him from other potential victims, that we must lock him away for the rest of his life. To do that you need only to find the accused, Liam Thorsten

Sanstrom, guilty as charged for the crimes of rape, sodomy, and aggravated assault."

As Rainey returned to his table a hush descended. Finally, Radford rose, appearing calm and composed. "Ladies and gentlemen," she began, "I'm sure every one of you found that story as disturbing as I did. What Mr. Rainey has described is every woman's worst nightmare. *If it were true*, even in the least, then there would be no doubt as to the outcome of this trial."

As she spoke Radford studied each juror. "What you *will* find, however, is that this story is full of holes, that there is more than one side to what transpired that night, that what began as an unfortunate misunderstanding rapidly escalated into disappointment, anger and vengeance, ultimately leading to these *patently* false charges.

"As Her Honor, Judge Gilmartin, has explained, the tale Mr. Rainey just spun is *not* sworn testimony. It is, at *best*, repeated hearsay. The prosecution *cannot* prove Liam guilty for the simple reason that *he isn't*. By the end of this trial, you will see that there remains *far more* than reasonable doubt."

Without turning to look she gestured at the opposing table. "For one thing, you'll hear conflicting testimony from the state's own witnesses. The prosecutor, Mr. Rainey, is quite aware of these inconsistencies, which is why he will introduce all manner of *irrelevant* evidence, the sole purpose of which is to confuse and prejudice you and cloud your judgement. Mr. Rainey's witnesses will include people who haven't the *remotest* credibility. You will meet *unbiased* witnesses for the defense, however, who will paint quite a different picture. Ms. Savage did *not* meet Liam by mere circumstance. You'll hear testimony from people who sat with Liam and his accuser that night that she was quite amorous, that she had quite a lot to drink and spoke openly of spending the weekend with him.

"Mr. Rainey has quite accurately described rape as a violent crime. But this is *not* a case of rape. It is a case of *defamation*, pure and simple. Men aren't the only ones who use sex to get what they want. As you will soon discover, Ms. Savage can become very angry and *very vindictive* when she can't have her way. When Liam and Ms. Savage left the concert that evening they went straight to his home where, *by her own admission*, they had consensual sex prior to the *alleged* assault. What Ms. Savage now tries to characterize as rape was, in fact, a fantasy game, a role play in which she *voluntarily* agreed to have Liam tie her up and *pretend* to rape her. Whatever you may think of such practices, they do *not* constitute assault for one simple reason. Ms. Savage *consciously and willingly participated* from beginning to end.

"Not until afterward, when Liam told her in full candor that he could not commit to a relationship, did she become angry and demand he take her home. In no shape to drive at that late hour, Liam did the only sensible and responsible thing. He offered to let her spend the night in his *guest* bedroom and would've driven her home in the morning. This conversation went on for some time. Then Ms. Savage stormed out, half-dressed. Liam called after her repeatedly before giving up and going to bed.

"Liam did *not* hear the police knocking at his front door for the simple reason he lay fast asleep. He hadn't *barricaded* himself in his bedroom. Why should he? He had no reason to suspect he'd be the victim of these scurrilous claims.

"Ladies and gentlemen, Liam sits before you today an innocent man unjustly accused. But for the grace of God, *his* fate could befall any of us. This is why our forefathers made it clear that the *government must prove* guilt beyond a *reasonable doubt*, something I promise you they *cannot* do.

"Already Liam's life is a shambles, and it is *he* who, in the end, must piece together his shattered reputation. I have no doubt that's *exactly* what he'll do. Liam is a man of strength and character. He has faced and overcome adversity in the past, and he will do so again when he walks out of this courtroom a free man. I am confident you will fairly and conscientiously carry out your sworn duties by exonerating him of these *unsubstantiated and specious* charges."

With that, Radford returned to her table.

* * *

"Mr. Rainey," asked the judge, "are you ready to call your first witness?"

"I am, Your Honor. The State calls Mr. Henry Massing." He shouted, as though the witness were somewhere downstairs.

A small, stoop-shouldered man tottered in with the help of a cane. When he finally took his seat, Rainey thanked him for his willingness to testify.

Massing scowled. "You sure took your sweet time. It's been almost two years. Why couldn't you have done this sooner? I always say *justice deferred is justice denied*."

Rainey gave the man a pained smile, and the judge admonished him to limit his responses to answering the questions.

"Mr. Massing," asked Rainey, "do you recall the events of that early Sunday morning, eighteen months ago, when you met Dina?"

"Of course, I do . . . I'm not senile."

"Could you recount for us what happened?"

The old man took a moment to compose himself. "I got up early, as always. I used to walk my cocker spaniel, Molly, every morning, before she passed away."

"Do you remember anything unusual about that morning?"

He took a deep breath, his voice softening. "Well, there came a knock on the door, and I answered it. I found a young lady there. She looked beat up, crying. Said she'd been raped. I invited her in. My wife Martha tried to console her while I dialed 911."

"So, you called the police right away?" asked Rainey.

"I called *911. They* sent the police and an ambulance."

On cross-examination Radford had two questions. "Mr. Massing, you said the *alleged* victim *looked beat up.* Did you actually see any bruises other than those on her wrists?"

"Well . . . no."

"While Ms. Savage was in your home you said she sat down?"

"Yes. As I recall she and Martha sat on the stairway while I went to the phone."

"Thank you, Mr. Massing. That's all, Your Honor."

The next witness, Cobb Police Sergeant Dave Landrum, had a light brown flat top and receding hairline, a deeply tanned face, and white ovals around his eyes shaped like aviator sunglasses. Tall and heavily built, he took the witness stand with the grace and ease of someone familiar with a courtroom.

Rainey picked a spot about eight feet in front of the jury box before turning to the witness. "Sergeant Landrum, I want you to recall for us the events of that Sunday morning, September 11, starting with the call you received from the home of Mr. Henry Massing."

Ramrod straight, the policeman leaned forward slightly, gazing not at the prosecutor, but at the jury, as he told his story. "I was on patrol in the vicinity of Paces Ferry Landing when I received a call to the residence at 2753 Morning Glory Circle. I arrived, joined by Officer Kim Kelly, also of the Cobb County Police."

"What did you find at the Massing home?"

"Mr. Massing met us at the door. He escorted us into his foyer where we met a woman who identified herself as Dina Savage. She said she'd been raped in a neighboring home by its owner, a Mr. Liam T. Sanstrom. While Officer Kelly interviewed Ms. Savage, I walked to Mr. Sanstrom's place, where I waited for backup. Officer Kelly and Detective Mark Samuels joined me there. Officer Kelly and I went around back to cover the rear exits. I took the deck and Officer Kelly stood outside the basement door. I heard Detective Samuels ring the doorbell and knock loudly several times, calling out to Mr. Sanstrom."

"Did you hear any answer from inside the house?"

"No sir."

"What did you do next?"

"Detective Samuels breached the front entrance while I pried open the sliding doors on the deck with a crowbar. Officer Kelly picked a lock and entered downstairs. We proceeded to search the house until we found Mr. Sanstrom hiding in a rear bedroom."

Radford jumped to her feet, like a pupil eager to answer a teacher's question. "Your Honor, I object. Unless the sergeant can see through walls he couldn't have known whether Liam was *hiding* or in bed sound asleep."

"Sustained . . . The witness will stick to what he knows."

Rainey asked, "Sergeant, could you tell us whether you found Mr. Sanstrom's bedroom door open or shut when you got there?"

"We found it shut."

"Did you knock on that door?"

"I did."

"Was there any response?"

"No sir."

"What did you do next?"

"I tried the handle."

"Were you able to open it?"

"No sir. I found it locked."

"And how did you get it open?"

"I stood back and kicked it."

"I see. Where did you find the defendant when you entered the room?"

"He was sitting up in bed naked."

"So, you placed him under arrest."

"Yes sir. I found a bathrobe for him. He put it on, and I handcuffed him and took him to the squad car."

Rainey turned to the bench. "That's all the questions I have for Sergeant Landrum, Your Honor."

Rising before Rainey had returned to his table, Radford asked, "Sergeant Landrum, when you arrested Liam, did he resist in any way?"

The witness hesitated. "No ma'am, he didn't."

"You said you found the bedroom door locked. Could you describe the type of lock it had?"

"I believe it had a standard residential passage lock."

"Did it look like this?" From a pasteboard box she pulled a doorknob assembly and approached the jury box, holding it up so the jurors could see it as she rotated the knob back and forth. With her back to the witness, she lowered the knob to one side and lightly flicked the button with her right index finger. Then she showed it to Landrum.

"I believe it might have looked like that," Landrum said.

"Your Honor, this is Defense Exhibit 1, already in evidence. It is, *in fact*, the doorknob to Liam's bedroom, the same one the witness says he had so much trouble unlocking. I'd like to ask Sergeant Landrum to examine it if I may."

The judge nodded, and Radford handed Landrum the knob. "I'd like you to show us how you tried to open the door with this knob," she said.

Eying it as though she'd handed him a gag present, Landrum gave the knob a vigorous twist. It didn't budge.

"Now, Sergeant, how difficult would it be for someone to accidentally lock this knob from the inside of the room . . ."

She never completed the question.

"Objection, Your Honor," said Rainey, "calls for speculation. Sergeant Landrum is not a locksmith."

"Sustained."

Radford set the knob on her table. For a moment it seemed she'd finished. Instead, she picked up a sheaf of papers and turned to an inside page.

"Sergeant Landrum," she asked, "you testified that you found Liam *sitting up in bed naked*. Is that correct?"

He gave the papers a look of recognition and blanched. "Yes ma'am. I . . . believe that's correct."

"You believe so? Are you sure?"

He paused. "Yes ma'am."

"Then why is it that, in your official crime scene report you said you found Liam asleep in his bed when you kicked in his door?"

Landrum hesitated.

Radford extended the paper toward him. "Would you like to read your report to us?"

He shook his head. "No ma'am. I'm sure that's what it says."

"Then please explain . . . were you telling the truth when you compiled the arrest report, or were you telling the truth just now, in this courtroom under oath?"

"It's, uh . . . been a couple of years. I guess I misremembered."

"I see. And what other details might you have *misremembered*?"

Rainey bounced up again. "Objection, Your Honor."

"Never mind, Your Honor. I withdraw the question," she said, turning back to the witness. "I have one more question, Sergeant. In your otherwise thorough search of Liam's home did you find any evidence of drugs?"

"He had plenty of time to . . ."

"Did you find any evidence of drugs?"

Landrum gave an embarrassed look. "No ma'am. I didn't."

"Your Honor, I've finished my cross-examination."

"Mr. Rainey," asked the judge, "would you like a redirect?"

"No thank you, Your Honor. My next witness is Officer Kim Kelly of the Cobb County Police."

As Landrum exited the courtroom, a short, muscularly built woman in a police uniform entered, her black hair pulled in a tight bun. She smiled at him as they passed.

Chapter Ten

Marietta, Georgia
Monday, March 18

As the bailiff administered the oath, Kelly sat erect, gazing straight ahead, as if she were standing at attention on a parade ground.

Rainey gave her a patronizing look as though expecting her to sell him a box of Girl Scout cookies. "Officer Kelly, how long have you been with the Police Department?"

"Twenty-seven months, sir."

"Thank you. Now, could you tell us what happened on that September morning, when you got to the home of Mr. and Mrs. Henry Massing?"

"Yes sir. Sergeant Landrum and I arrived at about the same time. While Sergeant Landrum took a statement from Mr. and Mrs. Massing I interviewed the victim, Ms. Dina Savage."

"Please summarize for us what Ms. Savage told you."

"She said she'd been to a concert, that afterward she and her date went to his home where he tied her to a bed and raped her."

"Did Ms. Savage name her assailant?"

"Yes sir. She identified him as Liam T. Sanstrom." As she spoke, Kelly gave Sanstrom a scalding glare.

"Did you notice anything unusual in Ms. Savage's appearance?"

"She had bruises on both wrists."

"Officer Kelly, I'm going to show you some pictures of Ms. Sanstrom taken at Kennestone Hospital and ask you if these are the bruises you're referring to."

Kelly studied the images and confirmed that they showed the bruises she'd described. Rainey then turned to the judge. "Your Honor, I'd like to allow the jurors to see the defendant's handiwork for themselves."

Through the disheveled hair and streaked mascara, Sax recognized the blonde he'd seen earlier in the corridor. Her outstretched arms revealed wrists wrapped in blue and purple bands, but he saw no other marks. As he started to pass the photos, he stopped for a closer look, seeing something out of character with the rest of the picture, a mixture of anger, sadness and perhaps a look of triumph in her eyes.

"Now Officer Kelly," asked Rainey, "what did you do after the ambulance left with Ms. Savage?"

"Sergeant Landrum and I proceeded to Mr. Sanstrom's home."

"And you were part of the entry team."

"Yes sir."

"Where did you enter Mr. Sanstrom's home?"

"The sliding glass door to his basement."

"And what did you find in Mr. Sanstrom's basement?" Rainey turned to the defense table with a smug look.

"Well, at first it was dark. I found a light switch and turned it on."

"What did you see?"

"I saw a single bed in the corner."

"Did you notice anything peculiar about the bed?"

"It had two long scarves sticking out beneath the mattress on either side. Each had a slip knot tied in the end."

"Is this the bed you're describing?" Rainey handed her two glossy photos.

Kelly cringed. "That's it."

"Your Honor, I'd like to give the jurors a chance to view these pictures also."

When they came to Sax, he noted the peculiar position of the bed frame, angled diagonally into the corner with two mattresses stacked neatly atop a box spring. A top sheet and blanket lay carefully folded on the floor, while the fitted sheet clung tightly to the bed.

Sax missed the prosecutor's next question as he studied the images, trying to imagine a man Sanstrom's size throwing a struggling victim onto the bed and jumping on top of her. Try as he might, he couldn't see how that could happen without pulling off the fitted sheet.

Rainey drew a pair of long scarves from an evidence bag. Handing them to the witness, he asked "Officer, are these the scarves you saw in the defendant's basement, the ones shown in the photos?"

"Yes sir."

He paced before the jury box, holding one of the scarves so the jurors could see them. In what seemed an absent-minded gesture, he ran his right hand through one of the loops, tugging so hard it pinched his fingers, turning them purple.

On cross, Radford requested the photos. "Officer Kelly," she asked, "Ms. Savage claimed that Liam picked her up, threw her onto *this* bed, pinned her down, bound her wrists and raped her. Is that true?"

"Yes ma'am."

"Did Ms. Savage mention anything about her ankles being tied?"

"No ma'am."

"Did you notice any bruising on her ankles?"

"No ma'am."

"Did you notice bruises anywhere else?"

"No ma'am."

"Now, as a police officer, I imagine you've, on occasion, taken physical descriptions of various people. Is that correct?"

Kelly gave her a blank look. "Yes ma'am . . . I guess so."

"Would that include approximate height and weight?"

"Yes ma'am."

"I'm going to ask Liam to stand up in a moment, and I want you to give me an estimate of how much he weighs."

Rainey shifted in his seat as though about to stand.

As Sanstrom stood, Sax noticed, for the first time, how tall he appeared.

"I don't know," answered Kelly. "Maybe 220 to 230 pounds."

"Very good, Officer. Liam actually weighs 222 pounds. And how much would you say his accuser, Ms. Savage, weighs?"

"Maybe 110."

Radford returned to her table and picked up a piece of paper. "According to her admission report at Kennestone, Ms. Savage weighed 117 pounds." She set the paper down. "Now, if my math serves me, that's a total of 339 pounds."

Kelly made no response. Radford let the implication dawn on the jurors.

"Now we've seen these two photos." She held them up for emphasis. "As you can see, the bed is pulled away from the wall. You'll also notice how neatly stacked the mattresses are and the fact that the fitted sheet is still on the bed. Does this look to you like a bed on which two people totaling 339 pounds . . ."?

Before she could finish, Rainey objected. "Your Honor, Ms. Radford is calling for speculation."

The judge pursed her lips, then sustained.

"One more question, Officer. In her sworn report, did Ms. Savage mention having *consensual* sex with Liam prior to the *alleged* rape?"

"Yes ma'am."

"How many times did she say she'd had sex with Liam?"

"Once."

Radford appeared startled. "Just once?"

"Yes ma'am. That's correct."

"Did she say where in the house they'd had the consensual sex?"

"In a guest bedroom."

"Did she mention ever entering the master bedroom?"

"No ma'am."

"Did *you* see any evidence she'd been in Liam's master bedroom?"

"No ma'am."

"Thank you, Officer. That'll be all."

The judge glanced at her watch and announced a one-hour recess for lunch. Again, she admonished the jurors not to discuss the case with anyone and to return to the jury room no later than one p.m.

The jurors filed out by a side door and down a short hallway. Retrieving their personal effects, they exited to the lobby and awaited an elevator. When it opened, Sax and the others squeezed aboard.

* * *

Colleen and Melanie stepped out for lunch at a beer and sandwich shop across the square opposite the courthouse. As they crossed Glover Park, a sudden cough overtook Colleen. It passed as quickly as it began but left her light-headed.

Melanie helped her to a low wall where Colleen sat for several minutes before getting back to her feet. In no time she'd put the episode behind her, despite Melanie's suggestion she have a doctor check her out.

Changing the subject, Melanie asked, "Radford seems to have handled Rainey quite nicely, don't you think?"

"Yeah, but she hasn't won yet."

Chapter Eleven

Marietta, Georgia
Monday, March 18

Sax returned by one p.m., as instructed. While waiting for trial to recommence, he pulled a report from his briefcase, stared at it and put it back, his mind returning to that morning's testimony.

He'd never understood why jurors deliberated so long, often acquitting defendants already convicted in the media. Now it seemed the prosecutor wanted to bias the jury with evidence unrelated to Sanstrom's guilt or innocence. For the first time, it dawned on Sax he might have to choose between sending a potentially innocent man to prison or putting a monster back on the street.

Moments later the bailiff announced the trial would resume. The jurors returned to find both attorneys, the defendant and judge already in their seats. Rainey called Detective Mark Samuels.

"Detective Samuels, could you tell us what happened the morning you arrested the defendant?"

"Well, I arrived at his home and went to the front door while Sergeant Landrum and Officer Kelly went around back to prevent Mr. Sanstrom's escape."

Radford objected, "Your Honor, why would Liam try to escape when, according to the police report, he lay in bed asleep?"

"Your Honor," Rainey countered, "Detective Samuels had no way of knowing, standing at the defendant's door, whether he was asleep or packing his bags."

"Objection overruled," the judge said, without looking at either attorney.

Samuels continued, "I rang the bell and pounded the door repeatedly. Finally, I took a sledgehammer and broke it down. Sergeant Landrum and I found Mr. Sanstrom in his bedroom. We placed him under arrest, read him his rights and allowed him to dress before taking him to the police station."

"I see. Who took Mr. Sanstrom in?"

"Sergeant Landrum . . . I stayed behind until crime scene technicians arrived."

"And while you were there, did you notice anything strange?"

"I saw a 9mm automatic pistol on top of Mr. Sanstrom's chest of drawers."

"Is this the weapon you found?" Rainey held up a clear evidence baggie containing a gun with its magazine missing and its slide fully retracted. A white tag hung from the trigger guard.

"Yes sir."

"Would you tell the court how you know this is the same weapon?"

"I had a crime tech photograph it on top of the chest of drawers before tagging it. He made a record of the serial number and sealed it in that evidence bag."

"Did you find anything else of interest in Mr. Sanstrom's home?"

"In the den I found a pair of women's panties." Samuels blushed as he spoke. "I photographed them as well, along with several other items. I carry a camera in my squad car for that purpose."

Rainey passed the photos to the jurors. In one, identified by Samuels as a shot of the den, a lace thong lay beside the couch in plain sight.

When Rainey had finished, Radford stood.

"Detective, I have here a copy of a crime scene report signed by you. If you'll look on Page Three, you'll see I've highlighted a particular finding you neglected to mention in your testimony. Would you care to read it for us?"

He took the paper, paused a moment and read. "The techs found what appeared to be fresh semen stains on the couch in the den."

"*In the den* . . . And you also found semen stains on the bed in the guest room. Is that right?"

"I did."

Sax recalled Officer Kelly testifying that Dina claimed she'd had sex with Sanstrom only once.

"The bed in the guest room, was that where you found Liam asleep?" Radford asked.

"Uh, no."

"In fact, you found him in the master bedroom, right?"

"Yes."

"Was there any evidence of sex in the bed where you found Liam asleep?"

"No."

"Did you find any of Ms. Savage's personal effects in Liam's bedroom?"

"No."

"So, as far as you know, she never entered Liam's bedroom."

"As far as I know."

Radford went to the table where the bag with the 9mm automatic lay. "Detective, you said you found this gun on top of a chest of drawers in Liam's bedroom, right?"

"Yes."

"Tell us the location of that chest in relation to the bed *where Liam lay asleep.*"

Samuels paused as though trying to remember.

"Maybe one of your *photos* will show us," Radford smirked.

"It was across the room from the bed."

"How far would you say that was?"

"About ten feet."

"Mr. Samuels, I had it measured. It's closer to twelve. When you found this gun *on the chest of drawers, twelve feet from the bed where Liam lay asleep*, did it contain any bullets?"

"Well, no . . . but he could have emptied it in a matter of seconds."

Radford gave him a look of utter contempt. "Detective, did you find 9mm cartridges *anywhere* in the room?"

"No."

"So let me get this straight." She paused as though carefully reconstructing from memory. "What I'm holding here is an *empty* weapon you found on the *opposite* side of the bedroom *twelve feet* from where *Liam lay asleep* when you arrived, a pistol that, for all you know, Liam's accuser *never saw* and had no idea he owned, because she never came into that room. Is that correct?"

Samuels sat in stony silence before answering, "Yes."

"One more question, Detective . . . As you searched Liam's home did you find any evidence of drugs?"

"No. I didn't. He could have . . . ."

"That'll be *all*, detective," she said, with a force that startled Sax. "Your Honor, I have no more questions for this witness."

Rainey then called Dr. Hyman Chen of Kennestone Hospital. The young physician appeared confident, almost cheerful, as he strode into the courtroom and took his oath. Yet he spoke in a voice so low the judge had to admonish him to speak up so the jury could hear him.

Rainey went through a series of questions establishing Chen's impressive credentials.

Chen said he'd been on duty the morning of September 11, when a Cobb EMT brought Dina into the emergency room reporting she'd been raped. He recounted in vivid detail, results of his pelvic examination, saying he found semen and signs of vaginal tearing. He also described bruises on Ms. Savage's wrists, consistent with ligature marks.

"Dr. Chen," asked the prosecutor, "did you run a blood toxicology screen on Ms. Savage?"

"I did."

"And what did you find?"

"She'd consumed a large quantity of alcohol and had traces of MDMA in her system."

"Is there a more common name for MDMA?"

"Ecstasy."

Rainey looked down for a moment and shook his head. "Might Ecstasy have clouded Dina's memory and judgment?"

"Certainly."

"To the point where she'd be unaware of her actions?"

Radford shifted in her seat as though ready to object but stopped.

"Yes," answered Chen.

"Thank you, Doctor Chen," said Rainey. Beaming, he turned to the defense table. "Your witness."

On cross-examination, Radford questioned Chen's experience with ligature bruises and asked if they could have resulted from some other cause, such as a fall.

The doctor gave her a condescending smile and said that the bruises he saw, in his professional opinion, could only have resulted from a forcible restraint, such as a knotted tie or scarf.

Radford asked if he had any idea how long the MDMA had been in Dina's body.

"Less than twenty-four hours."

"*Twenty-four hours?* So, she could have snorted it as much as a day earlier, perhaps Saturday morning or afternoon, before going to the concert?"

"It's possible, I suppose."

"Would you say you conducted a full examination of Ms. Savage, Dr. Chen?"

"Yes."

"And did you find bruises anywhere else?"

"No."

"So, as far as you know Ms. Savage had full, unrestrained use of her legs during this alleged rape."

His expression betrayed no emotion. "That's correct."

When questioned about the vaginal tearing Chen admitted it can sometimes result from consensual sex and doesn't necessarily indicate rape.

Sax glanced at the tattooed bartender, now seated beside him. In her notebook she'd written, "What a cunt! Somebody should tie her up, rape her, and see how she likes it." She'd underlined the word "cunt" three times.

On redirect, Chen reasserted his conclusion that someone had tied his patient by the wrists using a cloth material and raped her. Rainey turned to the jury with a look of satisfaction.

The afternoon's final witness, a thin, petite, conservatively dressed brunette took the witness stand without looking at Sanstrom or his attorney. She gave her name as Clarissa Smart. Sax guessed her age somewhere shy of thirty.

"Now Ms. Smart, could you tell the jury if you know or have *ever heard* of the victim in this case, Dina Savage?"

"No sir, I haven't."

"Do you think you might have met her somewhere?"

"I seriously doubt it."

"Why is that?"

"Because I live in Miami."

"I see." Rainey gave the jurors a confused look bordering on theatrical. "Well, do you know the defendant, Mr. Sanstrom?"

For the first time she turned to the defense table. "*I certainly do.*"

"Could you describe for the jury how you know Mr. Sanstrom?"

"Two years ago, I came to Atlanta on business. I met Mr. Sanstrom at an exhibit. We spoke after everyone else had left. He asked if I'd like to come to his house and see some more of his work."

"*To see some more of his work,*" the prosecutor repeated, arching one eyebrow. "What happened when you arrived at Mr. Sanstrom's abode?"

"Well, I'd had a fair amount of wine at the gallery, and when we got there he offered me a glass of cognac. I remember drinking the cognac, and then I must have blacked out. I awoke to find myself lying naked on a bed in his basement with my wrists tied down and him on top of me."

"*Who* was on top of you, Ms. Smart?"

Tears streaming down her face, she shouted, "*He was,*" pointing at Sanstrom.

"Please let the record show that the witness has indicated the defendant, Liam T. Sanstrom . . . What happened then, Ms. Smart? Take your time. I know this is difficult."

"I started screaming. I begged him *over and over* to stop, but he wouldn't. When he'd finished, he untied me. I got up, found my clothes and told him I wanted to leave. He wouldn't even take me home. I had to call Uber."

"Ms. Smart, did you report this incident to Cobb County Police?"

"No. I was hurt and embarrassed. I didn't want anyone to know. I went back to my hotel and returned to Miami the next day."

"Thank you, Ms. Smart." Rainey returned to his table.

"Ms. Radford," asked the judge, "do you wish to cross-examine?"

"I do, Your Honor. Ms. Smart, you said you had a fair amount to drink, and you don't remember all the events of that evening. Is that correct?"

"Yes."

"How much would you say you'd had?"

She paused for a moment as if trying to recall. "I had a few glasses of wine at the gallery and a glass of cognac at Liam's . . . Mr. Sanstrom's."

"Can you tell us exactly how many glasses you had before you blacked out?"

"No."

"Would you say enough to impair your memory?"

"I guess so."

"Do you recall using any recreational drugs with all that wine?"

"No."

"But you don't remember . . ."

"No."

"So, it's possible . . ."

Rainey objected and Gilmartin sustained.

"Ms. Smart," Radford continued, "you claim you have no memory of how you arrived in Liam's bed with no clothes on."

"That's correct."

"So as far as you know you might have disrobed willingly and en-gaged in consensual sex involving mock bondage."

Smart's eyes flashed. "I would *never* do that. It's demeaning and disgusting."

"Really?"

Radford walked back to the defense table and picked up two sheets of paper. "Ms. Smart, after that night, did you ever see Liam again?"

"No." She gave the papers a wary look.

"Ms. Smart, do you recognize either of these emails?"

With the judge's permission Radford handed them to the witness, who examined them, her face turning ashen.

Sax glanced at the prosecutor, who seemed preoccupied with his notepad.

"Now, I'm going to remind you again that you're under oath," Radford said gently. "Did you see Liam again after the night you just described?"

Smart continued staring at the emails.

"Your Honor," said Radford, "could you instruct the witness to answer my question?"

Before the judge could reply, Smart said, "Yes. I ran into him a couple of months later at an auction in New York."

"I see. Liam went to New York for an auction, and you just *happened* to be there. Didn't you spend the night with him on that occasion?"

Smart hung her head and sighed. "Yes."

"Did you have sex with Liam?"

"Yes."

"Did that sex involve S&M role playing?"

She stiffened. "*It did not*. I told him I wasn't interested. When he insisted, I got up and left."

"Okay. Ms. Smart, I want you to look at the emails I just handed you. Who wrote those emails?"

"I . . . I did."

"To whom did you send them?"

"Liam."

"You sent the first email about a week after your second date with Liam. Is that correct?"

"Yes."

"Could you read it to us?"

Smart began slowly. "My dearest Liam, I want to apologize for my abrupt departure the other evening. I was confused. I realize now you had no intention of hurting me. I felt uncomfortable with the things you wanted me to do. I'd like to meet you somewhere, next time you're in Miami, so we can talk this over. Please let me know a convenient time and place."

"I see. So, did you get back together for a third date?"

"Yes."

"Did you have sex on that occasion?"

"Yes."

"Did that sex include role playing and mock bondage?"

She pulled out a handkerchief to mop her tears. "I guess so."

"How did you feel afterward?"

Her face hardened. "I felt humiliated."

"When you engaged in this role play did Liam force himself on you?"

She replied in an inaudible whisper, and the judge asked her to speak louder.

"No," she said. "I don't suppose so. We were just pretending."

"If you felt humiliated, then why did you continue to contact him?"

"I guess . . . I wanted to be with him, and if *he* wanted to play games it would be okay as long as no one got hurt."

"*As long as no one got hurt* . . . Ms. Smart, in that second email, dated six months later, you asked Liam if you could spend the weekend with him at the very home where you claim he raped you. How did he respond?"

She began to sob. "He said we'd both made a mistake and he didn't want to see me anymore."

"Can you tell the jury how you felt then, especially after you changed your mind and went along with the role play?"

"I felt used." By now all emotion had drained away.

"You felt used. Did you feel so used and humiliated that you came here today to make false allegations against Liam?"

At this Rainey objected. The judge overruled.

"No. I did not." Smart's voice rose again.

"Ms. Smart, when did you first hear about Ms. Savage's allegations against Liam?"

"A few days after it happened . . . I read about it on the Internet."

"And you saw an opportunity for some retribution at Liam's expense?"

Rainey objected.

"Your Honor," said Radford, "I withdraw my question."

"Ms. Smart," Radford asked, "isn't it true that, shortly after this last email, you checked into a psychiatric hospital for evaluation?"

Rainey jumped to his feet. "Your Honor!"

"Ms. Radford," the judge said, "that is *enough*."

Radford smiled. "That's all I have, Your Honor."

Sax cast a sidelong glance at the defense table, catching a brief smirk on Sanstrom's face. *What a prick!*

After a long silence, Gilmartin asked Rainey if he had more witnesses.

"I have one more, Your Honor. I believe her testimony will take a couple of hours. If possible, I'd like to do it all in one sitting."

The judge consulted her watch. "I'm going to call a recess. The jurors need to be *back in the jury room by eight a.m. tomorrow*. Again, I remind you not to discuss this case among yourselves or with anyone else."

As he retrieved his briefcase from the jury room, Sax remembered his promise to meet with Cheryl and go over the paperwork from Simonton Duval. He called to say something had come up, that he'd call her in the morning. He struggled to put the day's testimony out of his mind, thankful the judge had recessed early. Tonight, he had an errand that demanded his full attention.

Chapter Twelve

Ron Dalrymple

Atlanta, Georgia
Monday, March 18

Ron Dalrymple ducked into a dimly lit pub on a Buckhead side street near Peachtree. Once the focal point of Atlanta's night life, the area had recently gone downhill.

Dalrymple frequented the place in its heyday, but the new owners had turned it into yet another seedy hangout for burned out losers with nowhere else to go. It had changed names so often Dalrymple lost track. Above the door hung a new sign advertising "Dan's Old Bar," the only part of the façade with a fresh coat of paint. Dalrymple found the place deserted but for a couple at the bar.

Standing in the doorway, he let his eyes adjust before spotting his latest client in a corner booth. He ordered a beer and casually made his way to her table, having exchanged the rumpled, brown suit for a blue polo shirt and loose-fitting jeans.

The pretty young blonde had arranged the rendezvous two days earlier by phone. Dalrymple didn't know her name but despite the ponytail and glasses, felt sure he'd seen her somewhere. He slid into the booth across from her and laid a large white envelope on the table. "They're all there, like you asked. I even got photos to match the names." He gave her an ingratiating smile, thinking this relationship might blossom into something else. "If you'd like, I can get a full background on them."

"That won't be necessary." She dropped the envelope into her purse and replaced it with an identical one. On closer inspection, an observer might've noticed it had grown thicker, three thousand dollars thicker, to be precise, all in twenties.

As she leaned across the table, Dalrymple caught the scent of her perfume. "In a few moments," she said, "I'm going to get up and walk out the front door." She slid him another twenty. "You will pay for my drink and wait at least twenty minutes before you leave. *Do not attempt to follow me.* Forget you ever met me or went anywhere near that courtroom today. Understood?"

Dalrymple, detecting something odd in her accent, nodded, trying not to stare at her ample cleavage and sheer lace bra.

As he glanced up he caught sight of a rear entrance which, he recalled, opened onto an alley beside the building. He stole a glance at her as she departed, left the twenty on the table and slipped out the back door, arriving out front just in time to see her climb into a black SUV with an unusual license plate. He memorized the number, went back inside and wrote it down on a paper napkin. Her instructions notwithstanding, Dalrymple intended to find out why she'd paid him so handsomely for so little work.

* * *

Dalrymple hadn't noticed the solidly built, mustachioed man seated at a booth near the door. Oleg Simonov, also known as Dirk Palme, nursed a neat Stoli with his left hand as he operated a small Go Pro hidden beneath a napkin. He'd pocketed the camera and left just ahead of the blonde.

* * *

An hour later Dina Savage and her date disembarked from his silver Bugatti at the entrance to Downtown Atlanta's Peachtree Plaza Hotel. Leaving the keys with a valet, they rode the glass elevator up seventy-two floors to the revolving Sundial Restaurant. There they enjoyed a panoramic view of the city, featuring a stunning sunset reflecting off of Stone Mountain in the east.

Dina sipped her Chardonnay and gazed into the candle-lit face of Pierce Flanders, whom she'd known for less than a month. They met at a sports bar she frequented near her office and discovered similar interests. Flanders and Dina had spent the past weekend at his houseboat on Lake Lanier and dined together four times in less than a week.

Flanders wore his blonde curls swept back in a pompadour and spoke with a soft Scottish burr. His olive-green Armani suit and Gucci shoes spoke of wealth and taste, a successful playboy with a hint of mystery about him. Dina watched him admire his reflection in the glass as he pushed a hair back into place.

Though, she knew little about the man, his explanations for his success seemed plausible, given their similar occupations. But his story of growing up in working class Edinburgh and attending the London School of Economics seemed too good to be true.

The soft buzz of his phone announced an incoming text, and he gave her an embarrassed look. "Sorry, my dear. This won't take long."

Dina smiled and assured him she didn't mind. As she took another sip she watched him tap in the code for his cell phone, 688791. After all these years she still had the gift and would remember that number for as long as she wished. For all she knew, it might come in handy.

Tonight, Flanders had reserved a room three floors below. They could drink as much as they liked and not have to worry about the drive home. That, Dina thought, could mean but one thing. He'd spend the rest of that evening banging her brains loose.

As they savored the cuisine Flanders inquired about Dina's past, saying he found her fascinating and wanted to know every minute detail.

She gave him evasive answers wherever possible and improvised as necessary, watching him slice his prime rib in the European style, fork held backward in his left hand and knife in his right. She could spend a lifetime with this man, collaborating on mutually profitable ventures. But never would she entertain the fantasies she'd had with Liam. Before she opened up to him, she'd find out more about him.

Shortly after Round Three in the sack, Flanders rose to use the bathroom. Unlike his previous trips, he closed the door this time.

Dina hopped out of bed and put her ear against the door, hearing him settle onto the toilet. Darting across the room to where he'd thrown his pants, she fished out his cell phone and tapped in the memorized code, attaching a small device she carried in her pocketbook. There she saw the photo of her spread out on his boat wearing her new bikini. She admired it as the progress bar crawled across the screen.

As the installation finished, she heard the toilet flush and water running in the sink. Returning the device to her pocketbook and the phone to his pants, she jumped back in bed just before the door opened. As Flanders climbed back on top of her she glanced at his trousers piled on the floor. Through the fabric she watched the LED wink out.

* * *

Jordan Oliver gazed in the restroom mirror as he shed his delivery uniform, shoved it into his book bag and changed into street clothes. At six-foot-two, he liked what he saw. He combed his blonde hair, sprayed himself with Axe and smiled, anticipating the evening before him.

As he reached for the back door of Pepper's Pizza, a loud knock startled him. He turned the knob to find Eric Saltzman, a sophomore half his size with raging acne and coke bottle glasses. Saltzman's black, wiry hair stood on end as he peered back.

"Thanks, Jordan," he said in his whiny voice. "I was afraid another storm might hit before I could get inside."

Jordan said nothing, shoving Saltzman as he stepped outside and let the door shut behind him. The earlier rain had cleared away, leaving the night air warm and humid. Ragged clouds streamed across the moonless sky, blocking the stars. The pizza joint's lone security light had burned out long ago, leaving Jordan to navigate toward his mom's minivan by sheer instinct.

He thought he heard something, like a boot heel grinding glass into the pavement. As he strained to listen more closely, lightning flashed. Quickening his pace, he wondered what had made him so jumpy.

He'd gotten over Misty Sax. If she wouldn't go down on him, then he'd find a girl who would. There were plenty who'd die for the opportunity to date a varsity quarterback, one of the most popular members of Walton's Junior Class.

Jordan's parents read him the riot act after police rousted them in the middle of the night. He couldn't believe they'd make such a big deal over a little slap on the face. Eventually they saw this for what it was . . . a lot of fuss over nothing. They brought in his dad's lawyer, a close friend of the juvenile judge, and in the end, Jordan walked out of the courtroom with little more than a stern warning. From now on he'd have to control his temper.

He'd phoned his parents from work saying he and his new girlfriend were going to Towne Centre. *Parents can be so gullible.* He had no intention of going to the mall. Instead, they'd find a deserted road near Lake Allatoona, and there she'd service his needs. If not he'd leave her there, as he'd done with Misty, and she could hitchhike home on I-75.

Halfway to the van, lightning flashed again, closer now.

A calm, deep voice called, "Jordan?"

Jordan jumped and turned to see a man covered in black motorcycle leathers with a matching helmet and gloves, his face invisible behind a tinted visor.

"Yeah, what do you want?" Jordan fought to suppress his mounting fear as he backed away. The man stood a couple inches shorter than him but thicker through the body. Jordan didn't like the fact that the man knew his name, or that he couldn't make out his face.

In his gloved hand he carried a dark cylinder, twenty inches long. When he whipped it downward, the retractable baton opened with barely a click.

Before Jordan could react, a steel pointed toe caught him in the groin. He let out a grunt as he collapsed to his knees. The baton came down on his right collar bone rendering the arm useless. Instinctively Jordan curled into a fetal position on the pavement, covering his face with his good hand, as shards of glass dug into his side.

The stranger calmly stepped around him and caught him on the right kneecap with the baton, breaking it with a loud snap. Shock gave way to excruciating pain, as Jordan let out a scream nobody heard. The man took his time. The baton came down again, more slowly this time, pressing against Jordan's throat so that he could barely breathe. Lightning flashed and then came the rain.

Jordan could smell the man's aftershave as his low, gravelly voice whispered in his ear. "I saw what you did to that little girl at the mall the other night. I want you to know I'll be watching. If you so much as go near her again or ever hit another girl, *I'll find you*, and I promise I won't be so gentle. *Understand?*"

Jordan wept but made no reply.

"I asked you a question, son. I suggest you answer it."

When Jordan replied he sounded like someone else, a ten-year-old kid submitting to a schoolyard bully. "Yeah, yeah, I understand," he choked.

"Good. Now you stay right there until I'm gone. Don't you dare move!"

The boy remained as still as possible, given his condition, and watched the stranger's boots walk around the dumpster. A moment later a motorcycle roared, rising to a crescendo and then fading into the night as quickly as the man had materialized. As Jordan lay, drenched, broken, bleeding, sobbing, the realization swept over him that he'd pissed his brand new jeans.

Thirty minutes later Eric Saltzman, on his way to the dumpster with a bag of garbage, spotted Jordan on the pavement. He knelt beside him and asked if a car had hit him.

* * *

Sax wheeled the borrowed motorcycle into a darkened rental unit in Sandy Springs. With great reluctance he'd dropped the retractable baton into a dumpster behind the Chic-fil-A on Johnson Ferry Road. The motorcycle and the garage belonged to Paxton Bailey, a fraternity brother to whom Sax had loaned ten thousand dollars a year earlier to cover his gambling debts.

Sax left the interior light off, fearing someone might see him. In the glow of a nearby streetlamp he shook off the black leathers, hung them in the corner and waited for the rain to slacken before dashing to his Miata.

As he dropped into the driver's seat, Sax remembered he hadn't turned on his cell when he left the courtroom more than five hours earlier. He'd missed three calls and a message from Cheryl.

"Sax, where the hell are you?" she demanded. "It's after eight and we need to go over those due diligence schedules."

The other calls, from Barbara and Misty, would wait. He'd phone them in the morning. He let out a deep breath, not believing what he'd done. The adrenalin subsided, and a cold shudder ran through him.

He waited until he got to the condo before calling Cheryl. The drive gave him time to concoct a good story as to why he hadn't called earlier.

She answered on the first ring. "Sax, where have you been?"

"I had a long call with Barbara and Misty," he lied.

"Are they okay?"

"Yeah, yeah, nothing serious . . ." He knew she wouldn't press him on a family matter but changed the subject anyway. "So, what was it you needed?"

"The due diligence stuff, but it's getting late. Will you be available tomorrow night?"

"Probably . . . Look, I'm sorry. I'll let you go. Text me if anything breaks. I'll call you in the morning on my way to the courthouse."

"Sure thing," she said. "Good night. Get some sleep."

* * *

A few miles away, at the Galleria office of Statham and Riley, a young woman trailed behind the cleaning crew as they crossed the lobby. She wore a baseball cap and heavy glasses. She glanced at the night security guard seated behind his desk watching a basketball game.

The rest of the crew got off on the second floor, but the stranger rode all the way to the top. Removing a stolen key card from her canvas bag, she accessed the suite and found Sara Radford's office unlocked. Though she wore latex cleaning gloves she took care not to touch anything. From experience she knew the slightest relocation of an object could tip off an occupant that they'd had an uninvited guest. Eventually they'd find out anyway, but she wanted to control the timing of that discovery.

She ignored the filing cabinets. Nowadays attorneys carried their most valuable information on their laptops. She found Radford's computer missing from its docking station, but her secretary's desk still had a tower. Seeing the photo of a toy poodle beside the monitor and a name emblazoned on a coffee mug, it took but a few keystrokes for the computer to boot up. Sure enough, the woman had used her dog's name as her password.

Inserting a thumb drive and clicking a command prompt, she gained full access to Sara Radford's files and correspondence. With no time to waste, she uploaded them to a cloud server temporarily commandeered for this purpose. She completed her work in twenty minutes and left. To avoid notice, she took a stairwell, exiting the building by a side door.

With light traffic Svetlana Argounova arrived at her Chamblee apartment in less than thirty minutes, keeping her vintage Volvo at the speed limit to avoid unwanted attention. She wondered, as she parked in a deserted corner and scanned the place, why anyone would call these *garden apartments*. They didn't remind her of any gardens she'd ever seen.

They served their purpose, though. These weren't the sort of neighbors who knocked on your door and introduced themselves. In a week or so, when Svetlana skipped on her lease, no one would remember what she looked like, not that her physical description would do the authorities any good.

Certain that no one had seen her, Svetlana made her way to the second floor landing. As she stepped inside the darkened living room, a gloved hand seized her from behind, clamping firmly across her mouth. A powerful right arm grabbed her by the waist, spun her around and pinned her against the wall.

Removing his hand from her mouth, Oleg asked, "What the fuck took you so long?" Kissing her hard on the lips, he pressed his body against her.

"What do you mean, asshole? I got in and out in no time!" she gasped. "What have you been up to?"

He felt harder than usual.

"Have you been on those porn sites again?"

He gave her a wounded look. "I've been working," he said in a thick Russian accent. "Our client wanted to discuss our latest findings. It took longer than expected. He is a very thorough man."

"So, what did you find?"

"I found that Ms. Dina and I share . . . *professional interests.*"

They ripped off each other's clothes and made love standing there.

Later, after removing her makeup, Svetlana showered, washing the dye from her hair and his scent from her body.

* * *

Oleg, meanwhile, pulled up the digital pictures he'd taken of Dalrymple and Svetlana at Dan's Old Bar. He considered emailing them to the police but decided to wait. Better to send them to Sanstrom's attorney anonymously. *How might she react?*

For now, he'd notify her of the break-in instead, using a phony email address routed through multiple servers. By morning, Radford and the police would be searching security images of Svetlana, images bearing an uncanny resemblance to Dina Savage.

Oleg went back over Dalrymple's list of jurors, stopping at DataScape Solutions CEO Jeffrey Sax. *A technology company.* Oleg perused the black-and-white photos Dalrymple provided until he found Sax. *My, my! What might I discover about this Mr. Sax and his DataScape Solutions? What would Dina look for?*

This time Oleg used the servers of Sven-Baud AB, subsidiary to Svenska Global Holdings, founded by Bjorn Sanstrom. The thought of implicating the old man brought a smile to his face. Moments later he'd wormed his way into DataScape's network. He discovered that Sax had fired his former VP of sales and marketing, Lance Barclay, for sexual harassment.

Oleg shook his head. *What is it with these Americans and their prudish attitudes about sex? So, what if a boss wanted to get a little poontang at the office?* It seemed to Oleg that such a fringe benefit might enhance productivity and employee retention.

Seeing that Sax had assigned IT Director Goldwyn Shah to scour Barclay's confiscated laptop for evidence of other misbehavior, Oleg had an inspiration. Locating the laptop's MAC address and static IP, he discovered that someone had left it logged onto the network. *If people are going to be so foolish, what can I do?*

As he commandeered Barclay's computer, Oleg crafted a plausible scenario in which Dina had met the hapless Barclay and exploited him for sensitive information about DataScape. Oleg changed the laptop's system date to three weeks earlier, opened it and transferred the photo Pierce Flanders took of Dina at Lake Lanier. For extra measure he created a Facebook account in Dina's name. Finding that too obvious, he deleted it and set up another under a *Lana Green*. Better that Dina should have an alias.

So far, Oleg's biggest disappointment was that he knew so little about Dina. Under different circumstances, they could've made quite a team.

He created a social media account for Barclay, and with a few clicks Barclay and Dina had embarked on a steamy relationship. For added measure Oleg sent an email from Barclay's new Facebook account to Ms. Green thanking her for their wonderful weekend and saying he hoped to see her again soon. In cyberspace, it seemed. Barclay could finally enjoy the office escapades Sax had so cruelly denied him.

With such fertile imagination, Oleg wondered why he hadn't become a novelist.

As he perused DataScape's other servers, he came upon a trove of customer data. *Why should Old Man Sanstrom care if I profit from this? What is he, a Bolshevik?*

Chapter Thirteen

Marietta, Georgia
Tuesday, March 19

Sax and Misty wandered among carnival rides, cotton candy stands and other attractions at the North Georgia State Fair. Barbara remained at home, for reasons Sax couldn't recall. The park echoed with squeals of roller coaster riders. Seven-year-old Misty clung to her father's hand, as instructed, until they came to the freak show.

"Daddy, Daddy," she pleaded, "Can I?" She gazed up at him, her face a brilliant mask of tiny freckles.

"Okay." He made her stand beside him as he purchased tickets, handing her one. Golden in the late autumn sunset, the tent swayed in a freshening breeze.

Gazing at the horizon, Sax saw it coming, a seemingly impenetrable wall of cloud. The wind rose, spinning dust devils about him. No one else seemed to notice as trash and debris swirled past. Banners, ripped from their moorings, took to the sky.

As he turned, Sax saw that the attraction had grown, engulfing the entire fair. The ticket-taker in his purple zoot suit and matching fedora leered at Misty. From somewhere in his past, Sax recalled the words to an old poem.

". . . and the little lame balloon man whistles far and wee . . ."

Struggling to catch up to his daughter, he tried to run, but his feet wouldn't move. Deep in the darkening halls he glimpsed her rounding a corner, her red curls lifted by the wind. Again, he tried to run . . . Suddenly, something loud and shrill sounding pierced the evening, perhaps a tornado siren.

Sax awoke to the insistent ringing of his bedside phone, his legs tangled in sheets. He glanced at the alarm, realizing he'd overslept. Freeing himself, he answered.

Without preamble Barbara said, "Tell me you had nothing to do with the attack on Jordan Oliver last night."

"Look, I can't talk now."

"Sax, the police were just here."

"*I can't talk.* I overslept and I'll be late for the trial."

He hung up before she could reply, showered, dressed and jumped into his car, praying he didn't get a speeding ticket on his way to Marietta, his mind returning to the weird dream. *What the hell did it mean?*

At the intersection of Roswell and Providence Road, he watched a yellow school bus full of teenagers make the left turn toward Walton High School, wondering if it carried his daughter. Then his mind shifted to the Sanstrom trial.

* * *

The long line of buses rolled to a stop. As Misty grabbed her books, a classmate said something, which she ignored. Stepping down onto the pavement, she gazed across the parking lot in time to see a blue pickup stop near the entrance. She recognized it even before she read the words "Oliver Landscaping" in white letters on the passenger side.

The door opened, and Jordan stepped out, resting gingerly on one foot. He slung his book bag onto his good shoulder before shifting his weight onto a pair of crutches, as best he could with one arm in a sling. Fresh bruises covered one side of his face and a bandage engulfed his nose. He winced with every step.

He glanced at Misty and their eyes locked, hers morphing from shock to regret, perhaps guilt, though she didn't know why. He stared back, smoldering with hatred. In that moment, without a word, they both knew.

As Jordan turned and hobbled off to his class, Misty ran to hers, anxious to avoid speaking with anyone.

* * *

Sax arrived just as the jurors filed into the courtroom, remembering too late that he'd promised to call Cheryl.

"You're pushing your luck, Mr. Sax," said the bailiff. We were about to come looking for you, and *that would not have been pleasant.*"

In the courtroom the judge, already at her bench, glowered at Sax over her reading glasses but said nothing. Opposing counsels sat at their respective tables, Radford deep in conversation with Sanstrom. Rainey, meanwhile, conversed with the attorney Sax had seen escorting the beautiful blonde the day before.

* * *

On her way to the courthouse to meet with the prosecutor and her personal attorney, Dina stopped by her office to submit a report she'd compiled.

She'd left Flanders snoring in his room at the Peachtree Plaza, a brief note beside his bed promising to call him later. Thinking back on the previous evening, a warm feeling came over her. She had to admit she enjoyed being with the man, though she knew so little about him. Accessing the spyware she'd loaded on his phone, she found him engaged in conversation. She had to leave now, but within hours she'd know a great deal more.

As she closed her laptop, Dina's thoughts returned to the trial. Rainey had asked her to get there an hour early, though he might not call her to the stand until after lunch. Driving north from Midtown Atlanta, she opted to leave the top up on her Alfa despite the beautiful weather, not wishing to testify with her hair askew.

* * *

Sax shifted in the jury box as the prosecutor called Elizabeth Strong, an Emory University psychiatrist specializing in assault-related trauma. After establishing her credentials, Rainey took her through details of her interviews with Dina. She described the long-term, devastating physical and emotional effects of Rape Trauma Syndrome, which she compared to Post Traumatic Stress Disorder.

On cross-examination, Radford did little more than question the witness' certainty as to her conclusions.

Next up, a gynecologist described, in graphic detail, the damage she'd found inside Dina's vagina. When questioned by Radford, she admitted the scarring could have happened much earlier.

Finally, Rainey produced a former colleague from Moore and Frye who recounted conversations with Dina regarding her experience. Radford objected to this as hearsay, and the judge struck the testimony.

As he finished, Rainey said he had one remaining witness whose testimony would take a a while, and the judge called a recess.

* * *

On his way to lunch, Sax checked his voice mails. Seeing one from Cheryl, he punched the play button.

"Sax, you're starting to worry me. You were going to call me this morning, remember? Look, I need to speak with you right away. Goldwyn just came into my office and said someone hacked our servers last night. He doesn't think they damaged or stole anything, but he's trying to trace it back to the source. Whoever this is really knows what he's doing . . . Call me."

"What's this about a security breach?" Sax asked when she answered.

"An unauthorized user hit our client servers. Goldwyn can't figure out who, but they seem to have gotten in through Lance's laptop."

"*Lance's laptop?*" Sax shouted.

"Yep. It seems one of Goldwyn's team, the one who ran the virus scan, left Lance's computer logged on."

"Ah shit!" Sax exclaimed, pacing the sidewalk outside a café. "And nothing's missing or contaminated?"

"As far as we can tell."

"Ah shit! If this gets out, we're ruined."

"Should we let the buyers know?"

Sax pondered. "We have to, but first, Goldwyn needs to search everything. I don't want to tell them one thing now and something else later. Wait until tomorrow, *then* we'll contact them. We'll also need to call the police."

"Okay," said Cheryl. "Do you think they were after credit cards?"

"Could be. Fortunately, they're on a separate server."

"Do you think it might have been Lance?"

Sax scoffed. "He wouldn't know how to do something like this . . . But still, have Goldwyn take a look. I want to know everyone Lance emailed and every file he sent or received in the past month."

"Sure."

"Do you have anything else?"

"Yes."

Cheryl walked him through the additional paperwork Simonton Duval had requested, and Sax said he'd come by the next day to sign it.

* * *

Crossing the courthouse lobby, Radford picked up a text from her boss, Managing Partner Herb Riley. She punched his number.

"Sara," said Riley, "Trey Anderson came by my office this morning and said he'd received an email about spyware on Valerie Jansen's desktop."

"Did he say who sent it?"

"It seems to have come from a bogus Gmail account, but Trey's seeing if he can trace it. Meanwhile, I had him check Valerie's computer. Sure enough, there it was, loaded last night around eleven p.m. We're not sure how it got there, but Valerie swears she logged off yesterday before leaving, as she always does. I contacted security. They have video of an unidentified Caucasian female disguised as a member of the janitorial crew. Our own cameras show her booting up Valerie's computer. She looked to be in her twenties or thirties with long, blonde hair. Trey says the spyware captures and transmits emails."

Radford's mind had already raced to the obvious conclusion. "Did you get a good look at the woman's face?"

"No. She kept her head down the whole time, but she had a blonde ponytail sticking out from the back of her cap."

"I need a copy of that video ASAP. If our intruder resembles Dina Savage, even remotely, I'm sure the judge will find this *most interesting*. In fact, if Trey could print out some still shots and send them to me right now, I'd appreciate it."

"Okay."

Chapter Fourteen

Horace Rainey

Marietta, Georgia
Tuesday, March 19

As the jurors and attorneys returned from lunch, the prosecutor announced, "Your Honor, the State calls Ms. Dina Savage."

Every head in the courtroom turned to see Sanstrom's victim enter, stunning in a canary yellow blouse, navy blue skirt and pearls, her shoulder-length hair tucked behind one ear. As she brushed back an errant lock with her left hand, her sleeve rose, revealing a multi-colored butterfly tattoo.

"Ms. Savage," Rainey began, "is it okay if I call you Dina?"

"Certainly." She spoke without inflection, her voice calm, but clear enough for anyone in the room to hear.

"First of all, please tell us what kind of work you do."

"I'm a market research analyst for the firm of Moore and Frye."

"What exactly does a market research analyst do?"

She paused, as though parsing her words. "I gather financial, sales, personnel and operational information about our clients' potential customers and competitors. Then I prepare reports explaining what I've found."

Rainey started to ask his next question, stopped and reconsidered. "What skills and experience does this work demand?"

"Basic computer knowledge and an understanding of corporate accounting, finance and management strategies."

"What degrees do you hold, Ms. Savage?"

"I have a Bachelor of Science in software engineering from Case Western Reserve University and an MBA from Harvard."

Rainey turned to the jury, eyebrows raised, then glanced at his notes before continuing. "Now, Dina," he said, his voice softening, "I know this has been painful, but I need you to recount, in your own words, the events leading up to, and including your date with the defendant, Mr. Sanstrom."

Rainey handed Dina a cup of water. She paused for a sip. "I met the defendant at an art showing in Roswell. He introduced himself and told me he'd painted several of the pieces on display. We had a long, pleasant conversation. As I started to leave he invited me to his house to see some more of his paintings."

"He'd just met you, and he asked you over to *see his paintings*." Rainey made air quotes with his finger as he spoke. "Did you take him up on this proposition?"

"No. I told him I'd had a long day and needed to go home. He then asked if I'd join him and his friends at the Harry Connick concert that following Saturday."

"And what did you say?"

"I thought about it and said yes. I'm a huge Connick fan."

"How did you get to Chastain?"

"Liam . . . Mr. Sanstrom came by my condo and picked me up."

"Tell us about the concert."

"We enjoyed it. We sat at a table near the stage with four other people."

"And what happened afterward, when the concert ended?"

"He took me to his place. We'd both had a great deal to drink. He offered me cognac . . ." Dina paused, stared at her hands folded in her lap, and sighed. "And then he talked me into snorting some white powder."

"Dina, did he tell you what this powder contained?"

"Afterward. He said it was Ecstasy."

"Had you snorted Ecstasy before?"

"No."

"So, you'd had a lot of alcohol . . . and then you snorted Ecstasy. Thinking back now, would you say you'd had enough to impair your judgment?"

"Yes."

"Just so we're clear, who provided you the drugs and alcohol?"

She pulled a tissue from her purse and wiped her eyes, for the first time staring at the defense table. Fixing Sanstrom in an icy gaze, she pointed. "He did," she snarled.

"Let the record show that the witness is indicating that the defendant plied her with illegal drugs and alcohol on the night in question," said Rainey. "Dina, I *have* to ask you this. Did you have consensual sex with the defendant that evening?"

"I did."

"How many times?"

Her voice choked. "I can't recall clearly, but I believe only once, in an upstairs bedroom."

"After that, did he want sex again?"

"Yes. But I told him I was tired and wanted him to take me home."

"How did the defendant respond?"

"He refused. He said I could sleep in his guest room if I wanted, and he'd take me home in the morning."

"Did you sleep in his guest room?"

"No. I asked him again and again to take me home. He finally agreed."

"Did he take you home?"

She began to sob. "No. He . . . he took me downstairs to his basement. He said he had something he wanted me to see. When we got there I saw a single bed with scarves pushed up under the top mattress. He told me he wanted to play a game. He wanted to tie me up and pretend to rape me. He said he'd be gentle."

"Did you agree to this?"

"*No! I did not!*" she screamed. "*I refused.*" She covered her face with her hands.

"Take your time, Dina. You're doing fine." He paused, offering her some water. "Now, tell us what he did when you refused to let him tie you up."

"Before I could move, he picked me up, threw me on the bed and jumped on me. When I started to scream he stuffed a handkerchief in my mouth. I bit down on his finger, but he crammed it deeper and deeper. Then he pinned my wrists with his knees and tied the scarves around them. I continued to fight him," she choked, "as he tore off my blouse and skirt, pulled down his pants and pushed himself inside me. Through the gag I pleaded for him to stop, but he wouldn't."

Perking up, Radford leaned forward, clinging to every word.

Burying her face again, Dina said, "When he'd finished, he left me there and went upstairs without a word." She shivered as she stared at the defense table. "After a while I worked the scarves loose and put on my clothes. I looked around for my underwear but couldn't find them."

"What did you do then?" asked Rainey.

"I didn't know where he'd gone and feared he might come back and kill me . . . that look on his face . . . like he was crazy. I ran out of the house and down the street. I saw a light on at the corner house and knocked. A nice man and his wife invited me inside and called 911."

She then described what little she remembered of her police interview and her trip to Kennestone.

Rainey concluded with a single question. "Dina, I wonder if you could describe how you felt after this experience."

She looked down and shook her head before turning to face the jury. "I felt damaged," she said, "humiliated, used."

As she spoke she made eye contact with each of the twelve strangers, stopping when she came to the lone Black male on the second row. "I grew up in a Mississippi trailer park," she said, "raised by a single mom, abused, neglected and mistreated by everyone in that community. I escaped, worked hard, got a college education and built a career, because I believed in myself. I knew I was *not* someone's toy, but a human being with dreams." Her voice faltered as tears flowed. "That man over there," she pointed at Sanstrom without looking at him, "tried to take all that away from me. He used me and used my body and then threw me away like a piece of garbage."

Rainey nodded. As he'd coached her, Dina focused on Carlton Beasley, who sat motionless, his expression impassive, eyes wet with empathy. Rainey quietly returned to his table.

Radford rose, approaching Dina, as a cat might stalk a bird. "Ms. Savage, you've testified that the events of that evening were . . ." She stopped to consult her notepad. ". . . a blur. And yet you gave graphic and detailed descriptions of your alleged rape. It seems you have a convenient . . ."

On his feet in a flash, Rainey shouted, "Objection, Your Honor."

"*Sustained,*" said the judge. "Ms. Radford, ask the questions and save your judgments for your closing statement."

Radford continued, "When you went down into Liam's basement with him, what were you wearing?"

Dina paused as though struggling to remember. "I wore a white cotton blouse and a tan skirt."

"Were you wearing shoes or were you barefooted?"

"I wore sandals."

"Now, according to your story, Liam picked you up and threw you on the bed. You say he managed to bind your wrists against your will, even as you thrashed around. Were you still dressed at this point?"

"At first I was," she said, her voice cold. "Then he tore my clothes off and raped me."

Rainey leaned forward, squinting at Dina.

"He tore off your blouse and skirt?"

"Yes."

"And removed your sandals?"

"I . . . I imagine so."

"And, all the while, you were trying to fend him off?"

"Yes."

"You were kicking at him?"

"Yes."

"Do you recall exactly what damage he did to your blouse or your skirt?"

Dina paused, answering now with less conviction, "I'm pretty sure he popped the buttons off of my blouse and may have torn it."

Radford beamed. "Was that the same blouse you wore when you went to the Massing's home and asked them to call the police?"

"Yes."

"The same blouse you wore to the hospital?"

"Yes."

"The same blouse that from that time until this morning has sat sealed in an evidence bag in police custody?"

Dina gave her a wary look. "Yes."

Radford strode to the table on which lay the evidence bag. From it she slid a blouse and held it up so Dina and the jurors could see it.

Rainey willed his heartbeat to slow and scribbled notes to hide his mounting anxiety.

"Ms. Savage," Radford asked, "would you point out, for everyone's benefit, the torn fabric and missing buttons?"

Dina froze, stammering, "I . . . I don't know. Maybe he didn't damage my clothes. It's been eighteen months since that night."

Radford picked up the skirt and the sandals. "Can you point out any other damage?"

Dina stared, her mouth opening and closing like a fish flopping on a dock.

"Do you see any damage, Ms. Savage?"

Closing her eyes, she answered, "No."

"But you testified under oath that you wore *these* clothes when you had sex with Liam in his basement."

Dina's eyes flashed. *"We did not have sex. He raped me. What part of that do you not understand?"*

"That'll be enough, Ms. Savage," said the judge. "Please answer the questions."

Dina glowered at Radford.

"Ms. Savage," asked Radford, "who removed your clothes?"

"He did." Again, she pointed at Sanstrom.

"Ms. Savage, you testified you'd had wine and cognac and snorted Ecstasy that evening. Did Liam force you or otherwise coerce you into doing this?"

Dina looked at Rainey as though seeking support. "No."

"You've described in great detail the events you say occurred in Liam's basement. Are you sure all that Ecstasy didn't cloud your memory?"

Rainey objected.

"Your Honor," countered Radford, "I'm following up on testimony Mr. Rainey introduced. It has a direct bearing on this case."

Judge Gilmartin paused. "I'm going to overrule the objection, Ms. Radford, but please get through this."

"I will, Your Honor." She repeated the question.

"*I was raped*," said Dina. "I remember it as clearly as if it just happened. I see him every night in my sleep." She stared wildly at Sanstrom as though seeing an apparition. Her voice morphed into a Southern drawl, "Every time I think about that lowlife redneck I smell his whisky breath, and I feel the pain of him inside me." She caught herself, as though suddenly aware of the sea of stunned faces. It seemed that whatever vision had materialized had just as quickly vanished.

The courtroom reacted in stunned silence. Rainey exhaled slowly, as Radford appeared to have forgotten her next question. She shook her head and gave the jury a perplexed look.

"Ms. Savage, you say he bound your wrists. Is that correct?"

"Yes."

"What about your feet? Did he tie them also?"

"No."

"No. In fact, there were only two scarves in the picture we saw."

Rainey shifted his gaze from Radford to Dina.

"So, your feet were free?" Radford asked.

"Yes."

"Ms. Savage, do you know a Mr. Kim Young Sun?"

"Yes."

"Can you tell us how you know him?"

"He's a Tae Kwon Do instructor."

"Isn't it true you're one of his students?"

"Yes."

"And what does *Tae Kwon Do* mean?"

"Hand and foot fighting."

"How long have you studied Tae Kwon Do?"

"Three years."

"What belt are you, Ms. Savage?"

"A black belt."

"In fact, you're a third degree black belt. Isn't that correct?"

"Yes."

"Did you have to pass an exam for this *third degree black belt*?"

"Yes."

"And did it involve breaking boards three inches thick with your foot?"

"Yes."

"And yet, with both feet free you couldn't manage to fight off a man preoccupied with binding your wrists and removing your clothes, removing them so carefully, in fact, they remained undamaged?"

"It's not the same thing," Dina pleaded. "I was drugged and afraid for my life."

Radford feigned surprise. "Did Liam threaten you as you had sex with him?"

"Repeatedly . . . He said if I didn't cooperate he'd kill me."

"And yet, when you had finished you want us to believe he allowed you to get dressed and leave the house?"

Rainey had had enough. "*Objection!*" he exploded. "Your Honor, Ms. Radford is badgering the witness."

"I withdraw the question, Your Honor. That's all I have."

"Mr. Rainey," asked the judge, "Do you have any more witnesses?"

"No, Your Honor, the prosecution rests."

"Ms. Radford, are you ready with your defense?"

Rainey turned as a young man entered the courtroom and, reaching across the rail, placed a manila envelope on the defense table. Radford opened it, removing several black-and-white photos.

The judge repeated her question. "Ms. Radford, is the defense ready?"

Looking up, Radford answered. "We are, Your Honor, but I anticipate a lengthy testimony from my first witness and request a recess until tomorrow morning . . . Also, Your Honor, I'd like to approach the bench if you don't mind."

"Okay. It's after 4:30. She turned to the jurors. "Please be here *promptly* tomorrow morning at eight."

Banging her gavel, she said, "Ms. Radford . . . Mr. Rainey . . ."

* * *

In her chambers, Gilmartin removed her robe, settled in behind her desk and removed her shoes before asking, "So, tell me counselor, what earth-shattering revelation you have that can't wait until tomorrow."

Radford handed her the envelope. "Your Honor, my office received several pictures last night, attached to an email, copies of which I have here."

A grainy shot showed a young woman, wearing glasses and a baseball cap, crossing a lobby with a plastic carry-all filled with cleaning supplies. In another she knelt beside a desk, holding a thumb drive and examining a computer. A yellow sticky note read, "Savage?"

"These images, Your Honor, came from the offices of Statham and Riley and the lobby of our building. The firm's IT manager has verified that someone breached our network."

Gilmartin examined the pictures before passing them to Rainey.

"Your Honor," said Rainey. "I can't tell who the woman is." His eyes narrowed as he spoke.

"But," added Radford, "there *is* a remarkable resemblance to Ms. Savage."

"Now wait a minute . . ." said Rainey.

"I can't tell either, Mr. Rainey," said the judge. "I don't want to jump to conclusions, but I find this very disturbing. Ms. Radford, I'll speak with the Cobb police chief personally. If I find out this break-in has anything to do with this case . . ." She glared at the prosecutor. ". . . I will have no mercy on the responsible parties. Understood?"

Blood rushing to his face, Rainey stammered, "Your Honor, I assure you . . ."

The judge raised a hand to silence him. "I'll look forward to hearing what the police have to say. In the meantime, Ms. Radford, this is *not* evidence in this trial, and I will *not* admit it."

"I understand, Your Honor."

Rainey returned to his table, stuffed his papers into his briefcase, pulled out his cell phone and dialed Dina's personal attorney. *If I lose this case due to her shenanigans, I'll arrest her myself.*

Chapter Fifteen

Marietta, Georgia
Tuesday, March 19

Exhausted, Sax climbed into his Miata, lowered the roof and headed home, relishing the cool breeze on his face. On the radio a local reporter announced, "A Cobb County jury today heard more testimony . . ." Sax switched to a Classic Rock station playing Bob Seger's *Night Moves*.

He arrived at the condo to find a Cobb Police cruiser and a blue F150 pickup parked out front. In the street stood two cops engaged in animated conversation with a middle-aged man in a blue work shirt and chinos. Sax recognized Officers Clark and Daniels, who'd interviewed his family following Barbara's 911 call. No sooner had he pulled into the garage than his doorbell rang.

"Mr. Sax, I need to ask you a couple of questions," said Clark. "Where were you last night about nine p.m.?"

Daniels remained in the street in a face-off with the other man. "Mr. Oliver," he said. "I told you to get back in your truck. If you don't, I'll have to take you into custody."

Scott Oliver had the look of an ex-jock, mid-fifties, wavy blonde hair going gray. He stood more than six feet tall and had at least eighty pounds on Sax, most of it gone soft around his middle. They locked eyes like two alpha males in a kennel, neither of them wavering. Clark stepped between them to block Sax's view.

"I was here all night," Sax lied.

"Can anyone verify that?"

"I don't think so. As you can see, I live alone." He shifted for a look at Daniels and Oliver. "What's this all about?"

"Someone attacked Jordan Oliver last night, a man he described as about your size."

"Is he okay?" Sax asked, feigning a sudden concern.

"As well as you might expect with a busted kneecap and broken collar bone. Mr. Sax, do you own a motorcycle?"

"No, I don't."

"Do you mind if I look in your garage?"

Sax hesitated for a heartbeat and gave the officer a confused look. "No . . . That'll be fine. We can come through here."

Seeing no motorcycle, Clark thanked Sax and apologized for any inconvenience.

Sax assured him he didn't mind, adding, "I hope you catch whoever did it."

By now, Oliver had left, but Sax knew he'd return.

As he scanned his sparsely furnished residence, Sax studied a small picture on a table beside the sofa, a shot of Misty at her Bat Mitzvah. How long had it been since he'd seen her smile like that?

Overwhelmed by a profound shame, Sax imagined the rage Scott Oliver must have felt. He closed his eyes, massaging them with his fingertips. *What the hell was I thinking? The boy deserved a beating, but not like that. What sort of man have I become?*

Then he remembered the call from Barbara that morning. As he reached for the phone it rang.

"Okay," she began, sounding calmer now, "I'm going to tell you how I feel about this, and you don't need to say a word. First, I want to you to know I find it noble, but more than a bit *frightening*, that you would go to such lengths to defend our daughter. I never would have expected this from you, Sax. Part of me is glad you did. The rest is thankful you didn't kill the little shit."

Sax said nothing.

"Look, I can only imagine what you're going through with this buy-out and your jury duty. I want you to know that, despite everything we've been through, I . . . I'm proud of you."

For a moment he thought she'd say, "I still love you." Sax didn't know what to make of this.

"You mean a lot to me, Sax. Don't you *ever* do anything like this again. You have far too much to lose, and you might not be so lucky next time."

Taking a deep breath, she added, "If you have time this weekend, why don't we meet somewhere, perhaps Starbucks. We can get a cup of coffee. We don't have to talk about any of this. You can tell me how your week went, and I'll tell you about mine. Okay?"

"Okay."

Sax heard what sounded like a muffled sob.

"Yeah. That would be great," he added, "Maybe we could meet somewhere for lunch."

After a long pause, she said, "Sure."

"I'll call you."

"Okay." She hung up without a goodbye.

As Sax returned the phone to its cradle, it rang again. He looked at the caller ID, groaned, and picked up the receiver.

"Hi, Mom," he said, trying to sound pleased.

"Hello, Jeffrey. I'm surprised you remember me."

"Mom, please don't start. It's been a long week."

"So, you're too busy to call your mother, Mr. Hotshot Business Mogul?"

"You know I'm selling the business, Mom. And on top of that, I've been on jury duty."

Her tone shifted abruptly. "Are you on that child molester case in Marietta, the one with that pervert priest? I saw it on the news."

"No, Mom. I'm on another case."

"The artist who raped that girl?"

Sax let out a long sigh. He heard her cover the phone as she shouted, "Myron, Jeffrey's on the jury in that rape case, the one with the artist."

"The what?" his dad yelled, sounding as though he were in another room.

"The rape trial with the artist!" she screamed.

Sax heard a muffled response as she returned to the phone. "So, tell me about it."

"Mom, I can't talk about it."

"Not even to your own mother?"

He wanted to say *especially not to my mother* but resisted. "No, Mom. I can't talk about it until it's over."

"So, when will it be over?"

"I have no idea . . . hopefully this week." He immediately regretted saying this.

"Good. Then you can come over for supper Saturday night. I'll cook a brisket."

"I'll have to see."

She waited a moment, before asking, "So how are you doing living alone?" Another subject he didn't wish to discuss.

"I'm okay, Mom."

"I tell you, that woman doesn't deserve you."

"Mom, will you lay off Barbara?"

"So how is my granddaughter these days? She doesn't call me either."

"She's doing fine," Sax lied. "She's been very busy with her home-work." He couldn't believe how lame he sounded.

"Well, she needs to spend more time with you and her grandparents. Maybe she can go to temple with us. When was the last time either of you went?"

Sax ignored the question. "I'll have to see, Mom." Before she could speak again he added, "Look, it's late and I've had a long day. Maybe I can call you tomorrow."

"Sure . . . fine. I'll wait by the phone. It's not like I have anything else to do."

Sax hung up.

Despite the early hour, Sax brushed his teeth and went to bed with a new Daniel Silva novel he'd picked up at the library.

* * *

Colleen arrived home tired from a long day. Desirous of some fresh air, she accompanied Tom on his evening walk with Bogie. As they strolled their neighborhood streets, fingers intertwined, Bogie sprinted about on his retractable leash, checking out the latest smells. In her other hand, Colleen carried a plastic grocery bag in case he decided to leave a gift on someone's new mowed lawn.

"So, tell me," Tom asked. "How's the trial going?"

Colleen stared at him in astonishment. "How did you know . . .?"

"That you were playing hooky this morning?" He smiled in smug satisfaction. "After all these years, Colleen Williams, you know better than to think I'd reveal my sources."

"Yeah, right! You spoke to Beth." Beth Franco had been Colleen's personal secretary more than five years. "I'll need to counsel her on the nature of confidentiality."

"I also spoke to Mitch earlier. He said he saw you there. He told me the TV stations are all over this. Who knows? Maybe you'll be on TV tonight. We'll have to rush home and see."

Colleen smirked, stood on tiptoes and kissed him on the lips.

Two boys, about ten years old, stopped and allowed Bogie to jump up and lick their faces.

"Hey, mister," asked one of them, "is it okay if we pet your dog?"

"Of course."

The boys knelt in the soft grass as Bogie took turns climbing on them.

"What kind of dog is he?" one of them asked.

"He's a German Shorthaired Pointer."

"My brother had a dog like this," said the other boy. "His girlfriend made him give it away."

Tom glanced at Colleen and gave the boy an astonished look. "Your brother chose his girlfriend over his dog? Sounds to me like he needs to re-examine his priorities."

The boy nodded, "That's for sure."

From somewhere down the street a woman called, and the boys ran home as Tom and Colleen walked on.

"You're lucky," she said, "that I love that dog as much as I love you."

"Yeah, but . . . do you love me as much as you love the dog?"

Colleen took in her idyllic surroundings, savoring the cool, dry air, cleared of pollen by the previous night's rain.

"From what Mitch tells me," Tom said, "Dina handled herself pretty well, despite Radford's trying to trip her up."

"I missed her, unfortunately. I had to duck out for an afternoon deposition. But Radford *shredded* Rainey's other witnesses. Tomorrow she gets her turn. Remember, she only needs one skeptical juror, and from what I saw on their faces she had at least a couple of them."

"I'd like to see this for myself."

"Nope. You're not allowed in that courtroom until Radford calls you to the stand."

Colleen stopped in her tracks and bent over, coughing violently.

Tom stroked her back as she slowly recovered. "How long has this been going on?"

"It's nothing, perhaps a cold."

"That doesn't sound like a cold. Promise me you'll go to a doctor. I'll call Kathy tonight and see who she recommends."

"I promise," Colleen managed.

Chapter Sixteen

Oleg Simonov

Chamblee, Georgia
Tuesday, March 19

Oleg sat alone at his laptop, the light of a fading sunset seeping through the curtains of his apartment. For no reason he could think of, his thoughts drifted back to his Moscow childhood. How his tastes had changed over the years! Back then he would have killed for a place like this.

Oleg's father had been a party member and a minor GRU officer. *So what? Moscow crawled with party members.* Oleg, his parents and two sisters occupied a two-bedroom walkup near the airport metro station.

At nineteen he discovered his father had another, much nicer, apartment nearer the Kremlin, one he shared with his mistress and *their* two children. Buried in his heaviest coat and fur hat, Oleg waited outside the place one snowy winter evening as the old man departed, crept up behind him and hit him over the head with a pipe, leaving him unconscious and bleeding on the sidewalk.

In time, Oleg came to accept his father's infidelity. With his stressful job, he'd earned such small pleasures. *He gave the best years of his life to Mother Russia, and for what? To be put out to pasture by Gorbachev and his toads.* Oleg quit the homeland, determined to become his own man, a citizen of the world, beholden to no one but himself.

Svetlana had gone out for the evening . . . no doubt spending what remained of Oleg's money. As soon as he collected his payoff from the

Swede he'd dump her and go somewhere warm, far from crowded apartment buildings and stale cooking odors. She could rot in this place for all he cared.

He finished off his supper of cold pizza as his phone vibrated, a message from the young man he'd hired to sit in the courtroom and take notes. According to the text, a commotion ensued at day's end, when the defense attorney received an envelope and handed it to the judge. Oleg thanked him and promised another payment in the morning.

Flush with success, he plotted his next step, pulling up a digital photo of Ron Dalrymple, clearly identifiable, chatting with Svetlana at Dan's Old Bar. Her face partially obscured, Svetlana could easily pass for Dina Savage. He attached it to another email destined for Sara Radford, along with a photo of Dalrymple leaving the courtroom on the day of jury selection, yellow notepad in hand. The email identified Dalrymple as a local private detective hired by Dina to compile backgrounds of jury members.

Once authorities discovered Dina's smiling face on DataScape's servers, the judge would, no doubt, declare a mistrial. Dalrymple, should the police question him, would never manage to identify Svetlana. *I taught her well.*

* * *

Sara Radford returned to her office to go over her notes for the next day. When she saw the email, she at first dismissed it as a hoax spawned by news of the previous night's break-in. *But who else would know about that besides Rainey, the judge and the perpetrator? Could Savage really be so stupid, or is this someone's lame attempt to discredit her? What could they hope to gain?*

She pondered how the sender might expect her to use this information . . . *and* how might it affect Liam's defense. The prosecution had a weak case, at best, as Radford had proven, and she couldn't risk blowback by overplaying these photos without a positive ID.

Then it came to her. *These pranksters, whoever they were, don't have to prove anything. All they need is to sow doubt, leading to an acquittal, a hung jury or a mistrial.*

Liam couldn't have done this. That left his parents, particularly the father. *Surely, the man knows better.* Radford had to turn this over to the court, as she'd done with the security photos and again express her misgivings. Meanwhile, she'd forward copies to Rob Alford, her investigator, to compare them with shots of Dina.

Radford studied the mousy little man at the bar . . . Ron Dalrymple? *Let's see what Rob can find out about him. Under threat of losing his license, he just might cooperate.* She texted Herb Riley, asking him to call her right away. When her cell rang two minutes later, she heard restaurant noises in the background.

"Look, I'm sorry to bother you . . ." she said.

"If it's about the Sanstrom trial don't be sorry."

She described the email and said she'd forward it to him. He cautioned her not to say anything to anyone until they had a chance to think about it.

* * *

At that moment, the object of Oleg's efforts sat alone in her Buckhead condo. Dina opened her laptop and checked the app she'd installed on Flanders' phone. As expected, it had dutifully recorded all his contacts, recent calls and texts.

She'd turned down another dinner invitation, telling Flanders she needed to catch up on some work. By now, she suspected, he'd invited another woman over to his place for dinner and a romp.

Among tonight's calls she noticed two names. One said "Dina," its time stamp coinciding with his invitation for dinner. The other indicated someone named "Ross." Scrolling back, she found that Flanders had made *seven* such calls in the past three days. *Does he swing both ways?*

Flanders sent the last text twenty-four hours ago, mentioning his date with Dina. So, Ross knew about Dina, but she knew nothing about him. *Maybe I could interest them in a threesome.*

Then she saw Sunday's text, with its attachment, the photo of her in her bikini on Flanders' boat. She needed to find out all she could about this *Ross*. Memorizing his phone number, she had another thought.

She dialed Flanders, and he answered immediately, the call registering on her monitor.

"Hey," she said. "I finished up early and wondered if that dinner invitation still stands."

"I just ate some leftovers, but that doesn't mean we can't get together. Why don't you come over for some . . . dessert?"

"Give me your home address."

Dina disconnected and, in seconds, saw another message to Ross. "Invited her to my place for dessert."

"Don't get used to it," the reply read. "You must maintain professionalism at all times."

What in the hell does that mean?

* * *

Twenty miles away, Christine Posner unlocked the front door of her empty, two-bedroom flat, her third night living there alone. On Sunday her ex-boyfriend, Shaun Gilbert, had come by to pick up the last of his things. Christine remained in the guest bedroom while a mutual friend, Cam Dorn, helped Gilbert move out. She watched them through a crack in the door as Shaun sulked back and forth under Cam's watchful eye.

Shaun had been out of work for six months, and Christine grew tired of supporting him, fighting with him and listening to him cry and apologize afterward. If she'd needed a dysfunctional child she could have adopted one.

Cam, like Christine, tended bar at Blue Moon Pizza in Smyrna. He stood six-six, with thick biceps, and provided a sense of protection in case Gilbert showed up drunk and belligerent, as he'd done so often over their two-year relationship.

Good riddance. If only she could find someone new. She closed her eyes and pictured Cam, muscles bulging beneath his tight-fitting shirt. He'd be perfect, she thought; strong yet so gentle. *Too bad he's gay.*

When the two men left, Christine sat staring at the walls. She'd taken the night off but decided to drop by work anyway. She could have a few drinks, then go home and turn in.

She'd been there little more than an hour when she said her good-byes and left. Tomorrow would be another long day of jury duty.

As she drove, she pictured the defendant, Liam Sanstrom, handsome, yet *cold, evil and arrogant.* Christine envisioned the many ways such a man could take advantage of a woman and looked forward to putting his ass away where he belonged. He could find out for himself what rape felt like.

143

Suddenly a thought came to her. *His house is . . . what, two miles away?* Perhaps she could check it out. *So, what if this violates the judge's orders? No one will know, and, besides, it'll give me a better understanding of the crime.*

She took Paces Ferry Road south to Vinings and turned right, across from the Overlook. Back among the neighborhoods she missed a couple of turns, wandering among winding streets before finding Overton Road. As she made the turn from Morning Glory Circle, a doe stepped into the splash of her headlights and froze, forcing Posner to jam her brakes. Not five seconds behind her came a young fawn, its coat dappled in white spots. Christine caught her breath as they bounded into the darkness.

Sanstrom's home sat at the end of the darkened cul-de-sac. Christine had brought her notebook from the trial, in which she'd written the address, mentioned by one of the policemen. Parking in the deep shade of an overhanging tree, she made the long walk down Liam's driveway. From either side came a loud chorus of insects and cicadas.

It seemed someone had repaired the front door after the police broke it down. A fixture beside it provided the only illumination. With the aid of a flashlight, Posner made her way around back. She rounded the corner and was startled when a set of overhead floods suddenly came on, apparently triggered by a motion detector. She glanced about, seeing none of the neighboring houses.

When she'd regained her composure, she peered into the basement through the sliding doors, beholding a scene even more horrific than she'd imagined. The bed sat just as it had in the photos the prosecutor showed the jurors. She stood for several minutes, trying to imagine that fateful night as Dina had described it.

She felt a chill despite the mild evening, and the empty place creeped her out. As she turned to run, a large spider web beneath the deck caught her in the face. She screamed and stumbled uphill to her car.

As she turned onto Morning Glory Circle, a Cobb Police car passed, turning into the cul-de-sac.

* * *

Unknown to Posner, a security camera on an interior wall had captured her visit. A signal, triggered by the same motion detector that activated the floodlights, went out to a monitoring station. Working late, Oleg had hacked the camera feed at Liam's security company. He stared at the jerky image. *Who is this?* he thought. In a moment he had it, pulling up the photos Dalrymple gave Svetlana at Dan's. *How thoughtful of him.*

Most were grainy, not nearly the quality of Oleg's work, but the young woman with short black hair and tattoos came through perfectly. *A dangerous looking woman*, thought Oleg, the kind he preferred, *Christine Posner, Juror Number 4.*

How serendipitous! This will throw yet another wrench into the Sanstrom trial. Oleg would have to demand more money from the old man. *Now. What will be the best way to play this?* He could email the images to Radford, as he'd done previously, or he could send her a text from a throwaway phone. But so far neither of his tactics had produced results.

This would require a much bolder approach, one that would capture the attention of many people and give the judge no choice but to declare a mistrial. He hummed an old Russian folk tune as he sought out Posner's Facebook account.

* * *

Perched on her knees, Dina Savage gasped and smiled down at Flanders. His chest heaved as he grinned back, continuing to thrust. Tonight, she'd refrained from alcohol, and her Glock lay in her open purse, within easy reach.

Dina started to say something when her phone rang. Annoyed, she glanced at it, recognizing the name of her personal attorney. She gave Flanders a sheepish look. "I'm afraid I have to take this. I'll get rid of him, and we can have some more fun."

Flanders ambled into the light spilling from his bathroom. The phone rang a second time. Punching it with her thumb, she answered, "Yeah. What is it?"

"Where were you last night?" her lawyer asked.

"What?"

"Where were you last night?" This time he spoke slowly, as if to an obtuse child.

"With a friend. Why?"

"Can this *friend* vouch for you?"

"Sure. Can I ask what this is about?"

"Someone broke into Sara Radford's office. Security cameras recorded a young woman copying data from the secretary's computer."

"What?"

"Word is she looks a lot like you, though I understand the image isn't very good. You know, if you get caught doing something like this, Eunice Gilmartin will throw this case out in a New York second. And then she'll prosecute you for burglary and obstruction of justice."

"Are you shitting me?" asked Dina, heat rising to her face. "Do you really think I'm that stupid?"

"I'm just saying . . ."

"It wasn't me, you dumbass, and I can prove it."

"Alright. If you say it wasn't you, it wasn't you." He paused, seeming flustered. "Look, I'm sorry I bothered you. Go back to enjoying your evening."

Enjoying my evening? Dina thought as the lawyer hung up. *What the hell did that mean?* She wondered what else the creep knew about her private life.

Her mind ran back over what the man said. She'd long ago stopped believing in coincidences. *Who would break into Radford's office and what would they want from her computer?* If Dina had wanted anything she could have gotten it without going anywhere near the place.

Flanders called her from the shower. But, no longer in the mood, Dina didn't respond. Someone had set her up. *Could it have been Radford?* That would be the logical place to start, but Dina had to move cautiously. First, she'd find out more about Ross and what he and Flanders were up to.

Chapter Seventeen

Sara Radford

Marietta, Georgia
Wednesday, March 20

Dina arrived for work early the next morning and updated the antivirus on her laptop. It took her a while to find the spyware in her registry. Her repeated attempts to trace it proved fruitless, but she knew it had something to do with Flanders and his friend Ross.

Paranoia had saved Dina more than once over her career. If authorities discovered her clandestine pursuits, it would wreck her career, her life. She erased all the bots from the servers she'd used, which alone took more than an hour, then deleted her files. She emptied her recycling bin, cleared her browser and reformatted her hard drive, which she would destroy later, along with her cell phone.

On her way out the door, Dina stopped and spoke to her supervisor, who had comforted and supported her throughout her ordeal. Realizing, perhaps for the first time, how much respect the firm had given her, Dina felt tears gather in her eyes.

Just as quickly, she dispelled them. Later, when she emailed her resignation, she'd make the excuse that she needed to get away for a while. Then she'd look for another job, perhaps out west, somewhere far beyond prying eyes. *For now, she would burn her bridges.*

* * *

Seated in the courtroom, awaiting recommencement of trial, Radford re-examined the photos her anonymous source had sent the previous day and reread his attached email:

The woman you see in the booth is Dina Savage. The man across from her is Ron Dalrymple, a private detective. He has just handed Ms. Savage an envelope containing names and personal information of every juror in the Sanstrom case, for which Ms. Savage has paid him handsomely. Ms. Savage makes her living in ways that, shall we say, go beyond the fringes of the law.

The photos gave clear depictions of Dalrymple's face, but the woman had her head turned in every shot, obscuring her features. Radford would hold off on going back to the judge until her investigator, Rob Alford, found out more about Dalrymple.

The bailiff announced, "All rise," as Judge Gilmartin, ashen faced, entered the courtroom.

"Ladies and gentlemen," she said, "Before we begin, I have tragic news. One of our jurors received word last evening that her son died. I hope you'll all join me in keeping Ms. Farmer and her family in our prayers. I've excused her from jury duty. We'll proceed without her."

Following a brief pause, she turned her attention to the defense table. "Ms. Radford, you may call your first witness."

"Your Honor, the defense calls Mr. Thomas Williams."

* * *

With a reassuring smile, Radford asked, "Mr. Williams, could you tell us what you do for a living?"

"I'm a retired newspaper reporter and freelance writer."

"Have you ever met the defendant, Liam Sanstrom?"

"Yes."

"Can you tell us how you know him?"

"We sat together at a Harry Connick concert about a year and a half ago."

"I see. Did Liam have anyone with him at the concert?"

"Yes, a Ms. Dina Savage."

"Had you met either Liam or Ms. Savage *prior* to that evening?"

"No."

Radford handed him a photo and asked, "Mr. Williams, do you recognize this picture?"

"I do."

"For the benefit of the jury could you identify the two people shown here?"

"Yes. That's Mr. Sanstrom, and that's Ms. Savage."

With the judge's permission, Radford handed the photo to the nearest juror, who examined it and passed it on.

"Who took this picture, Mr. Williams?"

"I did."

"You did an excellent job. Are you a professional photographer also?"

"Not really. It's more of a hobby."

"I see. Tell me . . . how would you describe the behavior of Mr. Sanstrom and Ms. Savage that evening?"

Tom pursed his lips. "I'd say they were pretty amorous."

"Could you give us more specifics?"

"Well, he had his arm around her shoulder, and she kept putting her head on his chest, as you can see in the picture. At one point she put her tongue in his ear."

A wave of suppressed laughter rippled through the courtroom as Tom, blushing, added, "From where I sat, I saw her stroking the inside of his thigh beneath the table."

When Radford had finished, Rainey declined to cross-examine. The judge dismissed Tom and allowed him to join Colleen in the gallery.

* * *

Radford's next witness, Matt Conroy, strode into the room wearing a broad grin. He wore his blonde hair swept back with gel and had a tattoo of a skull on his left arm. His rawhide face spoke of a life spent in the sun. Tom sensed something feral about him, like a weasel.

"Mr. Conroy," asked Radford, "what do you do for a living?"

"I'm a landscape contractor."

"Do you know the defendant, Liam Sanstrom?"

He leaned back and gave Sanstrom an exaggerated appraisal. "Nope," he said in a slow drawl. "Can't say I do."

"How about his accuser, Ms. Dina Savage?"

"Oh yeah. I know Dina." He leered and arched one eyebrow at the jurors.

"Did you ever date Ms. Savage?"

"You might say so."

"Mr. Conroy, please limit your answers to a simple 'yes' or 'no'."

"Yes ma'am." He leaned back with a surprised look as though chastened.

Rainey shifted in his seat.

"Mr. Conroy, did you and Ms. Savage ever engage in sexual role play when you dated her?"

"Objection, Your Honor," shouted Rainey. "This is *totally* irrelevant and prejudicial."

Radford asked to approach the bench. Out of Tom's earshot, the judge listened as the attorneys debated the point. When they'd finished, Rainey returned to his table, face flushed.

"Remember, Ms. Radford," admonished the judge. "I'm allowing only those *two* lines of questioning."

"Mr. Conroy, did you ever engage in rough sex with Ms. Savage?"

"Yes ma'am," he said, grinning and winking at Radford.

"Without getting *too* graphic, Mr. Conroy, could you describe the roles you and Ms. Savage played?"

"Yeah. Old Dina liked to tie me up and spank me for being a *bad boy*. I played along just so I could get a little afterward."

"On any of your *dates,* did you and Ms. Savage ever use any recreational drugs?"

A worried look clouded Conroy's face.

"Mr. Conroy you're not the one on trial here today. Just answer the question truthfully."

"Yeah . . . I guess we did."

"What kind of drugs?"

"Well . . . pot mostly. Sometimes a little coke."

"Did Ms. Savage say why she liked taking drugs during sex?"

"She said they helped her get her rocks off."

The courtroom erupted, and the judge pounded her gavel. "That'll be enough, Ms. Radford. Do you have any more questions of this witness?"

"No, Your Honor. I don't." Radford flashed the jurors a broad smile.

"Mr. Rainey?"

The prosecutor leapt to his feet before the words left Gilmartin's mouth. "Mr. Conroy, you testified you're a landscaper. Is that your sole source of income?"

Conroy gave him a confused look. "Man, I don't know what you mean."

"Isn't it true, Mr. Conroy, that you've been arrested on multiple occasions for drug dealing?"

"Well . . ." He looked to Radford, as if pleading for help.

"Mr. Conroy, let me refresh your memory." Rainey walked back to the prosecution table and removed a clip from a thick sheaf of papers. "According to your criminal record, you have twelve convictions for possession, everything from marijuana to methamphetamine. And you're currently awaiting trial for trafficking in Oxycodone and Rohypnol. Is that not true?"

Impassive, Radford studied her witness as his eyes darted between her and Rainey.

"I was framed. My lawyer says they don't even have a case against me."

Rainey beamed at the jury, and returned to the witness with an intimidating glare, as though about to ask another question.

"That'll be all, Your Honor."

"Ms. Radford," asked Gilmartin, "any redirect?"

"Yes, Your Honor." She rose suddenly with a smile. "Mr. Conroy, was Ms. Savage one of your regular customers?"

Rainey screamed, "Your Honor!"

"Your Honor, Mr. Rainey introduced this line of questioning."

"*Sustained*!" yelled the judge. "Ms. Radford, I warned you. You are on *thin ice*."

Radford nodded in submission. "I understand, Your Honor. I withdraw the question."

Her next witness, Preston Davidson, CEO of Silas-Burke, described his business as a *marketing intelligence firm*.

"Mr. Davidson, have you ever met Liam Sanstrom?"

"No. I have not."

"Have you ever met Dina Savage?"

"I'm afraid so."

"Could you please tell us what you mean by that?"

"Three years ago, Ms. Savage worked for Silas-Burke. She filed a sexual harassment complaint against her supervisor."

"Describe the nature of the complaint."

"She said he made unwanted sexual advances which she rejected repeatedly."

"How did you respond to these charges?"

"Based on initial questioning, we asked Ms. Savage's supervisor to resign."

"Were there further ramifications from Ms. Savage's claims?"

"Yes. The man she'd accused came out publicly, saying he was gay and had lived with the same partner for more than twenty years. He sued Silas-Burke, alleging defamation and mental anguish. Witnesses refuted Ms. Savage's claims, and Silas-Burke settled for an undisclosed sum along with reinstatement. He also demanded Ms. Savage's formal written apology."

"Did she make that apology?"

"Only when we made it a condition for her continued employment. We view sexual harassment *very seriously* at Silas-Burke. We take false allegations *just* as seriously."

"Does Ms. Savage still work for you?"

Davidson gave a sour look. "No. She left a few months later to join one of our competitors."

"Thank you, Mr. Davidson. I have no further questions."

"Your Honor," said Radford, "I have one more witness. His testimony will be rather long, and I'll need to use the overhead projector."

"If you'd like, Ms. Radford, we can take an early lunch break and hear from your next witness when we return." Gilmartin instructed the jurors and attorneys to be back in an hour.

* * *

"Your Honor," said Radford, approaching the bench when the courtroom had cleared, "there's something else I need to bring to your attention." She turned and looked at Rainey before handing the judge the envelope. "I've received *yet another* email with photos attached. I don't know what to make of them. Again, I'm *not* sure the woman is Ms. Savage . . ."

Gilmartin studied the contents before handing them to Rainey.

The prosecutor skipped the email and shuffled through the photos, his face coloring. "Your Honor, this woman could be anybody. I certainly hope this isn't some lame attempt by Ms. Radford to argue for a mistrial."

"Far from it, Your Honor. I'm as dubious of this as Mr. Rainey, which is why I've asked my investigator to see what he can discover about Mr. Dalrymple. I've also asked him to find out where this email came from, though I doubt he'll be able to. I simply felt obligated to pass it on."

Gilmartin sighed, pressing her forehead as if taken by a sudden headache. "Okay. I'll refer it to the sheriff's office. As bad as this smells, Mr. Rainey, it bothers me very much, coming on the heels of the break-in at Ms. Radford's office."

"This looks to me like the grade school theatrics of a defense attorney afraid she's about to lose her case," said Rainey.

Gilmartin broke off Radford's reply. "Mr. Rainey, you should be *very* careful before leveling accusations. We can find out quickly enough what this Mr. Dalrymple has to say. I'll keep this, if you don't mind, Ms. Radford. Meanwhile, let's get back to trying this matter, shall we?"

With that, she exited the courtroom, as Radford and Rainey, glowering at each other, departed for lunch and Radford's assistant connected his laptop to the projector.

Chapter Eighteen

Tom Williams

Marietta, Georgia
Wednesday, March 20

Tom and Colleen returned to the courtroom as Radford called her next witness. The slightly built man appeared to be in his mid-thirties with thinning blonde hair and wire-rimmed aviator glasses. He gave his name as Stan King.

"Mr. King, would you state your profession?"

He leaned forward, speaking earnestly into the mic. "I'm president of Sebastian Services, a home security business. We provide fire and burglary protection, as well as emergency alarms."

"How do you know Liam Sanstrom?"

"I've serviced his home for a few years now. Mr. Sanstrom has many valuable paintings, and he's concerned about the threat of burglary."

"Could you describe your services in more detail?"

"Besides the silent alarm, we have cameras continuously monitoring the perimeter."

"Do any of these cameras monitor *inside* the house?"

"No. We're looking for anyone trying to break *in*. Once they're inside we've already called law enforcement, and they're on their way."

"I see. Now most of Liam's paintings are in his basement. Is that correct?"

"I believe so."

"And Liam has a camera *inside* the basement pointing toward an exterior glass door."

"That's correct. We put it there to prevent a burglar from disabling it. It allows us to see anyone trying to get in."

Radford turned to the bench. "Your Honor, I'd like to have the witness explain to us some footage from Liam's basement on the night of Ms. Savage's *alleged* rape."

Gilmartin nodded, and the bailiff lowered the overhead lights. Radford's assistant powered up his laptop. The screen, positioned near the front of the courtroom, afforded everyone a view.

"Now Mr. King, can you describe to us what we're seeing here?" Radford asked.

"It's the interior view of the basement. The camera sits high on the wall opposite the glass doors."

"And there's no visibility beyond the doors."

"No ma'am. It's dark outside."

"What's this light reflecting on the inside of the glass?"

"It's coming from a ceiling fixture in the stairway going up to the main floor."

"Now, I've frozen the image at this point so we can get a feel for where we are," said Radford. "What are those numbers in the upper left corner?"

"That's a timer. We're at 4:18 on the morning in question."

"So, from this point until five a.m. would've been *forty-two minutes*. Is that correct?"

King smiled. "Yes ma'am."

"Okay. So, we're going to let the video run for a bit, and I want you to describe to me what you see. Before we do, I want to point out to the jury we've had these images digitally enhanced by a certified lab, so we can see more clearly what's happening. The action here is running a bit slower than normal so we don't miss anything. If necessary, we can pause it to examine any details."

Radford nodded to her assistant, who touched the mouse pad on his laptop. At first it showed no apparent changes besides the digital timer.

King leaned forward and studied the image as though afraid he might overlook something. An object appeared in the lower right corner of the screen.

"What we have here," he said, "appears to be a person's head. The hair's rather short. We can't determine its color in this black-and-white image, but it appears light. I can see just enough to conclude that it's probably a man's head."

"Could you tell us how tall this man is?"

Rainey objected that the question called for speculation.

Radford explained that King had positioned the camera himself and knew its *exact* distance from the floor, angle of view, and proximity to the subject. She added that, as a security professional, King could accurately gauge the man's height.

Gilmartin overruled.

King continued, "I'd put his height at roughly six-foot-two."

"Your Honor, I'm going to have Liam stand up for a moment if you don't mind."

Gilmartin nodded.

"Mr. King, how tall would you say Liam is?"

"Six-foot-two."

"Very good. He's six-two-and-a-half. So, let's continue. Please describe what you see now."

The head on the screen moved out of view, and in two seconds another materialized. This time the subject appeared shorter.

"This," said King, "is a second person crossing just below our line of view from right to left. The only reason you can see her is that she's farther away from the camera."

"So, she's walking *behind* Liam?"

"Yes."

Radford again signaled her assistant to pause the video. "Alright . . . Your Honor, as I mentioned earlier, we had this image professionally enhanced by Dexterity Labs of Boston, and they've provided a detailed report regarding their processes, which we can place in evidence if Mr. Rainey wishes.

"Now, we're going to zoom in so we can see the image more clearly." She nodded to King.

The assistant tapped another key. The image closed in on the sliding doors, revealing a dimly lit view of a young woman with light hair down to her shoulders. The face, though unclear, strongly resembled Dina Savage. Also visible were her hands, *unbuttoning her blouse*.

"This appears to be a young woman, about thirty-five . . ." King blushed. "She seems to be disrobing."

"Is Liam still visible in this picture?"

"No. He's not."

"Is anyone helping the woman remove her clothing?"

"No, Ma'am."

The assistant clicked the keyboard again. As the woman passed from view, the blouse slowly drifted from her shoulders to the floor. The assistant froze the video at that point. The jurors sat, mesmerized by the blouse suspended in midair.

"Your Honor," said Radford, "I have no further questions for this witness."

"Mr. Rainey, would you like to cross-examine?" asked the judge.

Rainey rose slowly and asked, "Mr. King, can you tell from this video who the woman is?"

"No sir. I cannot."

"With all of your *professional* skills at identification, do you think you could pick her out of a lineup of other women in their mid-thirties with light hair?"

The witness took a moment. "No sir. I'm not sure I could."

"Can you tell us what happened after the defendant and this woman, *whoever* she is, walked out of view of the camera?"

"No sir."

"Of course not . . . Were there any other cameras in that basement?"

"No sir."

"Thank you, Mr. King. Your Honor, I have no further questions."

Radford smirked as she stood and scanned the jury. "Your Honor, the defense rests."

"Given the late hour," said Gilmartin, "we'll recess until tomorrow. Please be back here by *eight a.m.* for closing arguments."

* * *

Dina concluded her meeting with her attorney, livid over what he'd told her about Matt Conroy's testimony, feeling violated yet again. *When this is over*, she thought, *that little worm will pay*.

Even more disturbing were Stan King's statements and the video evidence presented. Dina wracked her memory, unable to recall following Liam downstairs *or* taking her clothes off. In fact, she couldn't remember how she'd *gotten* to the basement. What she did remember, quite vividly, was his tying her to the bed and telling her she could scream all she wanted, but no one would hear.

The sonofabitch raped me, just as Dennis Ramsey did, and one way or another I will get my revenge.

She stormed out of the lawyer's office, seething. As she drove back to Midtown she spotted a convenience store near the Big Chicken. At the edge of its parking lot stood a twentieth-century relic, a *pay phone. So, what if it's traceable?* Dina no longer cared.

She dialed Ross' number from memory, shocked when a Russian-accented voice answered.

"Yeah, who is it?"

"Is this Ross?"

"What do you want?" he asked warily.

"Ross, or whoever you are, this is Dina Savage, *and what I want is for you to go fuck yourself.*"

She slammed down the phone before he could reply. Not smart, she knew, but she felt better.

Though Flanders had only once mentioned his employer, Burns and Kelly, Dina recognized the name. Tomorrow she'd call to verify his employment. *Why didn't I do this earlier?*

* * *

Meanwhile, in his darkening living room, Oleg wondered what to do next. *Where did Dina get this number?* She still didn't have his name, but she would before long. He punched in Flanders' number and, when the man answered, spoke three words in Russian, *"Get out now."*

* * *

Radford's phone chirped as she unlocked her apartment door. She fumbled it from her purse and read the ID, *Rob Alford.*

"What you got?" she asked.

"You were right. I ran a facial structure analysis on the break-in photos and those at Dan's Old Bar. They match perfectly . . . but she's *not* Dina Savage."

"What about Dalrymple?"

"Dalrymple's a small-time private investigator, way out of his depth. You want his number?"

As she jotted it down, Radford remembered, with relief, her expressions of skepticism to the judge. Then the anger set in. Bjorn Sanstrom set this up, but she couldn't prove it . . . yet. The sonofabitch couldn't trust her to get an acquittal, no doubt because of her age and gender. *He just had to screw with the system. If this comes down to a mistrial and the DA's office retries it, the Sanstroms can find themselves another attorney.*

* * *

An ochre sunset illuminated the storefronts of Roswell's Canton Street. Tom and Colleen sipped margaritas outside Ceviche, a local Mexican restaurant, as passing pedestrians, young and old, browsed the shops. A passing motorcycle momentarily drowned their conversation.

"So," Colleen asked as their food arrived, "tell me again what inspired you to drag me *all the way here from Marietta* when we have so many fine eateries in Midtown."

"I thought we could celebrate our courtroom experience with a little road trip."

"Bullshit." Leaning back, she read the sign above a storefront across the street. "Hmm . . . *Sally's on Canton* . . . Where have I heard that name?"

"Okay. So, I wanted to see the spot where Liam met Dina."

"Fine. We can go over there and check it out."

As they ate Colleen recounted for Tom the testimony that preceded his.

"I don't care what the police told Mitch. I'm already seeing skepticism, especially that software CEO . . . Sax."

"So, you think they'll acquit Liam."

"Who knows? He's not a very sympathetic defendant. He's rich, pampered and aloof, the kind of guy you can imagine drugging and raping a beautiful young woman."

"Listen to you. You'd have made a great DA . . ."

She wadded her napkin and threw it at him.

* * *

Sally Meister turned out to be a plump, pleasant-looking woman, perhaps mid-fifties. Judging from her placid demeanor, Tom figured she'd already enjoyed some of the wine and hors d'oeuvres provided for her guests.

"You have an interesting collection," Tom said. "I wondered if you had anything recent by Liam Sanstrom."

Sally's smile faded. "No. I don't."

"I see. Someone told me this is where Liam first met Dina Savage."

Sally scowled, as though she'd had some bad calamari. Through clinched teeth she said, "I don't know what that woman told you, but I wish I'd never met her. She waltzed in here one day, waving money around, saying she was decorating her condo in Buckhead. I should have asked her why she came all the way up here. She saw a photo of Liam beside one of his paintings and practically drooled on it."

"Really?"

"She asked if he ever came in the shop. I have events periodically, usually on Saturday mornings, where artists show up and talk about their work. Liam came in a couple of weeks later." Sally waved in a grand gesture, "And there she was, Ms. Dina Savage, *all over him*. They ended up leaving together. A week later I heard she'd accused him of raping her. Now I can't even show his paintings."

"I'm sorry to hear that. I testified at the trial today. My wife and I were at the concert with Liam, Dina, Bonnie Baron, and Bonnie's date."

"Oh my God! You're Bonnie's friend, the writer she told me about."

"Yes. After my testimony I stayed and watched the trial. You'll be happy to know Liam will probably walk. The prosecution's case looks shaky."

Pausing, Tom noticed, for the first time, a small group of eaves-droppers gathering about him, among them a very uncomfortable look-ing Colleen.

Sally gave a sigh of relief. "That's the best news I've had in a long time. I appreciate your coming by and telling me."

Colleen grabbed Tom by the arm and ushered him back to their car.

Chapter Nineteen

Mistrial

Marietta, Georgia
Thursday, March 21

Fred Connor settled in front of his laptop with a cup of coffee and a toaster waffle. He had a half hour to kill before leaving for the office. Posting on Facebook and slipping off to watch trials had become his obsessions. Connor needed to find a girlfriend, get a life and stop reading the random musings of people he didn't know.

On his timeline he wrote, "another day at the courthouse watching an interesting case, an artist accused of date rape." Then he scanned other posts, stopping to glance at attractive women, including a bartender who called herself "Illustrated Lady." Studying her face, he could swear he'd seen her recently.

He started to move on . . . then her latest missive caught his eye:

Stuck on jury duty . . . a rape case of all things . . . We are so going to crucify this jerk . . . I drove by his house last night and checked out his little pleasure pen through a rear window. What a creep!

Connor caught his breath, read the post again and brought up a mental image of her, seated in the jury box. An attorney himself, he hated getting involved, but had no choice. He clicked the printer icon, waited for the hard copy, then texted his office saying he had to run an errand on his way in.

Thirty minutes later Connor entered Gilmartin's courtroom. Trial had not yet reconvened. He handed the bailiff the printout. "I need to speak with Judge Gilmartin."

With a condescending look the man started to say something.

"*I believe*," said Connor, "*she'll want to see this.*"

The bailiff took one look at the highlighted Facebook message. "Wait here," he said. "I'll be right back."

Moments later he reappeared. "Follow me. Her Honor will see you now."

* * *

Rainey and Radford had already arrived. They noticed the young man addressing the bailiff and looked up in unison as he hurried back through the courtroom, head down, clutching his briefcase, minus the paper he'd had earlier.

The bailiff motioned them to follow him back to Gilmartin's chambers. The judge, without preamble, asked, "Ms. Radford, can you get me the phone number of the security firm owner who testified yesterday? I need to speak with him."

Dumbstruck, Radford replied, "Yes, Your Honor." As she started to speak, Gilmartin interrupted, handing her the Facebook post.

* * *

As the jurors waited, Sax tried to focus on the latest documents he'd received from Cheryl. Scanning the room, he read stress and fatigue on the faces. He wondered what kept the bailiff. Trial should have resumed already. When the man finally stuck his head in the door, he asked for one juror, Christine Posner.

The young bartender rose with a startled look.

"You need to bring your personal belongings, Ms. Posner." Sax detected something cold in his voice.

As she picked up her pocketbook and followed him out, the other jurors exchanged glances.

* * *

Seeing Posner stride out of the courtroom, her face a mask of tears, Radford glanced at Rainey. Before either could react, the bailiff came out and, in a low voice, beckoned them again to Gilmartin's chambers.

When they returned ten minutes later, Radford wore a broad smile. Rainey made no eye contact with her or Sanstrom, but instead gathered his papers, whispered at length to the police officer at his table with him, and left the courtroom.

Radford struggled to remain calm as she spoke. "Liam, you're a free man, at least for now. The judge will come out in a moment and announce she's declaring a mistrial. It seems one of the jurors, the woman who just left, posted an inflammatory message on Facebook, and the judge believes she may have tainted other jurors. Mr. Rainey *could* retry you, but I doubt he will. If he decides not to, you're done."

Liam's face registered bewilderment and then joy. Seated behind him, his parents overheard the conversation.

His father blinked, nodding slowly, but remained expressionless. "Does this mean . . ."

"We don't know yet what it means, but, for the moment at least, Liam's a free man."

Brigid turned her eyes heavenward, let out a deep breath and exclaimed, "Thank you, Father."

* * *

In the hallway, Rainey saw Dina and her attorney and beckoned them into a small conference room.

When he'd closed the door, he explained what the judge had decided. "I'm afraid, Ms. Savage, this is it. Given the way the testimony has gone and the opportunities this mistrial has afforded the defense, I don't see how we can continue to prosecute this case."

Dina searched his face, as impassive as those she'd seen on Mount Rushmore. She turned to her attorney, whose blank stare confirmed what she'd heard.

"No!" Her long, shrill scream echoed down the hallway toward the courtroom.

Rainey rose, extending a hand. She drew back, jumping up from her chair.

"There have been too many irregularities," said Rainey. "The defense has completely undermined . . ."

Dina glared at him. "Irregularities, my ass! Somebody orchestrated this stunt. I *did not* break into that lawyer's office, and I can prove it."

"I believe you, but I'm afraid nothing I do will reverse the damage. There's too much room for reasonable doubt."

Before he could say anything else, Dina rushed blindly from the room and straight to the elevator.

* * *

Still sitting in the courtroom, Tom and Colleen heard the scream. Tom glanced at two television reporters he recognized on the row in front of him. They looked at each other and shrugged.

The bailiff walked in and shouted, "All rise." The judge followed behind him, waiting as the remaining jurors filed in and took their seats.

"First of all, I'd like to thank each of you for your service to Cobb County. I know this week has been tough on all of you, and I pray you never have to go through this again."

She faced the gallery as Rainey returned and took his seat. "Due to the misconduct of a single juror, compounded by other circumstances, I find myself unable to continue these proceedings. For this reason, I'm declaring a mistrial.

"Mr. Sanstrom, I've spoken with your attorney, Ms. Radford, and with Mr. Rainey. I want to caution you that this *does not* preclude Mr. Rainey's retrying this case should he choose. Until he reaches a decision, you are free to leave . . ." She leaned forward, lowering her reading glasses, "under the condition, Mr. Sanstrom, that *you are not to leave the state of Georgia until you or your attorney hear from Mr. Rainey.*"

The gallery erupted. One of the TV reporters sprang for the door as the other made his way through the milling crowd surrounding the defense table. Tom followed in his wake.

"Ms. Radford," he shouted above the din, "Do you think we could get a statement from you and your client? I have a cameraman out front where there's more room."

Radford turned to Sanstrom with a questioning look. He glanced at his parents, then gave a slight nod. "Give us a few minutes," she said. When he'd left, she leaned over to discuss with Liam what he should say.

* * *

Sax packed his briefcase, stopping for a moment to stare at his notes, wondering what he should do with them.

As the other jurors argued the results, Sax made his way to the lobby. Waiting at the elevator, he recognized the newspaper writer who'd testified for the defense, chatting with a woman, perhaps his wife. Before the door closed, the defendant, his attorney and an elderly couple joined them. Sax moved to the back of the car to make room.

* * *

Dina discarded her high heels as she ran the short block to where she'd parked. Out of breath, she reached into her glove compartment and dug beneath the stack of maintenance receipts. The Glock's grip felt comforting in her palm as she dropped it into her pocketbook.

A feeling of detachment came over her, as though she were watching the inevitable ending to a long movie. As she retraced her steps a voice called out, "Ms. Savage! Do you have a moment?" Ignoring him, she picked up her pace.

Chapter Twenty

Looking exhausted and bewildered, Liam took in the sea of reporters, photographers, former jurors and spectators jostling each other. Two Cobb County Sheriff's deputies struggled to clear a path along the sidewalk.

His sudden celebrity only enraged Dina more. Head down to avoid detection, she elbowed her way to within five feet of him as her hand rose from her purse. The first shot caught him behind the right ear, the opposite side of his head exploding like an overripe tomato. Bystanders screamed, ducked and scattered, tripping over each other.

As Dina pivoted toward Radford, a deputy grabbed the Glock, sending the second shot ricocheting off the building. Before she could fire again, a male juror disarmed her and threw her to the ground, where she screamed, kicked, and tried to bite him. Within seconds she lay face down on the concrete, wrists cuffed behind her.

* * *

Sax had only wanted to get past the crowd and away from the courthouse. Standing behind Sanstrom as the first shot rang out, he staggered backward and fell. Time stopped.

"Sir, are you alright?" a voice called from the blur. "Don't move. Help's on the way."

Recovering but unable to speak, Sax stared at the blood and gray matter on his shirt, then turned and vomited.

A face came into view, the reporter who'd testified. A Marietta cop shoved him away, kneeling beside Sax as other officers disbursed the crowd. In time, attendants arrived, placed Sax on a gurney and rolled him to an ambulance waiting at the curb.

* * *

Sitting beside Colleen on a park bench across the street, Tom realized for the first time that he hadn't seen Bonnie at all during the trial. He couldn't imagine why, given her client needed her emotional support.

Above the melee rose the sound of a woman screaming. Tom looked to see Brigid Sanstrom, fists clenched, staring heavenward as her husband carefully folded her into him and hustled her into a black limousine.

* * *

Miles away, Ron Dalrymple answered a loud knock to find a pair of Cobb Police officers in the hall outside his Doraville apartment.

"Mr. Dalrymple, do you mind if we come in?"

"I . . . I don't suppose so. Can you tell me what this is about?"

Stepping into the cluttered, confined living room, they scanned the discarded pizza boxes, empty beer cans, graphic novels and murder mysteries stacked in every corner. Dalrymple reached for his remote to mute a cable news broadcast.

"This shouldn't take long," they said. "We have some questions about a woman you met recently at Dan's Old Bar in Buckhead."

Dalrymple started to say something but reconsidered.

"This is you. Right, Mr. Dalrymple?" asked the younger officer, handing him an eight-by-five black-and-white photo.

"Uh . . . yes."

"Can you identify the young woman seated across from you?"

Dalrymple stared at the image as if it were an ancient manuscript, shaking his head. "She . . . was a client."

"Did she, by any chance, give you her name?"

Dalrymple felt ill. "No. She arranged the meeting by phone and paid me in cash."

"For what?"

Not sure if he'd broken the law, he thought fast. "Should I call my attorney?"

"I don't know, Mr. Dalrymple. Have you done anything illegal?"

"Uh, no!"

The older cop gave him a tired but reassuring look. "Mr. Dalrymple, we're not investigating you . . ." He paused before adding, ". . . at this time. We just need to know who your client is."

Dalrymple tried to convince them he didn't know her name or where to get in touch with her. He described, to the best of his recollection, her appearance and the information he provided her.

"Let me show you another picture. Do you think this could be her?" asked the younger officer.

The attractive blonde staring back at him seemed familiar, perhaps someone he'd seen on television. "I'm not sure. The woman I met at Dan's wore sunglasses and had her hair pulled back."

"Mr. Dalrymple, it would be in your best interest to cooperate with us. The state board takes a dim view of investigators who obstruct justice, and so do we. I'm sure you'd like to hang onto your license."

The older officer's phone chirped. He checked the readout before answering.

"Daniels," he said. He listened, then hung up, turning to the other officer. "We gotta go."

"Thank you, Mr. Dalrymple," said the younger man. "These are the only photos we have, but we'll send you some fresh copies. We may want you to come down and identify this woman in person if you don't mind. In the meantime, *please don't go anywhere.*"

"I won't." said Dalrymple, voice trembling.

As they departed, Dalrymple wondered what could have interrupted them. Returning to the news broadcast, he got his answer. Studying the mug shot of Dina Savage, he realized she wasn't the woman he met at Dan's.

It took him an hour to locate the bar napkin with the SUV's license number beneath the old newspapers and food wrappers. Reaching for his phone, he dialed Rollo Witherspoon, a man who seemed to know everyone in Atlanta. Rollo had helped Dalrymple on several occasions, especially with tracing auto registrations. Rollo assured him he'd have an answer in twenty-four hours.

* * *

The Kennestone physician examining Sax concluded he'd suffered nothing worse than shock and recommended tranquilizers. Outside the emergency room, Sax tossed the prescription in a trash can.

He thought about Dina's visit here following her alleged rape, re-calling the photo of her wearing a hospital gown, outstretched arms, bruised wrists. He kept coming back, though, to the look in her eyes, the hurt, the anger. *Something happened to her.*

In his opening arguments, the prosecutor mentioned her traumatic childhood, but Sax couldn't recall it coming up during trial. *And what about that weird comment she made about a drunken redneck?* Did she simply snap when she heard of the mistrial, or had this been the latest in a long line of traumas?

Realizing he'd left his car at the courthouse, Sax considered calling Barbara, but punched up Uber instead.

* * *

Curled up on their sofa, Tom and Colleen watched local coverage of the shooting. As it cut to the entrance of the courthouse, they heard a muffled noise, off camera, followed by one gunshot, then another.

The image blurred as the cameraman spun to find two police officers wrestling Dina to the ground. A large Black man Tom recognized as one of the jurors held her feet as she tried to kick him. As the image closed in on Dina's face, Tom noticed that, with all her struggling, she seemed calm, detached.

The camera turned back to where Liam lay on the concrete, partly shielded by a distraught Sara Radford, blood and gray matter spattering her white cotton blouse. For a moment Tom caught a glimpse of Liam's face, covered in red, head pushed out of shape, eyes staring into eternity.

Colleen gasped. "They could have spared us that."

The story cut to an impromptu press conference in Glover Park. Cobb District Attorney Butch Lowry confirmed that the sheriff's office had placed Dina under arrest for murder and that she'd remain in custody, pending arraignment. When asked, he refused to rule out the possibility of a death penalty.

Next up, Christine Posner's attorney, a short, balding man in a rumpled tan suit, hotly denied reports she'd posted Facebook comments about the case or gone anywhere near Liam's home. Someone, he claimed, had hijacked her account.

A reporter summarized events of the trial, including the break-in at Radford's by a woman resembling Dina and rumors she'd paid a private detective for jurors' background information.

Tom turned to find Colleen staring at him. "Oh no," she said. "I've seen that look before. You're going after this story."

"Of course, I am. It's too good to pass up." He thought for a moment. "Let me ask you something . . . Do you know anyone who works at Harvard, perhaps in the registrar's office?"

Colleen leaned back, eyes narrowing. "What are you thinking?" she asked.

"All we know about Dina is that she went to Case Western, then Harvard. I'm thinking they'd have her high school transcripts."

Colleen started to shake her head, then stopped. "You remember my best friend from childhood, Isabella Castro. Last I heard, she was working in the Harvard registrar's office. But I can't ask her to risk her job by giving out confidential information."

"No one has to know. Besides, how long do you think it'll be before Butch Lowry knows who she is?"

Colleen gave an exasperated sigh. "What if I have my investigator look into it?"

"That would be great."

* * *

Trembling and crying, Sara Radford set her shower temp as hot as it would go and stepped in, hoping to wash away the stench of death. In time, the water ran cold.

Drying off and wrapping herself in a white terry cloth robe, she tried to come to terms with Liam's murder and her own close call. She considered going out for a drink but instead went to the kitchen for a glass of Merlot.

Her first reaction had been overwhelming anger. If she could have gotten her hands on that gun, she'd have turned it on Dina and saved the state a trial. Liam walked out of that courtroom, for all intents a free man, only to lose his life on the courthouse steps.

This would have been the case that launched Radford's career. She walked into that courtroom confident she could get an acquittal the old fashioned way, by destroying the prosecutor's case, by sowing reasonable doubt in the minds of twelve fair and honest citizens.

Wracked by waves of guilt, she laid her face in her hands. For months she'd thought only of winning an acquittal. Not once had she pondered what it had been like for his parents. Now they'd seen their child gunned down only inches away.

Unconsciously, she reached for her remote. A local newscast led with the shooting. Again, she heard the shots, the screams, and saw Liam's blood and brains splattered against the wall. A closeup showed her stunned look as officers wrestled Dina to the ground.

Radford turned off the television and sipped her wine. Nothing in law school, nothing in her brief career, could have prepared her for this.

Knowing she should walk away and get on with her life, she kept returning to the thought that someone working for Bjorn had manipulated the trial to create the impression of jury tampering. She had to find out for sure. *She hated loose ends.*

Radford pictured throngs of reporters, trying to reach her for comment. Without looking, she pulled out her phone and shut it off.

The Cobb deputy who'd whisked her back into the courthouse after the shooting seemed genuinely concern for her well-being. He gave her his card and asked her to call him when she felt like talking. She turned her phone back on and dialed.

"Gaines," he answered.

"Deputy Gaines, this is Sara Radford. I spoke to the judge about this yesterday. Night before last I got an email with photos of a man meeting a woman at a bar in Atlanta, supposedly Dina Savage."

"Yes, ma'am?"

"I understand the man's a private investigator, Ron Dalrymple."

"Yes ma'am. Judge Gilmartin turned the matter over to Cobb Police. They interviewed Mr. Dalrymple this evening."

"Any word on what they found?"

"No, ma'am."

Rather than pressing him further, she said, "Well, thank you anyway."

She pulled out her laptop and brought up the anonymous emails. In the pictures at the Buckhead bar, Dalrymple's positioning and demeanor indicated he had no idea anyone had photographed him. What, besides a setup, could have motivated the photographer? Draining the Merlot, she dialed the number Rob Alford gave her.

The voice on the other end sounded reticent. "Hello."

"Is this Ron Dalrymple?"

"Yes."

"Mr. Dalrymple, don't hang up. This is Sara Radford, attorney for Liam Sanstrom, and I believe you've been the victim of a scam."

"Yes?"

"I received photographs of your meeting with an unidentified woman, supposedly Dina Savage, at Dan's Old Bar."

"Yes."

"Did you know anyone had photographed you?"

"No."

"Do you have any idea who did this?"

"No."

"How did they contact you initially?"

Dalrymple relayed the story he'd given Cobb Police earlier, that a woman had contacted him and refused to give him her name or number. She offered him cash for information on the jurors in the Sanstrom trial and told him to meet her at Dan's.

"And you had no idea who she was? Did you notice anything strange about her?"

"Yep. At first her Southern accent seemed overdone, then, later, she sounded more European."

"European? Scandinavian perhaps?"

"I don't think so. More like . . . Russian."

"Anything else?"

"Nope."

"Could you call me if you remember anything?"

"Sure."

Chapter Twenty-One

Bonnie Baron

Decatur, Georgia
Friday, March 22

Bonnie's phone rang in her pocketbook, its tone, appropriately enough, *Bad Day* by Daniel Powter. She retrieved it, read the screen and punched the green button.

"Hey, Tom."

"Bonnie, I'm so sorry. I can't even imagine what you're going through."

She closed her eyes. When she finally replied her voice caught. "I wasn't there for him, Tom. He needed my support, and I didn't even show up."

"Bonnie, you couldn't have done anything. I *was* there. I saw the whole thing. It happened so fast no one could have stopped it, not even the police."

"That's not what I mean," she sobbed. "His lawyer asked me to testify. I told her I'd scheduled a trip out of town and couldn't change it. That was a *lie*." Bonnie took a pull from her cigarette. "It was that damned rape charge. Liam had become a pariah, and all I wanted was to get as far away from him as possible."

"Bonnie, none of that would've have made any difference. Liam didn't need character witnesses. If there hadn't been a mistrial, he'd have walked."

"How do you know that?"

"Colleen was there. She said Radford took Dina apart. She had her on video, for God's sake, taking her own clothes off. Outside the court-room, before Liam came out, Colleen told me the prosecutor would *never* retry that case."

Bonnie stared at the floor. "I should've been there," she repeated. "I thought he was guilty, Tom. I knew for sure he would go away for the rest of his life." Her sobs turned to anger. "God, I hope that bitch gets the needle."

"Who knows? She might. There won't be any reasonable doubt this time."

"Look, I have to go," she said. "All of a sudden, I'm busy as hell. After his arrest no one would touch Liam's paintings. Now my phone won't stop ringing. These art collectors are like vultures. It's Liam's notoriety and the fact that he'll never paint again. Now everyone wants a Liam Sanstrom . . . Sometimes I could *scream*."

Bonnie stared absently at Liam's portrait of a young girl painting her toenails. "Listen, thanks for the call. It means a lot to me."

* * *

Rollo Witherspoon returned Dalrymple's call the next day as prom-ised. He explained that the vanity plate Dalrymple saw outside Dan's belonged to a Gwinnett County resident who'd reported it stolen. Under police questioning, the man finally admitted he'd parked outside a mas-sage parlor on Cheshire Bridge Road the night before Dalrymple's ren-dezvous at the bar.

Dalrymple thanked him and hung up. It seemed the matter had reached an impasse. His thoughts returned to his interview with the two officers. They hadn't called back, but he knew they would. Never in his life had Dalrymple known a cop who could tolerate loose ends.

He recalled the threats they'd made and tried to imagine his life without a PI license. Maybe he'd get a job at the Walmart down the street. He'd have to sell his car, but he could always walk to work. Anxious to put such thoughts out of his mind, he pulled out the card the older cop, Daniels, had given him and dialed.

The call rolled to voice mail. Dalrymple left a message with the number of the stolen tag, a description of the SUV and the name of the tag's owner. He prayed that might placate the man for now. An hour later Daniels called back and agreed to meet him at the White House Restaurant in Buckhead for lunch.

Dalrymple arrived early and took a table near the back with a clear view of the door. Daniels came in carrying a thick manila folder, looking as though he'd been up all night. From the envelope he pulled the picture of Dalrymple and the woman at Dan's. "So, any ideas who she might be?"

"No. but I saw the Savage woman on the news last night. I'm pretty sure it's not her. This woman has a more angular face."

"Maybe this'll help," he said, pulling out another shot of the blonde with the ponytail climbing into the passenger side of the black SUV. Her face stood out more clearly in daylight. In the background, Dalrymple saw himself peering around the corner of the building.

"Yep. That's her. How'd you get this?"

Daniels pursed his lips, scanning the room for anyone listening. "You didn't here this from me. I got it from an FBI friend who's been tailing this woman on an unrelated matter. He heard about the Sanstrom case and somehow made the connection. He couldn't give me her name or what the FBI wants with her. But he gave me a picture of her last known associate, this man. I'm hoping you might identify him."

The next photo showed a squarely built man with curly brown hair and a moustache. "This guy left Dan's Old Bar just ahead of your lady friend. We believe he drove the SUV."

Dalrymple stared at the photo. "If you know who he is, why don't you pick him up?"

"The agent couldn't give me his name either, or his whereabouts. Just said he's a suspected Russian hacker known as the *Commissar*. Do you recognize him?"

"Nope."

"And you're sure you don't remember seeing him inside the bar?"

"No." Dalrymple recalled his conversation with Sara Radford. *Is this the guy who took my picture?*

Daniels put the photos back. "Yet somehow this woman knew *you* well enough to call and arrange a meeting at a neighborhood bar." He tapped the envelope with his right index finger as he spoke.

"I've already told you," said Dalrymple. "When she contacted me she wouldn't give me *her* name or how she'd gotten mine. She asked if I wanted the job or not. I've checked around since, and nobody remembers talking to her."

Daniels gave him a bland smile. "What we have here, Mr. Dalrymple, looks like obstruction of justice. And it's now material to a murder case. We have two suspicious characters, very little idea who they are, and no idea where they went or what they're up to. The one person we do have . . . *is you.* I'm sure you can appreciate your predicament. If you find out anything about this woman, call us. You really need to protect yourself. Stay in touch."

With that, Daniels stood, paid his tab and left.

Dalrymple had no idea how to locate a Russian hacker. In desperation he called the first person he could think of, Rollo. The phone rang five times before he answered.

"Hey, man. Whazzup?" Rollo's voice slurred.

He's stoned. That's just great. "Hey. I need your help."

"Anything man. You name it."

"You know that stolen tag?"

"Yeah."

"I think I know who stole it. I just need to find out where he is."

"Okay. I'll see what I can do."

"The guy's a Russian hacker."

"A hacker?"

"Breaks into other people's . . ."

"Yeah, man. I know what a hacker is." Rollo sounded offended. "I'm just not sure how to find him. That shit's *way* outta my league." He paused a moment. "There *is* this one person I know might be able to help. Weird dude, but *damned good* at this stuff."

"Anything. I'm in a jam here. The cops are breathing down my neck."

"Sure. I'd call this guy myself, but I'm on my way out to visit one of my lady friends, if you know what I mean. Here, I'll give you his number."

Dalrymple grabbed a napkin, pulled a pen from his pocket and jotted it down. He called but got no answer. He'd try again later.

* * *

Mark Winston felt his phone buzz in the pocket of his Cobb Police uniform. He frowned at the caller ID. "Tom Williams . . . tell me you're not calling about this Savage woman. I already told your buddy Danner . . ."

"Now Mark, how long have we known each other?"

"Long enough for me to know this ain't no social call." Winston glanced down the hallway to see if anyone might overhear him. "Sorry, man," he muttered, "I can't help you. Word gets out I'm talking to a reporter they'll have me directing traffic out on Powder Springs Road."

"Mark, you know I'm retired."

"Bullshit. You guys never retire. You just get old and die."

"Okay. Okay. Tell you what, why don't I ask some questions, and you can say 'yes' or 'no.' But don't nod your head. That doesn't help me over the phone."

"Alright," he whispered, "but nothing about the murder, okay?"

"Okay . . . So, is it true you guys interviewed this man . . . Dalrymple, who supposedly met Dina Savage at a Buckhead bar?"

"Uh huh."

"And he spells his name like the street up there in Sandy Springs?"

"Yup."

"Is it true he's now saying it wasn't Savage but another woman?"
Winston glanced around again. "Uh huh."

"Did he give you the other woman's name?"

"Nope."

"Mark, what do you know about Dina Savage's background?"

"Not a thing."

"Surely *somebody* knows whether or not she has prior arrests."

"I'm sure somebody does, but that somebody wouldn't be me."

Williams paused and said, "Thanks, Mark. I appreciate your help."

"No problem."

Winston slipped the phone back into his pocket and strolled down the hall humming to himself.

* * *

Sax awoke Friday morning, having slept precious little the night before. Images of Sanstrom's head exploding and the photo of Dina in the emergency room still haunted him. He called Cheryl to say he'd be back at work on Monday.

They spoke for more than an hour. Filling him in on latest developments in the buyout, Cheryl said the new investors wanted to come by the office the following week. Sax agreed but asked her to hold off on scheduling it until he came in on Monday, so he could call them himself.

When she'd hung up, he laid the phone on the bedside table and wondered what he should do. Then it rang again. He answered on reflex, without checking the ID.

"Hey," Barbara said. She sounded out of breath. "I saw you on the news this morning. My God, Sax, you could have been killed. I called to see how you're doing."

"A little tired, but I'm okay."

"How could that woman just walk up to the courthouse and start shooting like that?"

"I don't know. It happened so quickly I had no time to think. Next thing I knew I found myself in an ambulance on the way to Kennestone."

"And you're sure you're okay?"

"Yeah. Yeah. At first the officer thought I'd been hit . . . I tried to explain it was Sanstrom's blood all over me."

"You poor baby! When I saw you on TV I thought I would die."

"I'll be okay."

That's great, Sax thought. *I'm all over the news. How long before Mom and Dad find out? I'll have to call them.*

"You want to go somewhere and talk about this?" Barbara asked.

Sax recalled their previous conversation about a lunch date. "Sure," he said. "How about Marlow's?" He glanced at his clock . . . almost ten.

"Sounds great. You sure you can get away?"

"Yeah. I took the day off. Let me get up and shower. I'll meet you there at 12:30."

"It's a date then." She sounded more cheerful than she had in a long time.

* * *

Sax ordered a sandwich and a glass of water, Barbara a salad and a Malbec. He filled her in on the case, including the mistrial and the shooting.

"All I thought about was getting out of there. Now I feel like shit."

"Now that you can talk about it, do you think Sanstrom raped her?"

"I have no clue, *really*. In a way I'm glad we didn't have to decide. I never imagined it would end so horribly. I couldn't stand the guy, but the State never proved him guilty. Every one of their witnesses fell apart on cross-examination. Some of the other jurors seemed ready to string him up. Hell, we'd probably still be there arguing if it hadn't been for that crazy bartender. My gut tells me Sanstrom either raped Savage or she sincerely believed he did."

Before long, the subject turned to the buyout. "Cheryl has everything under control over there, but I've got to get back. I'm about to go stir crazy."

"You work too hard, baby. I've been telling you that for years."

"Yeah. Cheryl keeps telling me the same thing."

Barbara's expression soured. Sax knew he'd said the wrong thing. She pursed her lips and nodded. "Yep. Sounds like Cheryl takes good care of you."

"I've told you, Barbara, it's not like that."

"Yeah, right. I've seen the way she looks at you. That woman wants something . . ." Barbara caught herself before reopening an old and painful subject.

Switching gears, she said, "Once the sale goes through you could take some time off. The company can get by for a few weeks without you. *Cheryl* can run things while you're gone."

Sax shrugged. "Maybe so." His voice lacked conviction.

Gazing into Barbara's eyes, he asked, "So . . . how are things at home?"

"*They suck. Really.* Thanks for asking."

The waiter returned, and Barbara ordered another Malbec as she recounted her latest arguments with Misty.

"Is there anything I can do to help?"

"Like what, start acting like a father?" Catching herself, she said, "Look, I'm sorry. That's unfair. It's . . . just . . . been rough not having you around."

"No, no, no. It's my fault," he said. "I've let this buyout, and now the trial, consume me. For years I've worked late hours and weekends. Maybe we can get together and . . . you know . . . go somewhere." He felt foolish as soon as the words tumbled out, expecting another sharp retort. Instead, she smiled and changed the subject.

"Of course . . . Say, you'll never guess what your daughter wants now."

"What?"

"She says she's sick of Walton and wants to go to a private school."

"You're kidding!"

"Nope. Apparently she's become distant from her friends. She's had a rough time this year. I thought that . . . with that big payday you have coming . . ."

"Sure. I mean Walton's a good school, but there are some excellent private ones in the area." Sax suppressed a smile. "How about the Emmaus School?"

"*Are you shitting me, Sax?* You want to send our daughter to some Christian madrasa?"

His blossoming grin stopped her.

"You asshole!" she said, kicking him under the table.

He held up his hands, palms out. "Just kidding. We could check out Walker or Atlanta International."

As their conversation rolled on, hours passed. Barbara ordered and finished a third glass of wine. Sax could see its warmth rising to her face.

She studied him for a moment. "You know . . . there *is* one thing you can do for me."

"What's that?"

She pulled at her lower lip. "The faucet in our bathroom sink is dripping again. I planned to call a plumber . . ."

"Don't. It's a waste of money. I'm sure I still have that set of washers in the garage. I'll come by and fix it."

"Really? That would be great."

"In fact, I could come by right now if that's alright."

"Sure."

They finished their meals and Sax paid the bill. He followed her to where she'd parked, climbed into his Miata and trailed her home, worried a cop might pull her over. Instinctively, he parked in the garage beside her Mercedes and closed the door.

He found the wrench and washers and followed Barbara to their master bath, where he opened his shirt collar, rolled up his sleeves, and, in no time, had the faucet working properly.

190

As he worked, Barbara stood in the doorway silently watching. Glancing up, he saw a strange look come over her. She smiled and wrapped her arms around his waist.

"You know," she said. "I have another plumbing job for you."

* * *

The school bus stopped at the entrance of the narrow, shaded street, and Misty disembarked. Lost in thought, she walked the short distance to her home, books clutched tightly to her chest. Two other girls strolled behind her, engaged in animated conversation. One of them shouted to Misty as she turned into her driveway. Never looking back, she simply waved.

As she let herself in, Misty wondered why her mom had closed the garage. Maybe she'd gone to the gym or the grocery store . . . *What's that sound upstairs?* Misty dumped her books onto her bed and heard it again. *Okay. She's home.*

Remembering something she needed to tell her, she opened Barbara's bedroom door without knocking. There in the middle of the bed lay her parents, naked.

Misty gasped, slamming the door behind her. Stunned and confused, she stumbled to her room and shut herself in.

Moments later, she heard a soft knock.

"What?!" she yelled.

"Hey," her dad replied through the door.

Misty shivered. "Are you decent now?"

"Yes."

She turned the knob and stepped back.

"Hey," he said. "Can I come in?"

She didn't answer. He moved tentatively inside.

"You wanna talk?"

"Not really . . . *Not about that*."

Apparently relieved, he stood there as though fumbling for something to say.

"Okay. So, if you do, call me . . . Love you."

She let him kiss her on the forehead. "Love you too," she said.

From the bedroom Misty heard her mother, laughing hysterically. Staring at the ceiling she posed the question so common to teenage girls, *"Why me, God?"*

Chapter Twenty-Two

Decatur, Georgia
Saturday, March 23

At the door to The Baron Agency a young woman greeted Tom and Colleen. It took him a moment to recognize her. Two years had passed since they met Heather. Since then, she'd shortened her hair and carried herself now with an air of confidence.

She ushered them to a back room that served as Bonnie's gallery. A long, horizontal window high up the wall provided northern light. A table in the corner held an espresso machine. The only other furnishings, besides a sink and four lavender armchairs, were art displays. Heather offered them a seat and a cup of coffee. They declined both, electing to browse the paintings instead.

What struck Tom repeatedly were the three-dimensional effect and panoramic view created by Liam's use of diffused illumination and reflection. One work, *Midnight in the Potting Shed*, created a downward view of a concrete walkway in a darkened green house. Plants lined either side of a narrow path. Leaves from hanging baskets added depth, and a puddle in the center reflected the windows above and a full moon beyond.

Another painting showed a priest seated at his desk writing a sermon. Behind him, a stained-glass window cast multi-hued light across his scribbled notes. Colleen gasped.

Finally, they came to a canvas of a middle-aged, mustachioed man with a cheap-looking toupee mixing a drink at a wet bar. He wore nothing but a towel around his waist. Gray and white hair blanketed his sagging chest. Behind him lay an unmade hotel bed and beyond that a sliding door onto a sunbathed balcony. A young woman leaned against a railing wearing nothing but a bikini bottom.

She'd turned her head, presenting a clear profile, sea breeze combing back her blonde rivulets. It took Tom and Colleen but a moment to recognize Dina Savage, seconds longer to identify the old man as Horace Rainey.

A voice interrupted their reverie, "Liam painted that while awaiting trial."

Tom and Colleen turned to find Bonnie Baron behind them. She'd acquired a hardened, weary look.

"Bonnie, it's good to see you. How are you holding up?" Tom asked.

"Better than expected under the circumstances." She forced a wry smile. "I guess staying busy helps."

Heather threaded her arms around Bonnie's waist and laid her head against her shoulder.

Suddenly, Colleen broke into a coughing spell.

"Are you okay?" asked Bonnie.

Colleen nodded.

"Can I get you some water?"

"Thanks."

Heather grabbed a cup from the espresso table and filled it with filtered water from the sink.

"You promised to see a doctor," said Tom. "What about the one Kathy recommended?"

Colleen took a long sip. "I have an appointment on Tuesday," she gasped.

Bonnie continued to stare at the painting. "That's the last piece Liam completed. With everything that woman put him through, he still obsessed over her."

"How well did you know Liam?" Tom asked.

"As well as anyone, I guess," said Bonnie, "besides maybe his parents."

She gave Tom an inquisitive look. "I suppose you're asking if I believe he raped her. Liam was a complicated person. He had remarkable empathy when it came to his paintings. It's like you can see inside his subjects and hear what they're thinking. But when it came to real people, especially women, I think Liam saw them as objects. When he wasn't painting, all he wanted was pleasure, which he got through manipulating other people."

"You make him sound like a sociopath," said Tom.

"The word that comes to mind," said Bonnie, "is *narcissist*. I don't believe he ever meant to harm anyone. He never thought about it. I'm not sure he was capable of rape, in a figurative sense. He could be so persuasive and, from what I've heard, he liked role play. Maybe Dina changed her mind at the last moment. She started to object, and he considered that part of the game. Liam had trouble reading other people's cues."

"Where do you think that started?" Tom asked.

"He grew up in the lap of luxury, his mother's only child, small, shy and awkward. She doted on him. His father's the opposite, cold, distant and demanding. Liam probably suffered from autism. He failed miserably at academic pursuits. His parents hired tutors, to no avail. So, he retreated into his drawings and paintings, which his mother indulged. She paid for private lessons from the best art instructors in Europe . . . And then Liam grew up tall and handsome."

Bonnie bit her lower lip, staring at the painting. "The greatest irony of all is that he turned out more like his old man than his mom."

"Well, for what it's worth," said Tom, "Liam's attorney made it seem that Dina went along with the role play then became angry afterward."

"Or perhaps during," added Colleen.

Bonnie gazed at the painting some more, before conducting an extended tour of Liam's collection, most of which came from his now infamous basement.

* * *

On the drive home Tom asked, "Suppose for a moment Dina did agree to bondage, initially, and then changed her mind in the middle of the act. Is that what you think happened?"

"Perhaps . . . Nobody knows but Dina. Hell, as much wine and blow as she'd had, I doubt even *she* remembers."

"If she *did* change her mind in the middle of the act would it then become rape?"

"I guess that depends on how quickly he pulled out."

"It's a shame that security camera didn't point at the bed. Then we'd know."

Colleen smiled. "I think that would give the camera a different purpose, don't you?"

"How do you get to the bottom of a case like this? How could a jury figure out what really happened?"

Colleen stared at him, incredulous. "Are you asking how we could determine the *truth*?"

"Well . . . Yes."

"Tom, darling, nobody gives a shit about the truth, least of all trial lawyers. In a case like this, the truth is whatever twelve people decide it is. You have a prosecutor selling them one truth and a defense attorney selling another. It *helps* if the jurors believe your story, but they don't have to. They simply choose the version they like best and go home thinking they've made the right decision."

"*That's* a cynical view of American justice."

"Believe me, it's been years in the making."

"By the way, you said you'd check into Dina's background."

"Oh! I meant to tell you. Sammy got back to me yesterday. One of his sources found records of a Dina Savage at Case Western. She'd changed her name from Dawn Sawyer, but her high school transcript came from a small town in Mississippi . . . Clewiston, I believe."

"I need to get over there before someone in the DA's office leaks it."

"Tom, you're not thinking of . . ."

"It'll only be a couple of days. You can come with me if you like."

"To Clewiston, Mississippi? I'll pass. Are you sure you can even find the place?"

"Garmin can find it."

"What are you hoping to discover?"

"I don't know." He let out a long sigh. "I just want to get to the bottom of this."

"There you go again, thinking you're going to make everything okay by discovering the truth. Trust me, Baby. The truth will *not* set you free. *There is no bottom to this*."

"Maybe, but . . . who knows . . . It's worth a try. I want to find out what motivated her . . . Rainey said something about her coming from a broken home."

"*Don't even go there*. Next thing you know, you'll start blaming *society*. I've heard that crap all my career. I've even used it when I had to, but that doesn't mean I believe it. *Society* didn't pull that trigger, Tom. *Dina Savage* did. And now she'll have to answer for it."

* * *

Sax stared at his phone. He'd promised to call Barbara but couldn't think of what to say. He picked it up, started to set it back down, took a deep breath and dialed.

"Hey," she said.

"Hey . . . How are you?"

"Confused, mostly."

"Me too." He grasped for something to say. "How's Misty?"

"Oh, she's *very* confused . . . not that she wants to talk about it."

"Do you think . . ."

"Jeff, I don't know what to think."

"Maybe . . . maybe we could get together for lunch . . ."

"Yeah. So, you can ply me with alcohol again and take advantage of me?"

He cracked a smile. "Well . . ."

"Let me think about it. I'll call you tomorrow."

Chapter Twenty-Three

Alpharetta, Georgia
Monday, March 25

Sax stepped off the elevator to find his entire company waiting to greet him. Cheryl, with help from HR and Marketing, had decorated the lobby with flowers, yellow ribbons and balloons. Across the opposite wall a red and gold banner read, "Welcome back, Jeff!"

Suppressing emotions, he expressed his gratitude for their compassion and support. "It's because of you that we have this deal, and I promise your hard work will have its rewards."

Escaping to the solitude of his office, he sipped coffee and went through emails he'd missed over the past week. Cheryl came in, shut the door and perched on the corner of his desk.

"You had quite a week," she said.

He gave her a fleeting smile.

"Do you feel like talking about the trial, now that you can?"

He thought for a moment. "I guess so, as long as we don't have to talk about the shooting."

"I can imagine. So, what exactly happened in the courtroom? Do you think Sanstrom raped her?"

"I don't know. I don't think anybody knows. It was your typical *he said, she said.*"

"I understand Savage is up for arraignment this morning."

Sax shook his head.

"What do you think made her do it?" Cheryl asked.

"I have no idea . . . anger, vengeance, a sense of injustice. Who knows?"

"It should make an interesting trial," she said. "Some folks will think Sanstrom raped her and had it coming."

"Maybe."

Cheryl tilted her head and studied her boss, swinging her feet back and forth. "What do you think you'll do when this is all over? The last time you worked for someone else you were waiting tables in college, right?"

He stared out the window, focusing on a point somewhere beyond the tree line, picturing Barbara and Misty. "I'm not sure. I have too much to think about right now. Besides, I told the new partners I'd stay on for a year. After that, who knows?"

"Whatever you do," she said, "you need to take time off, travel, have some fun."

Sax realized, for the first time, that he'd never contemplated life after DataScape. *What would retirement look like?*

He looked up, startled to see Goldwyn holding Lance Barclay's laptop.

"I thought you might want to see this, Boss. In one his emails, Lance refers to, um, an assignation between him and this young woman about a week before he left."

"So?"

Goldwyn gave Cheryl an embarrassed look. "*They did it on his desk.*"

"That's okay. I'm sure housekeeping took care of it."

"There's more."

Sax browsed Barclay's emails, stopping at one addressed to a Lana Green in which Barclay invited her to dinner at a nearby restaurant followed by a tour of the office.

"I wonder where he met this woman," asked Sax.

"I have no idea. Let's check his social media."

Sax opened Facebook using the password saved in Barclay's browser. There, among his many posts, he found a photo of a young woman on a boat wearing a string bikini. A broad-brimmed hat shaded the upper part of her face, but the smile gave her away, the same smile Sax saw in the picture of two people enjoying an outdoor concert.

"Guys, I want you to meet Ms. Dina Savage. Goldwyn, I need you to find out everything you can about her and her employer, Moore and Frye. I believe we've found the source of our break-in, but I doubt we can prove it."

* * *

Transferring scribbled trial notes onto his laptop, Tom took in the lingering aroma of supper. From the kitchen came sounds of Colleen rinsing plates and placing them in the dishwasher. Tonight, he'd prepared linguine and mussels in a white wine reduction.

Bogie sauntered onto the enclosed sleeping porch Tom had converted to a home office, curling up on an old blanket beside the chair. Absentmindedly, Tom scratched him behind the ear. From the kitchen he heard Colleen stifle a cough.

"Hey, Baby," he called out. "I can postpone that trip to Mississippi and go to the doctor with you on Tuesday."

"No need. It's not a big deal. Maybe a touch of bronchitis."

From the living room flowed the sweet, haunting melody of Janis Ian's *Society's Child*, part of an MP3 collection Tom had compiled for Colleen, featuring female artists from the first three years of their marriage, with a bit of Indigo Girls thrown in.

Tom scanned the list of jurors' names and phone numbers Colleen's investigator obtained, not wanting to know how. He called Christine Posner, who refused to talk on advice of her attorney. He thanked her anyway and moved on to Carlton Beasley, who sounded as though he were in a rush.

"Mr. Beasley, this is Tom Williams. I believe you were on the jury for the Sanstrom trial."

"Yes."

Given Beasley's wary response, Tom added, "Now that the trial's over it's okay to discuss the case. I don't know if you remember, but I testified for the defense. I wanted to get your impressions for a story I'm writing. I won't use your name if you don't want me to."

Beasley paused. "Sure, but we'll have to make it quick. I'm starting a new job."

"I understand. Did you think the prosecutor made a good case against Sanstrom?"

"Not really. I mean, I didn't like the dude, and I'm sure he was guilty of something, but . . . it's like the prosecutor fucked up from the start then tried to put it off on Chris."

"Chris?"

"Yeah. Christine. They kicked her off the jury, and now she's afraid they'll prosecute her."

"They said she discussed the case with other jurors . . ."

"That's bullshit, man! She didn't talk about nothing. They just wanted to drop the case. I bet that rich boy's daddy bought off the DA and the judge too. Chris is a good person. Hell, she got me this job at the bar where she works."

"Wow! Congratulations. Thanks."

Beasley had already hung up.

After striking out with another juror, Tom took a break. He invited Colleen for a walk with him and Bogie, but she begged off, saying she wanted to stay home, relax, drink her wine, and listen to the music.

As he reached for the dog's leash, Colleen launched into another coughing spasm. He poured her a cup of water and forgot about the walk.

* * *

Sax left work early, still pondering the discovery of Dina's picture on Lance's laptop. Preoccupied, he glanced in his rear-view mirror. Like a mirage, the dark blue pickup materialized, accelerating toward his rear bumper. Instinctively, Sax braced against his head rest anticipating an impact. Instead, the truck swerved into the oncoming lane. Sax recognized the Oliver Landscaping sign.

Up ahead a van turned right from Wills Road, bearing down on them. At the last moment, it veered onto the opposite shoulder, avoiding a head-on collision.

Scott Oliver's expression radiated mindless rage. Sax slammed his brakes before the man could run him into the ditch. He reached into his console for a can of pepper spray, cupping it in his right hand as he opened his door.

Fifteen feet ahead, Oliver pulled over and climbed out. The van driver remained in his vehicle, stunned, no doubt, and dialing 911.

Sax studied Oliver as he staggered toward him. *Ah shit, he's drunk.* Waiting for him to come within reach, Sax came up with the canister and emptied its contents into Oliver's face. He screamed, clawing at his eyes.

Sax took a half step back and planted his right foot, full force, into the larger man's groin, doubling him over and dropping him to his knees. This made his next move, a round house kick to the side of the face, much easier.

Confident he had him down, Sax moved as close as he dared.

"You stupid motherfucker! You *will* pay for any damage to my car, and if you or your shit son ever come near me or my family again I promise *I will shoot you like a dog*. Am I making myself clear?"

Writhing on the pavement the man coughed up blood and spit out a molar. Sax kept a wary eye on him as he waited for Roswell Police.

They arrived in less than ten minutes with an ambulance in tow. With help from the van driver, Sax made his case to the officer, who promised to file a report and gave him a number to call in case he wanted to prosecute. Fearing a reinvestigation of his assault on Jordan, Sax declined.

Returning to his empty condo, heart pounding, Sax warmed some leftover chili, poured a glass of red wine and settled onto his sofa. He'd just turned on the news when his house phone rang. The ID read "T. S. Williams." Sax stared at it, reluctant to answer, but relented out of curiosity.

After promising not to quote him, Williams moved right into his first question. "Let's start with the obvious. Do you think Sanstrom raped Savage?"

"I don't know. I think *something* happened, but her testimony didn't help. The security video showed her undressing, but it didn't *prove* a thing. We *don't* know what happened later." Sax sighed and ran his fingers through his hair. "With all that reasonable doubt, I'd probably have voted to acquit."

"Do you think the other jurors felt that way?"

"I can't speak for anyone else. We never discussed it. Once it finally ended, I just wanted to get out of there. I know that sounds terrible, but my company's going through a buyout . . . I saw at least one juror sobbing during Dina's testimony . . . And then that bartender . . . what's her name?"

"Christine Posner. You know she's claiming someone hacked her Facebook account, right?"

"Yeah! What a surprise!" Sax started to mention the DataScape attack but thought better of it.

Tom moved on. "So, tell me about your experience after the mistrial."

Sax took a deep breath. "I stood so close to Sanstrom I could have touched him without straightening my arm. I even got some of his brains on my clothes. I threw them out as soon as I got home. I never even saw the gun, it happened so quickly. My only glimpse of Savage was when they wrestled her to the ground."

"Yeah. My wife and I were about three feet behind you. I saw Sanstrom's head snap back."

"Wow! This must have been quite a blow, seeing your friend gunned down."

"More like a *friend of a friend*. Colleen and I sat at a table with him at the Harry Connick concert."

Refocusing, Tom asked, "What do you think about that private detective selling your personal information to the woman at the bar? Has anyone spoken to you?"

"No."

"According to my sources, she wasn't Dina Savage. What do you make of that?"

"I have no idea. The whole thing sounds screwy to me."

"Why would someone else, made up to look like Dina, want information about the jurors?"

Sax smiled. "Perhaps another journalist working on a story."

Tom laughed. "Could be."

"Do you think someone working for Sanstrom's parents wanted to discredit Savage?" Sax asked.

"Who knows? I have two daughters. Given similar circumstances, I'd do whatever it took to protect them."

When the call ended, Sax sat for a while replaying their conversation, wondering what the Sanstrom trial had to do with the breach at DataScape. His thoughts returned to Williams' comment about doing whatever it took to protect his daughters. *Did I go too far with Jordan Oliver? Did I do it out of guilt over separation from my family?* He picked up the phone and dialed.

"Hey," Barbara said. "I was about to call you."

"Sure, you were. They say they'll respect you in the morning, and then you never hear from them."

"You have some experience with that, do you?"

Sax laughed. "So, what do you think?"

"I don't know, Jeff. Let's take it one step at a time. How's that?"

"Sure." Remembering his earlier conversation with Cheryl about retirement, he added, "Maybe I can take some time off and we can go somewhere."

"That would be nice."

They talked about Misty, about his parents. Sax chose not to mention his run-in with Scott Oliver. Instead, he told her about the surprise party his staff had thrown and the discovery of Dina Savage's picture on Lance Barclay's laptop.

"That sounds fishy, Jeff. Of all the businesses in Atlanta she just *happened* to pick one owned by a juror in the Sanstrom trial."

"It doesn't make sense to me either, which is why I haven't reported it yet."

"You sound exhausted," she said. "Get some sleep."

"Good night."

"Good night."

Fly Away: The Metamorphosis of Dina Savage

* * *

Music blared and strobes flashed as Miranda Diaz, stage name Carmen Cardinal, strolled onto the dance floor at the Tattletale Lounge, grabbed a pole and began her number. Though she'd been at it less than a year, Carmen considered herself a rising artist. She awoke every day at noon and practiced for hours in front of a mirror to Lady Gaga's *Born This Way*. Closing her eyes, she parted her lips as she slowly untied and dropped her scant clothing onto the polished floor.

Carmen hated looking out at the patrons, such pigs, but she had no choice. Each overgrown adolescent had to believe that she danced especially for him. Their tips and the money she made hustling overpriced drinks comprised her sole income. They had no appreciation for the talent and conditioning her act required. She turned tricks, of course, but only with a select clientele. One day she'd kiss this all goodbye and return to school.

Wearing nothing but a garter and high heels, she lifted her left leg into a split and swung in a full circle around the pole. From the corner of her eye, she saw an overweight man settle into his customary seat at the edge of the stage. Her stomach lurched, yet she managed to gaze at him and smile.

None of the girls knew his real name. One of the bouncers said that people called him "the Penguin." With his beaked nose and thinning, greasy hair he made a taller, fatter version of Oswald Cobblepot, the Danny DeVito character in *Batman Returns*.

He watched her intently, licking his lips as she turned upside down, one knee bent, the other pointing skyward. His lips hung open at one corner in a perpetual sneer, making it difficult to tell if he were smiling or grimacing. His expression never changed.

* * *

The Penguin felt a vibration in his groin, ignored it, then felt it again.

Annoyed, he pulled the phone from the pocket of his loose-fitting Bermuda shorts. Only five people had this number, and *they* knew better than to call during recreational time.

He frowned at the readout. Six people apparently . . . Someone would pay dearly for this. He started to reject the call, but the interruption had broken Carmen's spell.

"What?!" he screeched.

Over the din he barely made out the voice on the other end.

"This is Ron Dalrymple. I'm a friend of Rollo Witherspoon's . . ."

"So?" The Penguin started to punch the off button. But as he moved the phone from his ear he heard something that made him stop. "What did you say?"

"I said don't hang up. Rollo said you might have information about the Commissar."

The Penguin took a moment to reply. He stared at Carmen as she leaned toward him and cupped her breasts, pursing her lips. "Wait a minute," he said.

Reaching into his wallet, he pulled out a five, slowly caressing her thigh as he pushed the bill into her garter. Normally he'd have strung her along with a bunch of ones, but he needed to take this call.

Stopping at the entrance, he said, "I'll be back in a second." The bouncer recognized him and nodded.

"Why do you want to know about the Commissar?"

"I think he just screwed me over," Dalrymple said.

"Yeah? Get in line."

"Look, I'm in a jam with the cops. I need something I can trade, like information."

The Penguin took a second to connect the dots. "You want to avoid prosecution by giving the authorities information on the Russian."

"Well, that, and I also don't want to lose my license."

"As what?"

"I'm a PI."

For the Penguin this presented an ethical dilemma, but he and the Russian had a long history. The thought of putting him out of commission had a certain appeal.

"Whatever I give you, it didn't come from me. Understand? If this guy finds out, losing your license will be the least of your problems. I will fuck you up in ways you can't even imagine."

"I understand."

Hearing the tremor in the man's voice, the Penguin said, "Give me a day or two. I'll get back to you at this number." He smiled at the thought of payback for the man who'd scammed him out of a hundred grand in marketable personal data.

"And, by the way . . . Don't ever call this number again, and don't give it to anybody. I'll have a little talk with Rollo next time I see him." Foregoing a reply, he shut off his phone and strolled back into the club.

Chapter Twenty-Four

Clewiston, Mississippi
Tuesday, March 26

A cloudless periwinkle sky faded to a white haze at the horizon. Beneath it, rows of young cotton plants blanketed the Mississippi Delta, outlined in thin strips of black earth like so much corduroy.

The air, grown warm, clung to Tom Williams like damp underwear, as he rolled up the windows of his aging Mercedes and turned on the air conditioning. Bug splats dappled his windshield despite the best efforts of washer fluid and wiper blades. Among them, clearly outlined in blue, fluttered the severed wing of a large butterfly. Tom slid in a CD and relaxed to the strains of Vivaldi's *Four Seasons*.

Three hours in, he felt the pavement change. Cracks and potholes jarred his spine. A passing sign advertised "Banks County." A second read "Clewiston 8." From the distance came a black car, headlights on in midday. Tom pulled onto the soft shoulder and allowed the cortege to pass.

Clewiston, he soon discovered, comprised three blocks of storefronts huddled around an ancient brick courthouse, behind which stood a much newer jail. A single stoplight marked the intersection of the state highway and a narrower county road. Downtown, such as it was, boasted three churches, a brightly painted thrift shop and a John Deere dealership.

To the right, along a parallel street, sat a row of vintage two-story homes, set back with long driveways and well-manicured lawns. They ranged from quite stately to merely impressive. To the left, behind the cotton warehouses and a feed store, ran a railroad track. Beyond it, tarpaper shanties cringed among stunted trees. In many ways Clewiston resembled the town in which Tom spent the first eighteen years of his life.

Further down, on the right, stood a truck stop restaurant with an unpaved lot. Beside it, a pink and purple cinderblock building with a neon sign proclaimed, "Happy Tails Exotic Dance Club."

Tom pulled over and consulted the directions Colleen's investigator had given him. He turned left onto an unnamed dirt track and followed it to a dead end, where six mobile homes, in varying states of decay, encircled a large Chinaberry tree. He stopped in front of the last one on the right.

The sagging screen door rattled as he knocked repeatedly. Its aluminum frame had oxidized to a solid white under years of relentless Mississippi sun. Beneath the warped plank steps an old dog worked up the energy for a single, half-hearted woof. A stiff breeze blew an empty plastic grocery bag across the tiny, grassless yard.

Seeing no one else around, he knocked again. As he turned to leave, the inner door opened a crack, and a bloodshot eye squinted at him through the narrow opening.

The woman sounded middle-aged, with the rasp of a heavy smoker awakened from a deep sleep. "What do you want? You better not be a salesman."

"Are you Sheila Mitchell?"

"Who wants to know?"

"Ms. Mitchell, my name's Tom Williams. I apologize for bothering you. I tried to call, but I got a message saying your phone had been disconnected. I drove over from Atlanta hoping I could speak to you about your daughter."

She regarded him in silence for a long time, but the door remained ajar.

"You a reporter?"

"Kind of . . . I'm writing a magazine article about your daughter's trial, and I thought maybe you could tell me . . ."

"What trial?"

"Dina, I mean Dawn, shot a man she accused of raping her."

"What?"

"Your daughter, Dawn Sawyer, changed her name to Dina Savage before moving to Atlanta. I met her and her date at a concert. She later accused him of raping her. When a jury failed to convict him, she gunned him down on the courthouse steps."

The door opened enough for Tom to make out her face. Any shock at hearing about her daughter seemed to have melted away. "How much you paying?" she asked.

Tom debated the journalistic ethics of paying a source.

"All I have is a ten."

"Get the hell out of here. I don't wanna talk to you anyway."

"It'll only take a . . ."

"Get the fuck out of here before I call the police," she shrieked and slammed the door.

As he ambled toward the Mercedes, Tom glanced over his shoulder in time to see a boney hand pull back a lace curtain behind a small window. It closed just as quickly.

He climbed in, shut the door and cranked the engine. He'd already put the car in gear when she appeared on the stoop and motioned to him to come back.

Tom studied her, wondering how badly he wanted this interview. She might've been pretty once, perhaps beautiful, but years of hard living had taken their toll. Calculating based on Dina's age, he guessed the mother's at somewhere around fifty.

She looked older . . . a lot older. Clearly this woman had given up *exotic dance*. Tom pondered for a moment what she did now to support herself and just as quickly dispelled the thought. As he crossed the threshold, a bouquet of stale cigarettes, spilt alcohol and cat urine overpowered him.

"Sorry." Her languid tone spoke of late nights in smoky bars. "I don't normally get up this early and I'm afraid I came off a bit grumpy." Her hair stuck out in every direction. She had bags under her eyes and wore no makeup. "By the way," she said. "I'll take that ten now. I'm used to getting paid beforehand."

This, to Tom, seemed like a "best practice" in Sheila's profession. He reached into his wallet and extracted the bill.

She cleared a spot on the worn, stained sofa and sat on a stool across from him. Perhaps her sudden change of heart came from the realization she might get her name in print, perhaps an appearance on "Oprah" or a book deal.

Tom tried to resurrect a Southern drawl he'd spent decades erasing, "Ms. Mitchell, I'm putting together some background on your daughter, and I have a few questions, if you don't mind." He retrieved a small notebook from his pocket.

"I saw something on the TV about a shooting over there in Georgia. I had no idea that was Dawn." She lit a Marlboro and tugged at her frayed house coat. "Hell, I hardly remembered I had a daughter. It's not like she stayed in touch. She got herself a scholarship to that fancy school up north and that's the last I ever saw of her."

Sheila waved her left hand as she spoke. "She never wrote or called or anything. The day she left we had a big fight. I told her, 'Don't let the screen door hit you where the sun don't shine.'"

She gazed out the window revealing the remnants of a classic profile. "Later on, I tried to reach her by phone a couple of times, but they

213

said nobody lived there named Dawn Sawyer. You know, I tried to be a good mother to that girl, but she was one mean little . . ." She took a deep drag and let the unfinished sentence linger in the acrid air.

"So, you raised Dawn by yourself?"

"Who the hell else do you think she had? I couldn't recall her daddy's name. I was pretty reckless in those days. I picked out *Sawyer* 'cause it reminded me of a man I knew once . . ." She smiled at the memory. "He was real nice."

Throughout the conversation Sheila never made eye contact. She picked something from her teeth and deposited it on the cluttered coffee table.

"Was Dawn ever in trouble as a girl?"

She considered this for a moment, shook her head, took another pull and watched a smoke ring rise to the ceiling. "She never had run-ins with the law, or in school, if that's what you mean. I'm sure she went off and did things, but Dawn knew how to protect herself." She sounded almost proud.

"Do you remember any other kids picking on her?"

"Nope."

"Do you know if she had any friends?"

"She had this one girl she used to hang out with, Cindy something. I don't remember much about her."

Tom wrote down the name. "You say Dawn got a scholarship to a school up north. Did it pay for her entire education?"

Sheila shrugged. "I suppose it did. She never asked me for any money, not that I had any to give."

"She must've been a smart girl, going to schools like Case Western and Harvard Business School."

"I guess so. As I recall she had good grades," Sheila smiled. "She must've gotten that from her daddy."

214

Tom glanced about at the tiny living room, no photographs of Dina in sight. "I don't suppose you have any pictures of her as a child."

Sheila thought for a moment. "Just a sec." Gathering her faded house dress around her, she disappeared into an adjacent bedroom.

Tom took in what appeared to be a kitchen. Somewhere beneath the pile of greasy dishes he pictured a sink of some sort. The bathroom door stood open, revealing a row of assorted underwear hanging on a line above a rust-stained tub. A black and white cat peeped from beneath a battered recliner.

Sheila returned, clutching a faded grade school photo that read, "PROOF" in diagonal white letters. Time had washed away most of the color, but Tom could still make out the toothy half-grin of a frightened-looking little girl. She bore no resemblance to the confident and beautiful woman he knew as Dina Savage.

"Would you mind if I borrowed this? I promise I'll return it when I'm through."

Sheila gave him a nonchalant look, hand shaking as she took another drag from her cigarette. "Knock yourself out, sugar. I'm sure there's more where that came from." As she glanced away, Tom caught the glimmer of a tear in the corner of her eye.

He thanked her, returned to his car and set out in search of lunch.

* * *

Hamilton's Diner, across from the courthouse, appeared to be the only eatery in Clewiston. It reminded him of Sandy's Café in his hometown, Monrovia, Florida. A lunch crowd had gathered, business owners, attorneys, farmers, and local government officials.

A peroxide-blonde waitress sauntered over. Pulling a damp, ragged cloth from her pocket, she gave the table a superficial swipe. From her care-worn face Tom guessed her age at somewhere around mid-forties. On closer inspection she appeared younger, perhaps thirty-five, tall and thin with the build of someone who'd once been an athlete. Her smile revealed tobacco-stained teeth, one of them chipped. "What can I getcha, hon?"

"I'll have a BLT with mustard, no mayo, some fries, and a Diet Coke."

"Sure thing . . ." She studied him closely and smiled. "You're new here. What brings you to Clewiston?"

He considered for a moment and decided he had nothing to lose by telling her the truth. "I'm a writer from Atlanta. I'm here researching a story about Dina Savage . . . uh Dawn Sawyer. You may have heard about her murder trial."

She dropped the cloth as if about to swoon. "Murder trial?"

A middle-aged woman at the next table cocked her head in Tom's direction. *Great*, Tom thought. *Now everyone in town will know.*

Ashen, the waitress eased into the booth across from him.

"Did you know her?" Tom asked. He glanced at her name tag. It read "Cissy."

She paused and glanced away. "Yeah, me and Dawn were best friends growing up." She shook her head. "We got in more trouble together . . . Actually, I was the one got in trouble. Dawn would've too, except her mother was a stripper, and a whore, who spent all her time drunk out of her mind. Most days that woman didn't know whether Dawn was alive or dead." Cissy pursed her lips and gave the table another wipe.

"Listen," Tom asked, "Do you think you might have time for some questions when you get off work? I won't have to quote you or any-thing."

She gave him a wry smile. "Honey, I ain't got nothing but time, and you can sure as hell quote me on that. I go on break in a few minutes."

Finishing his meal, Tom opened his wallet to pay, then remembered he'd given his last ten to Sheila Mitchell. Instead, he used a credit card, leaving a generous tip. He got a free refill on his Diet Coke and returned to the corner booth.

He didn't have to wait long. When the crowd had thinned, Cissy joined him. She told him how Martha, her mom, used to work a second job at night. When they were in high school, Cissy and Dawn would put on Martha's makeup and dress up in her finest clothes to appear older. Then they'd *borrow* Martha's car and drive over to Greenville to visit the honky-tonks.

A wistful look came over her. "I was about the only friend she had. A lot of folks looked down on her because her mom turned tricks and all. Shit! Half the men in town spent time out there in that little trailer, including the mayor and the police chief."

Cissy laughed. "You know, Dawn was one homely girl. She had bad teeth, a flat chest and zits so bad her face looked like a big straw-berry. It took just about all my mom's makeup to make her look half-way decent."

"Wow! That would have been rough for anybody, especially an awkward teenaged girl in a small town. How did she deal with all that?"

"Dawn used to have this saying, whenever she wanted to put some-body down." Cissy leaned over and looked Tom in the eye. "She'd ask them, 'Do you know the difference between a worm and a caterpillar? I may be a caterpillar, but someday I'll be a butterfly . . . And you'll still be a worm.' I suppose that's why she went and got that tattoo on her shoulder."

Something tugged at the back of Tom's mind, eluding his grasp. "What drew you to Dawn?"

"Well, it sure wasn't sympathy. I mean, I felt bad for her and all, but that wasn't why we became friends. What I always liked about

Dawn was the way she stood up for herself when other kids picked on her. The girl was smart, too. Hell, I'd have never graduated from high school if it hadn't been for Dawn. She'd come over to my house and help me with my homework."

Cissy stared at the tabletop and sighed. "She was probably the only friend *I* ever had, the only one I spent any time with. My mom used to let her spend the night. Sheila sure as hell didn't care."

"When did you last see Dawn?"

Cissy thought for a minute. "About the end of our senior year. She asked me to make her up to look older, like we used to do. Only this time, she went off by herself with a bunch of tip money she'd stolen from Sheila. The only reason I knew was because she asked me to drop her off at the Greyhound station in Greenville. She didn't want anybody in Clewiston to see her all dressed up like that. When she left I asked the man behind the counter where she'd gone. He looked at me kind of funny and said 'Tunica.'"

"Tunica?"

"Yep . . . Dawn had a thing for cards . . . poker, blackjack, you name it, like she always knew what other folks was holding. I figured she'd gone over there to try out her luck in the casinos. She must've done alright. She wouldn't talk about it when she got back. I didn't see much of her after that. She left town as soon as school got out and never came back, as far as I know. She didn't even show up for graduation."

"As far as you know?" Tom had his notebook out, jotting notes as fast as he could.

Cissy stopped as if she'd said something she didn't mean to. "No. I don't suppose she ever came back."

"Could you imagine her shooting a man who'd raped her?"

"I don't know. She had a quick temper. She got in fights all the time in school. Little as she was, she'd take on damned near anybody when she got mad. *I* sure wouldn't have messed with her."

Tom had interviewed enough people in his career to know when they were holding back. Still, he smiled, thanked her, and rose to leave. As he returned the small notebook to his pocket he couldn't resist one more question. "You were the only friend Dawn had?"

"Yeah, pretty much." Cissy paused as though remembering something. "There was this big Black man nicknamed Shorty, a bouncer over at Happy Tails. That's the strip club where Sheila danced. When Dawn was little, Sheila used to let her hang out there after school. I guess old Shorty felt sorry for her. He's the one taught her how to play cards."

"Do you know where I might find this Shorty?"

"I'm sure he's retired now. He'd be pretty old. He lives on a dirt road out there just before you get to the club, on the other side of the track."

Cissy gave Tom some vague directions, including the location of a long-gone gas station. He thanked her and had turned to leave when another question came to him.

"You said Dawn always did well in school. Do you remember any particular teacher she was close to?"

"Nope. Dawn got by pretty much on her own. Most of her teachers just ignored her . . ." Cissy caught herself again. "Actually, she had this one English teacher in the eighth grade, Ms. Mullen. Lord, I haven't thought about that woman in years."

"Do you think she might still be teaching?"

Cissy shrugged. "I guess so. She must've been pretty young back then." She laughed. "Hell, all the teachers looked old to us, but I suppose she was in her thirties or so. That'd make her about fifty now."

"Where would I find the school?"

"Go down here two blocks and take a right. It'll be straight in front of you."

Chapter Twenty-Five

A lone yellow bus pulled out of the dusty schoolyard. Anxious to avoid suspicious staff or teachers, Tom stopped the first student he met, a young man about twelve, and asked where he might find Ms. Mullen's room.

As it turned out, Cissy had accurately estimated Jane Mullen's age. She appeared to be in her mid-fifties, her dark hair now streaked in grey and hard lines crowding the corners of her face. She wore the tired look of someone who'd wasted her best years trying to inspire her pupils, only to suffer disappointment time and again. *Probably counting the days to retirement*, Tom thought.

"Ms. Mullen, do you have a moment?"

"Who are you?"

"My name's Tom Williams . . ."

"What are you doing here?"

"I thought I might ask your help with something."

"Did you check in at the office?"

Tom gave her his most contrite smile. "No ma'am. I apologize. You see, I'm a friend of Dawn Sawyer's."

A curious look came over her face. "Well . . . you're supposed to check in at the office. They don't just let people walk in."

"It'll only take a moment."

"So, how's Dawn?" she asked.

"She calls herself 'Dina Savage' now. My wife and I met her about eighteen months ago, at a concert. Later, she accused her date of raping her. Now she's in jail for murdering him."

Mullen gasped, "I saw the story on TV this morning. I'd never have recognized her."

"I'm researching her background, trying to find out as much as I can, anything that might help people understand her better." Tom couldn't believe how maudlin he sounded. "I understand you had a tremendous influence on her."

His guess paid off as a look of profound sadness swept over her. "Yeah. I had Dawn in my eighth grade class, the kind of student you get maybe once in a lifetime . . . if you're lucky. I'm not supposed to tell you this, but she had an IQ just shy of 180. You never forget a student like that, especially when they come from a dysfunctional home. Dawn sat in the back of the class, never asked questions or spoke unless I called on her, and yet she followed every word I said.

"One day I asked her to stay after class. I told her if she ever needed anything I'd be glad to help or just listen. I started giving her rides home. Nowadays I'd lose my job for that.

"Midway through the year, something happened. She missed several days of school, and when she came back I couldn't get her to talk to me. She never again stayed late. But, you know what? Her grades never faltered. If anything, they got better."

Mullen bowed her head and folded her hands in her lap. Through gathering tears, she said, "When Dawn came to me late in her senior year and said she'd been accepted to Case Western I broke down and cried. She probably didn't have anybody else to tell. Most folks around here would think Case Western was a brand of cheap whisky."

Throughout her oration, Tom simply nodded. Not anxious to press his luck, he said, "Ms. Mullen, I appreciate your time. You've been a

big help. Would it be okay for me to call you later, as the trial pro-
gresses?"

"Please do."

* * *

Tom's watch read 4:30, 3:30 Central. He didn't know if Hamilton's
had closed, but he needed to talk to Cissy. He caught her walking to her
car.

"Cissy," he blurted out, "something happened to Dawn when she
was thirteen, something so bad she missed several days of school. What
could it have been?"

"How should I know?" Her eyes darted back and forth as she spoke,
telling Tom she'd lied.

"You said you were her only friend."

"I don't know what you're talking about."

What could have been so horrible she won't tell me about it? "You
know exactly what I'm talking about. Did somebody molest Dawn in
the eighth grade? She's on trial for murder. People need to know who
she is."

Cissy grasped the door handle, then stopped. For a long time, she
gazed down the empty street toward the dusty horizon. Tom studied her
face. She turned back, as though she'd reached a decision.

"Dawn had a tough life," she said. "One night Sheila came home
with one of her regular customers. After she passed out from booze and
pills he went into Dawn's room and raped her. The girl was thirteen
years old, for God's sake. She walked all the way to my house and
knocked on my window. I had to climb out to help her inside. We snuck
into my hall bath, and I cleaned her up. The whole time she just stood
there with her teeth gritted. Despite the pain, she refused to cry. When

my mom woke up the next day, I told her Dawn had gotten sick, that Sheila had went off and left her by herself. My mom wanted to take her to the doctor, but Dawn refused. That doctor would've called Family Services. They'd have taken Dawn away and I'd have never seen her again."

"So, nobody reported it?"

Cissy gave Tom a smile reserved for people too idiotic to deserve an answer. "Now, who the hell do you think was gonna call the cops, Sheila? Nobody would've listened. Who cares about a little white trash girl, especially when her mom's the town whore? It would only have gotten Dawn in more trouble, especially when the john's one of the wealthiest men in Clewiston."

"Can you give me his name?"

"Nope." Cissy's face hardened. Without another word she climbed into her aging Pontiac and drove away.

* * *

Tom finally found the home of Shorty Watkins, a tarpaper shanty at the end of a dirt road. When he mentioned he had news about Dawn Sawyer, Shorty invited him to sit on his front stoop and offered him a malt liquor, which Tom politely declined.

"I have a long drive ahead of me. I don't need to be drinking."

"I know that's right."

As Tom told him about Dina and Liam, Shorty could only shake his head. Neighbors peeped from windows of nearby homes, no doubt wondering what brought this white man to their neighborhood.

"Yeah, I remember Little Dawn." Shorty smiled, shaking his head. *"She sure was a pistol."*

Shorty must've aged *years* since his days as a bouncer. Tom could see it in his eyes. Despite all that, he looked like a man who could take care of himself. The golden mid-afternoon sun shone on his bald scalp, and he spoke with the ease of someone who'd seen so much misery yet had somehow reconciled to it. He stared down at his shoe and dug his heel into the soft black dirt. "I tell you one thing, that little girl sure was smart. She could learn anything she put her mind to, like she saw something once and never forgot it."

"I understand you taught her how to play cards."

"Oh yeah, I taught her alright. Pretty soon she could beat *me*. She could count 'em better than anybody I ever saw. She got good grades too. She'd come around after school, and I'd ask to see her report card . . ." He shook his head. "Didn't seem like nobody else cared. She made straight A's every time, like nothing I ever seen."

"When did you see her last?"

"She disappeared right after high school, went off up north somewhere."

"And you never saw her again?"

"Well . . ." He gazed upward as though remembering something. "There was this one time . . . I'm pretty sure it was her, but she looked a whole lot different. I'd gone uptown on a Saturday afternoon to pick up something at the store, about a week or so before the big tractor pull. They had a big parade downtown, all them rednecks crowding around the courthouse in their pickups. I wasn't hanging around there too long if you know what I'm saying. Anyway, she kinda looked out of place, like a lady whose car broke down on her way to the big city, dressed up all nice, her hair done up just right. Folks stared at her, but I don't think any of 'em recognized her." He took a deep breath. "Man, I can't believe she'd go and kill somebody like that, not the Little Dawn I knew."

"You have a pretty good memory for something that happened so long ago."

He cocked his head as though the thought had never occurred to him. "Yeah, I remember it, wasn't long before that white boy, Dennis Ramsey, went and disappeared. It would've been the fall of 2002."

"Disappeared?"

"Yeah. They found his body a month or so later, back up in the woods. Somebody stabbed him a bunch of times and dumped him there."

"Wow! Did they find out who did it?"

"Nope. From what I knew about him, he had it coming. He was one *mean* dude. Used to hang out at the club all the time . . . get drunk . . . get in fights. I had to throw him out more times than I can remember."

Tom's eyes narrowed. "Tell me about this Ramsey."

"Like I said, he was an asshole."

"A rich asshole?"

"One of the richest in town."

"Would he have been capable of rape?"

"He'd a been *capable* of just about anything."

Tom nodded, extending his hand. "Shorty, I appreciate your time. I'll have to come back and take you up on that malt liquor."

The man grinned. "You be sure and do that, hear?"

* * *

On his way into town, Tom had passed a small newspaper office a block east of the courthouse. He couldn't imagine how a place so small could support a local paper.

The storefront window read *Clewiston Gazette*. Out front, two elderly men sat on wooden crates smoking cigarettes. One wore an old-fashioned snap-brimmed hat, the other sported coveralls and a cap so stained Tom couldn't read its logo. Neither of them spoke. They simply nodded to him as he passed.

Tom nodded back.

Inside he found a young lady, perhaps early thirties, with straight brown hair down to her shoulders. She had large, brown eyes framed by round wire-rim glasses and sat at a Formica-topped counter reading a novel. Her dress looked like a hand-me-down from her favorite grand-mother, and, though Tom couldn't see them from where he stood, he figured she wore square-toed, sensible shoes.

"Good afternoon," she said as she stood and laid the paperback carefully to one side. The cover, turned towards Tom, read *Fifty Shades of Grey* by E.L. James.

"Good afternoon," he replied, gazing through an open door leading to a storage room.

She smiled. "I suppose you're wondering where we keep the presses. We haven't printed the *Gazette* here in years. It comes from a publisher over in Birmingham now. All we do now is sell ads, post notices and take letters from folks who like to see their names in the paper. We don't even do much of that anymore." She waved her hand dismissively. "I guess this is what passes for a local paper these days."

"I can imagine," he said. "I've worked for newspapers all my life and I've seen the same story time and again."

"By the way," she said, "I'm Delia Crabtree." She extended a slen-der hand so white it looked like she'd bleached it.

"I'm Tom Williams."

"Nice to meet you, Mr. Williams. I can tell you're not from around here. What brings you to Clewiston?"

"I'm a reporter in Atlanta, and I'm researching a story. Do you keep a library of prior editions here?"

"I don't know that I'd call it a library, but we have files going back forty years. What are you looking for?"

"A story from the fall of 2002 about a big tractor pull and the disappearance of a young man."

"That was long before my time, but I know the one you're talking about."

"How'd you end up in Clewiston?"

"I studied journalism at Mississippi State. I dreamed of being an investigative reporter, or perhaps a great writer, like John Grisham or Eudora Welty. My parents died in a car wreck two months before I graduated," she shrugged. "I had to take the first job I could get."

"I'm sorry to hear that." Tom thought of his own parents, who'd died when he was eleven.

"I suppose it worked out well enough." She gazed out on the main street and managed a smile. "I actually like it here. When I started, the current owners had just bought the paper from a man named Buster Crouch. It had been in his family for years. I had a chance to meet the old man before he passed away, quite a character."

"What happened to him?"

"One morning before he sold the paper he came in looking like he'd slept under a bridge. He said aliens had abducted him and bestowed on him the secrets of the universe, not to mention those of some of Clewiston's most respected citizens."

"You're kidding."

"I wish I were. Old Buster set to work printing some of the vilest stories you could imagine. *Some of them weren't even true.*"

"Did people sue him?"

"A couple of them did, but by that time he'd gone broke and had to sell the paper. It seems that while circulation kept climbing, thanks to his wild stories, his ad revenues dried up. He died about a year later. It turned out he'd taken up furniture refinishing, working late nights in his basement, and the paint stripper fumes had addled his brain."

"Wow." Tom laughed. It sounded to him like the folklore that collects in small communities like hairs on an old brush.

"Oh!" she said. "You were asking about our old files." She disappeared into the back and returned with a white file box marked "2002: June-December."

"That was quick."

"I keep the place pretty neat. It's not like I have much else to do around here. I arranged the old boxes by year in case anybody wants to see them."

"Do people go through them very often?"

"So far you're the first one."

Tom thanked her and took the box to a folding table in the corner, settling into a plastic chair that might've been red once but had faded to a dull pink in the sunshine flooding through the picture window. He rummaged through old editions until he found one dated Thursday, September 12 with the headline, "Local Man Disappears." Its tag line read, "Tractor Pull a Huge Success."

Dennis Ramsey, last seen on Friday afternoon, had taken care of customers at his dad's John Deere dealership before leaving work. Friends and family expected to see him the following day at the annual tractor pull and became concerned when he failed to show. According to rumor, he'd travelled out of town for the evening on personal business. The story quoted authorities as saying they did *not* suspect foul play.

Tom scanned subsequent issues. For the first couple of weeks, Ramsey's disappearance continued to make front page news. By the third week, it had moved to Page Three. The next week's paper didn't mention it.

Then came the headline. On Saturday, November sixteenth, a deer hunter in a neighboring county came upon Ramsey's body in a thicket near an unpaved road. The story said he'd died from multiple stab wounds to the groin and abdomen and that Police Chief Gene Tilley would spearhead the investigation.

Tom jotted notes as he read. He looked up to find Ms. Crabtree once again enthralled in *Fifty Shades*. He carefully placed the newspapers back in the box, took it to the counter. and cleared his throat.

"Did you find everything you wanted?" she asked.

"Yes, I did. Can you direct me to Chief Tilley's office?"

She shook her head. "Chief Tilley passed away three winters ago from pancreatic cancer. Don Parquet's the chief now."

"Sorry to hear that."

Tom thanked her and took a short walk down the street.

* * *

He found Parquet locking up, apparently on his way home for the day. At first, he seemed annoyed at the intrusion, but when Tom mentioned Dawn Sawyer, he invited him back into his office and offered him a Coke.

Parquet, a heavy-set man in his mid-thirties, had graduated a year ahead of Dawn from Clewiston High.

"I saw the story on TV," he said. "but I'd never have recognized Little Dawn. She must've done something to herself. I gotta tell you, she was one *ugly* girl. I don't suppose I should be talking to a reporter, but I can't see what a murder in Atlanta has to do with Clewiston. She left here a long time ago."

"Actually, I'm not writing about the trial. I'm researching her background, her childhood."

229

Parquet regaled Tom with stories about Dawn, her mother, and the troubles they'd had.

"I spoke earlier today with a waitress named Cissy. She said she was a childhood friend of Dawn's," said Tom.

"Yeah. Cissy Johnson. Didn't I see you at Hamilton's around lunch time?"

"Yep. Cissy said one of Sheila's johns raped Dawn when she was about thirteen, that Sheila had passed out drunk in the next room."

Parquet gave him a disgusted look. "I wouldn't doubt that a bit. Sheila's about as worthless as they come. Hell, an alligator would've made a better mother."

"Cissy wouldn't tell me who raped Dawn, only that his dad was one of the richest men in Clewiston. Who do you think that would be?"

Parquet pursed his lips. "Claude Ramsey. Owns the John Deere dealership down the street. It's the only large business left since the tire factory shut down."

"The father of Dennis Ramsey?"

"Yep."

"I understand Dennis was a rough character and a regular patron at Happy Tails. Do you think he could have raped Dawn?"

"Could have. Dennis was a worthless piece of shit. I could see him raping a little girl. He thought, just cause his old man owned half the town, he could do whatever he wanted and get away with it." Parquet shrugged. "I don't know what good that does us now. Ramsey's dead."

"Yeah. I read about his disappearance and murder. I understand you never caught anyone."

Parquet let out a long sigh. "Chief Tilley did the best he could, but he had nothing to go on. Only reason he worked on it so hard and so long was because of Dennis' daddy. A man like that has a lot to say about who gets elected and who gets appointed in a town like this, if you know what I mean."

"I know exactly what you mean."

The two men remained silent for a moment before Parquet asked the obvious question. "You don't suppose Dawn had anything to do with Dennis's murder? I mean . . . she was a teenager. She left town long before Dennis' murder, and nobody's seen her here since."

Tom chewed his lower lip for a moment, facing a moral dilemma. "Not exactly," he said. "I understand Dawn may have been here the weekend before the tractor pull. Nobody would have recognized her with all that cosmetic surgery."

Tom didn't mention who'd told him this, and Parquet, for some reason, didn't ask. Instead, he stood, picked up his jacket and led Tom to the door. "Mr. Williams, I appreciate your coming by. This has been a *most* interesting conversation, but my wife hates it when I'm late for supper."

Parquet didn't look like a man who missed many meals. Outside on the street he asked Tom for a business card. Tom reached into his wallet and retrieved one so old it had become dog-eared and dingy.

"I may need to contact you later," he said. "I hope you don't mind."

"Not at all."

They said goodbye, climbed into their cars and drove in opposite directions.

* * *

Tom got as far as Columbus, Mississippi, on the Alabama line, before exhaustion overtook him. He had a late supper at a Cracker Barrel and checked into a Hampton Inn. He called Colleen to say he'd be home in the morning.

"Honey, you were there all day," she said. "Are you writing a feature or a biography?"

"I'll get back to you on that. Tell me, do you recall any mention during the Sanstrom trial of Dina being raped by someone else?"

"I think Rainey said something about that in his opening arguments but never mentioned it again. I kept wondering why."

"I think there's a story there. Dawn Sawyer's mother was a stripper and a prostitute. One of her rich clients raped Dawn at age thirteen. He turned up dead a few years later, right after Dawn, now Dina, suddenly reappeared in Clewiston."

"Oh my God!"

"I don't want to make too much of it yet . . . Tell me about your trip to the doctor's office."

Colleen took a moment to reply. "Oh, he listened to my chest and ran some x-rays. They should be back tomorrow or the day after." She stifled a cough.

"Maybe I should come home tonight. I'll just get some coffee . . ."

"No, you won't. You stay there and get a good night's sleep. I don't need you dozing off behind the wheel. I'll see you tomorrow."

He started to argue but knew she was right. Instead, he said good night and called the front desk for a five a.m. wakeup.

He'd just turned in when, suddenly awake, he switched on the bedside lamp and grabbed a writing pad and pen. He wrote a single sentence. "How did Cissy know about the butterfly tattoo if Dina got it in college?"

* * *

Sitting alone in the dining room of his latest abode, a shabby, one-bedroom apartment, Oleg Simonov decrypted and downloaded credit card numbers. His only illumination came from a small night light in the mildewed bathroom. Oleg liked working in darkness. It made him feel less conspicuous.

The Swede's last payment had arrived more than a month ago, most of it gone by now, and Oleg had his needs. The old man had promised him more work but hadn't called, and now Oleg had no way of contacting him. The Sanstroms had returned to Sweden to bury their son and, in all likelihood, would never return.

Svetlana had gone out. They'd argued earlier, and Oleg had slapped her so hard he knocked her across the room. Now she wouldn't speak to him and made him sleep on the couch. His back hurt every time he thought about the worn upholstery and broken springs.

By the time he heard the scrape of her key in the door, he'd uploaded the compressed CSV file to his friend in Minsk. Svetlana breezed past and into the bedroom, slamming and locking the door behind her.

He shrugged and began browsing porn sites. He especially liked the ones from Thailand with the younger girls. Tomorrow he would harvest more credit cards and Social Security numbers to fund such pleasures.

In a few days, he would receive a large deposit into his Bahamian account. He'd pack his bags and leave Svetlana to rot in this hole, while he escaped to Bangkok . . . which had always struck him as a most appropriate name.

The screen flickered, and it seemed that the laptop's performance had slowed.

* * *

The Penguin also preferred working in the dark. Leaning away from his monitor, he permitted himself a grin. *I've got you, you bastard.*

He'd known of Oleg's proclivities for young girls from a raid he'd made on the Russian's personal computer years earlier. The Thai porn site, with its Trojan horse, worked like a charm. By morning he'd know the Russian's location and everything he'd been up to.

Chapter Twenty-Six

Don Parquet

Clewiston, Mississippi
Wednesday, March 27

Notwithstanding his cool response to Tom Williams, Parquet had lain awake all night thinking about Dawn Sawyer being in town the week before Dennis Ramsey went missing. Dialing the North Mississippi Regional Crime Lab in Batesville, he revisited the notes he'd taken years ago at the murder scene.

"McLean," a voice answered.

"Clyde, this is Don Parquet over in Clewiston."

"Don, what can I do for you?"

"You remember a case we had here some years back, unsolved murder? Victim named Dennis Ramsey, aged twenty-seven at the time. A deer hunter discovered his body over in LeFlore County . . . estimated to have died three weeks earlier."

"Yeah. I understand his daddy's some big deal over there."

"Big as they come."

"Don't tell me you've cracked the case."

"Not exactly. I did get some interesting intel though. As I recall, your guys found some DNA in his abandoned car."

"We did. Wasn't much. Looked like somebody tried to get rid of it with Clorox."

"We didn't have anybody to match it to back then," said Parquet "but I may have somebody now."

"Really? I suppose we need to get on this right away."

"No rush. I don't think she's going anywhere for a few weeks."

"She? What do you mean?"

"You been following that case over in Atlanta, the woman who shot her ex-boyfriend on the courthouse steps?"

"Sure. What's the connection?"

"Turns out she's from right here in Clewiston. Called herself Dawn Sawyer back when I knew her. Now she's Dina Savage."

"No shit."

"I got this from a reporter from Atlanta. Who knows? Might not come to anything, but then again . . ."

"Wow."

"You suppose that DNA's still any good?"

"Of course." McLean sounded offended. Scandals had plagued Mississippi crime labs for years, including lost or tainted evidence.

"Why don't I call our friends over in Georgia and see what I can find out?" asked Parquet.

"Why don't you? We're swamped here. Might take a while to get back to you, but I'll see what I can do. In the meantime, why don't you see if you can me get some of Ms. Savage's DNA?"

"I think I'll do that. Thanks."

Parquet hung up. By now it'd be late afternoon in Atlanta. He could call the Cobb County DA in the morning.

He pictured Dawn Sawyer, the skinny little trailer trash girl everybody ridiculed. Looking back, he cringed to think how he and his friends tormented her. If, in fact, Ramsey raped her, which Parquet could easily imagine, then the bastard got what he deserved. Hopefully, the DNA match would prove negative. Still, as an officer of the law, he had to pursue every lead, no matter where it took him.

Williams said somebody recognized Dawn when she visited Clewiston. Parquet couldn't recall any friends Dawn had besides Cissy.

Perhaps he'd have a chat with her in the morning. He had shut down his computer and turned out the lights when the phone rang. Tom Williams again. The man seemed to have a knack for calling at suppertime.

"Chief, I have something for you. I'm not sure what it's worth."

"Shoot."

"When I was in your fair city yesterday, I told you I spoke to Cissy Johnson."

"Yep."

"She mentioned that Dawn had a butterfly tattoo on her shoulder."

"Uh huh."

"I didn't remember it at first, but when we were at the outdoor concert with her, my wife commented on it. The thing is . . . Dina said she got it in college. If that's true, then Cissy lied when she said she hadn't seen Dawn since high school."

Parquet made a note on his desk blotter. "Well, obviously one of 'em's lying. You got anything else?"

"Nope, just thought I'd let you know before I forgot. I hope I didn't catch you on your way out the door."

"No problem. Thanks a lot. If you think of anything else don't hesitate to call."

* * *

As Colleen stood from behind her desk, a dizzy spell came over her. Over the past several nights her recurring cough had kept her awake, and last night she'd taken a suppressant.

Her phone gave a soft buzz. She fished it out and froze. The ID read "Walter McCall," the pulmonologist Kathy had recommended.

Colleen pressed the receive button. "Walt?"

"Colleen, are you where you can sit?"

237

"Yes."

"I'm afraid it's bad news. We received your PET scan results and there are spots on your lungs, liver and spleen."

Colleen closed her eyes. "What does that mean?"

"We'll need to get you in for a biopsy right away. I won't sugarcoat it. This doesn't look good. I don't think surgery's much of an option at this point. Depending on what we find, you could be looking at chemotherapy. You'll want to talk to an oncologist."

Colleen took a deep breath and nearly choked. "I'll call Kathy right now." She sat for a while, struggling to process the news. "We're talking *Stage Four*." It came out more as a statement than a question.

"We need a specialist to make that call. Colleen, I am so sorry. I keep going back and looking at it, hoping I'm wrong somehow."

"What's my prognosis?"

"I can't tell you that. The important thing for you to know is that I don't give up. I hope you won't either."

It took her a moment before she could speak. "Thank you, Walt. I won't," she said softly. She hung up, folded her arms and laid her head on her desk.

A cold shiver ran up her spine. All her life she'd trusted in God in moments like this. Now she pictured her father, a lifelong smoker, spending his final months hooked to an oxygen tank.

Looking up, her gaze fell on an old photo of Tom and the girls, Kathy eight and Marie six. Standing at the end of a dock, they squinted into the setting sun, grinning, Marie with her front teeth missing, Kathy proudly displaying a small fish she'd caught. Colleen thought about her grandchildren and never seeing them grow into adulthood.

How could God let something like this happen? She scanned her well-appointed office, thinking back on her long, successful career, and realized now how little it all meant. How much time did she have left?

What could she do now to make a difference in the world and for her family?

She pictured the coming months as an unending nightmare. She laid her head on a stack of papers and wept. Whatever it took, she thought, she'd make the most of what time she had left. *I will not give in to this.*

* * *

Ron Dalrymple stared into his refrigerator, trying to recall how long the half-eaten sandwich had sat there. As he tossed it in the garbage, his phone rang. He'd saved the Penguin's number, not knowing his real name.

"Hey."

"I've got something you might be able to use," he said without preamble.

Dalrymple tried to mask his relief, afraid the man might raise his price. It'd been hard enough coming up with the two thousand he'd demanded.

"I have it on a thumb drive, and I'll give it to you once I have your money in hand. Meet me at the parking lot behind the old Swanson's furniture warehouse on Monroe Drive. You know the place, right?"

"Yeah. Off Piedmont at I-85."

"Eight p.m., not a minute late or a minute early. And have the money with you, nothing but twenties, neatly wrapped in a cardboard box."

* * *

Dalrymple arrived, thinking the man couldn't have picked a more secluded spot anywhere in the city. The lot backed up to a steep hill overgrown with kudzu, no other buildings in sight, and, more importantly, no people.

The rusted-out Corolla might have been dark blue once, but Dalrymple couldn't tell. The driver side door stood open, and the tall, obese man squeezed in behind the wheel made an incongruous sight. Even more incongruous were the small caliber hole in his forehead and the trickle of blood pooled in his left eye socket. His mouth gaped open as though struggling to say something. Dalrymple knew the look of a body assuming ambient temperature.

He spun about, frantically searching for whoever had fired the shot. Relieved to find himself alone, he turned his car around, heading for the narrow driveway running alongside the building.

As he rounded the corner, a brown Chevy sat parked at an angle leaving him no room to get around. He started to back up, when he saw a man standing in the shelter of a doorway, solid build, brown curly hair and thick moustache, holding a pistol. The first bullet caught him in the right eye. He never felt the second.

* * *

Oleg picked up the spent cartridges, as he'd done when he shot the Penguin, rolling them between his gloved fingertips, relishing their residual heat. When they'd cooled, he dropped them into his left pocket beside the thumb drive he'd found on the Penguin. Reaching into Dalrymple's car, he removed the shoebox containing two grand in twenties. As he drove away, he silently thanked the Penguin for choosing such a convenient spot.

Once he detected the Trojan horse and traced it back to the fat man, it took Oleg less than fifteen minutes to determine his location. Finding the Penguin's apartment building protected by a security intercom he'd followed him to the drop site. Now, with the Penguin's keys, he could search the apartment for any other incriminating evidence.

* * *

Two hours later, seated in an interrogation room, Rollo Witherspoon disclosed what little he knew to a Lieutenant Paxton Davis, promising to call him if he thought of anything else. As Rollo beat a hasty departure, Davis executed a search warrant on the home of David Curry, a.k.a. the Penguin.

The ransacked apartment yielded an external hard drive, duct-taped to the back of a toilet, and a security camera cabled to a computer in a locked, air-conditioned closet, which Davis sent to a lab for examination.

* * *

Svetlana ground the gears of her aging Toyota as she turned into the apartment complex in Tucker. Following another fight with Oleg, she'd stormed out and remained gone all day. The clock on her dash read 10:30 p.m.

Two weeks earlier, Oleg moved them here and abandoned their previous vehicle, which at least had automatic transmission. He purchased this piece of crap from a used car dealer, under a false name, for cash.

Oleg gave no explanations for such decisions. Svetlana learned long ago not to question him. But now everything had gone to shit, and Svetlana needed a backup plan, one that didn't include Oleg.

Rounding a corner, a strange sensation overcame her. A DeKalb County Police officer blocked the middle of the drive in his fluorescent vest. A crowd of neighbors stood opposite Svetlana's building, staring and pointing, awash in blue, pulsating light. A news cameraman, his cap turned backward, captured the unfolding story from just beyond the yellow tape.

Svetlana had no time for an emotional response. Her instincts screamed *run*. With some difficulty, she coaxed the car into reverse and backed away, trying not to arouse the policeman's suspicions. In her rear view mirror, the officer stared at her. As he spoke into the radio on his shoulder, Svetlana took a deep breath and drove.

She didn't stop, except for traffic lights, until she reached Jimmy Carter Boulevard, where she found a Wachovia Bank and parked in a darkened corner. There she pulled a scarf over her head, donned thick glasses and tried to ignore the security camera. In minutes she'd emptied the bank account she set up without Oleg's knowledge.

She didn't want to think about what happened at the apartment. There'd been sirens in the night many times, a common feature of life in Atlanta. She tried to tell herself tonight's episode had been nothing . . . but she knew better. Somehow this involved Oleg, and she'd narrowly escaped.

* * *

Svetlana drove further out I-85 as far as Beaver Ruin, where she turned south, ditched her car behind an abandoned fast food restaurant and checked into a nondescript hotel with a fake ID and cash.

The tiny room reeked of mildew. She grabbed the TV remote and scanned the channels looking for a local news broadcast.

"Maria, we're live at Regency Apartments on Mercer University Drive, where residents can finally return to their homes following a police standoff that has left one man dead and a DeKalb police officer seriously wounded. I'm told they life-flighted the officer to Grady Hospital, where he's in critical condition. The dead man, according to his identification, is a Swedish citizen named Dirk Palme. Police believe he's actually a Russian named Oleg Simonov."

Svetlana let out a gasp and doubled over.

"According to sources, Atlanta police wanted to question Simonov in the shooting deaths of two local men, David Curry, known to associates as *the Penguin*, and Ron Dalrymple, a private detective with connections to the recent trial and shooting death of artist Liam Sanstrom. Curry's occupation and his relationship to Dalrymple are unknown at this time."

Svetlana ran to the bathroom, little bigger than a closet, lifted the toilet lid, and vomited until she had nothing left. Fighting to regain control, she rinsed her mouth and splashed cold water on her face. Staring at her mirrored image in the sickly fluorescent light, she felt like a walking corpse. *What will I do? Where will I go?*

Never in her life had she lived alone. She'd escaped an abusive stepfather in Ukraine, only to end up in a codependent relationship with Oleg. She had to think fast.

Before long, police would begin searching for the young woman described by nosy neighbors as Oleg's live-in companion. They'd find the Toyota, which would then lead them to this motel. As a child growing up on the streets of Kyiv, Svetlana developed a healthy respect for the tenacity and resources of policemen, especially when victims included their own.

Fishing her phone from her purse, she scrolled through her contact list. What was that effeminate little prick's name? Olsen? Olafsen? Locating his number, she punched the call button only to get his voicemail.

As she spoke she slipped back into her native accent. "Kurt, if you have been watching the news, you will know who this is and why I am calling. And *you had better fucking listen*. Call me back immediately. If I get caught, I'll have no choice but to reveal information damaging to you *and* our mutual friends."

Now she'd wait and pray the Swede made the right decision. Watching the rest of the broadcast, she heard no mention of her . . . yet.

She'd begun to doze when her phone rang. She caught it just before it went to voice mail.

"This is Kurt."

He sounds afraid, she thought. *Good.*

He started gibbering.

"Shut up and listen to me," she hissed. "Tomorrow you will meet me at Lenox Mall outside Macy's at 11:30 sharp. Come alone and bring your phone. I am sending you a photo, with which you will create a passport. You will bring me a prepaid Visa card for one hundred thousand dollars U.S. Is that understood?"

"But I don't think . . ."

"You had better start thinking, little man. Think about what will happen to you when the Americans question the ambassador and his lovely wife. How would you like to wind up back in Stockholm massaging fat, hairy-assed old men?"

"Okay! Okay!"

* * *

As the Lufthansa gate agent gave the final boarding call, a young woman presented her boarding pass for the flight from Atlanta to Frankfurt. In her translucent blouse and turquoise miniskirt, she appeared no older than twenty and could have stepped off the cover of *People* magazine. Hoop earrings set off a bright red pageboy haircut.

From behind her oversized glasses and lavender lenses, Erika Bergen, formerly Svetlana Argounova, scanned the surrounding passengers. A lecherous old man smiled and stared at her breasts as she made her way down the jetway to tourist class, her only luggage a fringe backpack and a small purse.

Chapter Twenty-Seven

After waiting two weeks, Parquet again dialed the crime lab. McLean answered on the third ring.

"Hey, Clyde. Just following up on our conversation a couple of weeks back, wondering what you might've found out."

After a long pause McLean said, "Don, I'm afraid I owe you an apology. I've been meaning to call. We haven't been able to locate that DNA from the Ramsey boy's car." He let out a long sigh. "There's no excuse for this shit. Some of these folks here couldn't find their way out of an outhouse if you gave 'em a map. I wonder sometimes why I bother anymore. They're still looking. I'll get back to you as soon as I hear something."

Parquet shook his head. He hated unsolved murders, but the last thing he wanted was to drive all the way to Atlanta to bring Dawn Sawyer back for trial.

"No problem, Clyde. I appreciate your looking into it."

Hauling himself out of his swivel chair, Parquet opened a small file cabinet. The top drawer contained cold cases, the bottom a flask of bourbon and an unwashed plastic tumbler. Parquet poured a drink and pulled out the Dennis Ramsey file. By now the pages had yellowed. Brown smudges showed the fingerprints of multiple investigators.

Last seen on Friday, September 6, 2002, Ramsey left work saying he planned to meet a business acquaintance. The next day police discovered his empty car at the Colony Inn outside Greenwood. Weeks later, a deer hunter happened upon Ramsey's body where his assailant had dumped it, leaving a wallet with more than a hundred dollars sitting in his hip pocket. *What, besides robbery, would motivate someone in Greenwood to murder a scumbag from Clewiston? What kind of anger could drive a person to stab him twenty-nine times?*

Chief Tilley had questioned the hotel owner, his manager and several guests, none of whom remembered seeing Ramsey. Ramsey made no credit card purchases in Greenwood. *Does returning to the scene after all these years make any sense?*

Parquet closed his eyes, picturing the dump site. It sat beside a trail too rough for a car and too narrow for a truck. From there it looped through the woods before ending at an unpaved road. Ramsey's killer must have hauled in his body with an ATV, then dragged it back into the woods. By the time the hunter stumbled on it, weather and animals had obscured the tracks.

Ramsey stood about six feet tall and weighed roughly two hundred pounds. *Could Dawn Sawyer have carried him that far by herself? She was . . . what . . . five-three and a hundred pounds?* It didn't make sense.

Without the DNA from Ramsey's car, Parquet had reached a dead-end. He'd never link Dawn, or anyone else, to the murder. He picked up the phone and dialed the Leflore County sheriff, Tyler Brown, whose predecessor, David Hodge, helped Chief Tilley in the investigation.

A cheerful female voice answered. Brown, she said, had stepped out to lunch and would return shortly. Parquet gave her his number.

The mere mention of lunch made him glance at the clock on his office wall . . . 11:38 . . . close enough. As he sauntered down the sidewalk greeting friends and neighbors, Parquet wondered how so many people could have seen Dawn on a sunny Saturday morning and not recognized her, despite her cosmetic surgery. In those days, before the tire plant closed, downtown Clewiston had bustled with traffic.

Who might have seen through her disguise? Parquet could think of only three people, Shorty Watkins, Sheila Mitchell and Cissy Johnson. He could talk to Shorty and Sheila later, but right now he had a standing appointment with Cissy. At Hamilton's, the regulars had begun to arrive as Parquet spotted Cissy wiping down a table. *Why would she lie about something as seemingly insignificant as a tattoo, unless . . .*

She looked up with a smile. "Good morning, Chief."

"Hey, Cissy."

"The usual?"

"Yep. I might even have a slice of that pie today."

As she hustled behind the counter, Parquet settled into the last booth on the outside window, staring down the street at Ramsey's Farm Implements. Even in the noonday sun, the place felt dark and gloomy.

When Cissy returned with a hamburger and Pepsi, Parquet stopped her.

"Cissy, do you remember the week Dennis Ramsey disappeared?"

It seemed like an innocent enough question, but he couldn't help noticing her flicker of panic. Recovering, she said, "Sure . . . Who doesn't?"

"Yeah. I'm sure we all do, but some of us might remember something other folks don't."

"Uh huh," was her only response as she spied an imaginary spot she'd missed and gave the tabletop a swipe.

Parquet pictured Cissy and Dawn in high school. They'd reminded him of Mutt and Jeff; the brunette Cissy, at five-eleven the more athletic of the two, the shorter Dawn with her washed out blonde hair. At one time he'd found Cissy rather attractive. Even now, with some makeup, she could have any man she wanted. And yet, in all the time he'd known her, Parquet could not recall seeing her with a male companion.

She seemed to have aged badly in recent years. Her face had become gaunt, lines forming around the eyes and mouth. And yet, as recently as ten or eleven years ago, she'd been a champion body builder. Parquet recalled newspaper pictures of her in area competitions. He and one of his officers even watched her compete on occasions. With her hair pulled back, skin oiled and muscles flexed, Cissy could become a totally different person.

"Cissy, you were pretty close with Dawn Sawyer. Do you remember her returning to Clewiston after she went off to college?"

"Nope."

"Would it surprise you to hear someone saw her right out there on that sidewalk the week before Ramsey disappeared?"

She clutched the wet towel between her fingers and forced a smile. "I don't reckon much of anything surprises me anymore, Chief."

"Me neither . . ."

With that he tucked into his hamburger, eyes focused on Cissy as she took another customer's order.

* * *

Shorty Watkins gave up little in the way of new information. With some coaxing, he admitted seeing Dawn in Clewiston the Saturday before the tractor pull but never spoke to her.

The trip to Sheila Mitchell's trailer proved a complete waste of time. The woman had no knowledge of her daughter's visit and hadn't spoken to Dawn since she left home. Staring out of his office, Parquet counted the passing cars, trying to picture Dawn Sawyer as he remembered her from school, small and thin. She might have grown a bit taller and put on some pounds, but she still couldn't have overpowered Dennis Ramsey by herself. *Would she have had an accomplice?*

His thoughts drifted back to the long, narrow, rutted-out trail and the thicket where they found the body. At the time it hadn't occurred to him, to Chief Tilley or to the Leflore County sheriff to investigate reports of missing ATVs.

Leflore County's new sheriff hadn't returned Parquet's call, so he tried again. The same female voice answered and said the sheriff had stepped out. When Parquet explained what he needed, the woman said she'd let him know. An hour later, the phone rang.

Brown, a deputy at the time of Ramsey's murder, had located a theft reported on Thursday, September 5, 2002. The vehicle turned up a few weeks later behind an abandoned farmhouse. Sheriff Hodge simply returned it to its owner, thinking some teenager had taken it for a joy ride. The farmhouse, as it turned out, sat less than a quarter mile from the dump site. Parquet doubted, after all these years, there'd still be physical evidence linking the ATV to Ramsey, but Brown offered to take him out to question its owner.

Two and a half hours later they knocked on the door of a weathered farmhouse. Brown explained that the ATV had, at the time, belonged to sixteen-year-old Michael Skinner. Skinner died in Iraq three years later, but his widowed mother still lived here. Brown rang the doorbell, and, from inside, Parquet heard someone turn off a vacuum cleaner.

The woman could've been anywhere between forty and sixty. She had a pleasant, but care-worn and sun-beaten face, and wore her graying hair pulled back in a bun. She managed a brief smile for Brown and cast a wary eye at Parquet. "Good morning, Sheriff. What brings you out this way?"

"Doris, this is Chief Parquet from over in Clewiston. I hate to bother you, but I wondered if you still had that ATV. Your son . . . Michael . . .

reported it stolen a few years back, right before they found that man's body out in the woods. There might not be any connection, but Chief Parquet would like to see it."

She studied Parquet for a moment and then shrugged. "Sure. It's out in the shed . . . I never got around to selling it."

The *shed* turned out to be a small pole barn behind the house, built by the son on a six-inch concrete slab he'd poured and leveled by himself. A neat array of tools and small parts lined the walls. In the center, under a dust-covered tarp sat the ATV, clean and free of scratches, where Michael had parked it the day before he shipped out. Clearly, it had been the love of the young man's life. Parquet considered calling in a crime scene team to go over it, but knew he'd be wasting resources.

"Ms. Skinner," he asked, "do you recall what time of day the theft occurred?"

She thought for a moment. "It must've happened on that Wednesday night. Michael and I went to church. When he got up the next morning, he found it gone. That sort of thing hardly ever happened out here. We didn't even lock our doors back then. At first Michael thought one of his friends borrowed it. A couple of weeks later someone found it behind an abandoned house near the backside of our farm."

Parquet knelt behind the machine, examining its carrying rack, just the right size for a large buck . . . or a grown man. He pictured it backing up to a truck or a hatchback, and someone of moderate strength, perhaps a woman, hauling a body onto it. She could have tied it down and wrapped it in a tarp in case anyone came by. Three or four bungee cords would've done the job. The hardest part would have been dragging it off the trail and into the woods, something a sufficiently motivated person could have managed.

He shook his head. "Mrs. Skinner, I apologize for bothering you. I appreciate your time."

"No problem," she said.

When she'd gone back inside, Brown turned to Parquet. "Whaddya think?"

Parquet gazed across the expanse of cotton fields. "I didn't come here expecting to find the killer's fingerprints or DNA. I just wanted to get a picture of how someone could've moved a body all that distance . . . and, for what it's worth," he smiled, "I think I have."

On his way back to Greenwood, Parquet strung together a theory as to how the crime played out. Someone at the Colony Inn discovered Ramsey's car on Saturday, September 7. No one remembered seeing him at the bar the night before, but there could've been a crowd. *Well, I've come all this far. I might as well ask.*

The manager, an effeminate, well-dressed man in his early thirties, introduced himself as Brian Bailey. He'd been a desk clerk in 2002 and worked the evening shift the night Ramsey disappeared.

"Do you remember if you had a big crowd?" Parquet asked.

"Pretty busy, as I recall," said Bailey. "Otherwise, I'm sure we'd have noticed the abandoned car much sooner."

"Did you have some kind of event here?"

Bailey placed his right index finger to his chin, striking a thoughtful pose. "Well, we had some sort of business meeting that day . . . And oh yes! A wedding reception . . . No, a rehearsal dinner . . . in the banquet room across from the bar."

"Would you still have a record of it?"

"Sure." Bailey retreated into his office and returned minutes later with a screen printout. "We rented it to a Mr. and Mrs. Powers, parents of the groom." Below their names he had a local phone number.

"Mind if I borrow that?" asked Parquet.

"I don't suppose so. You are, after all, an officer of the law."

* * *

John and Shelby Powers lived in a small three-bedroom brick ranch near the edge of town. They seemed more than willing to help but recalled little of any use to Parquet.

Mrs. Powers offered him a seat on her flower print couch while she went in search of pictures from the rehearsal dinner and wedding. Mr. Powers explained that their son and daughter-in-law had moved to Biloxi, where he ran a pharmacy, and she taught sixth grade. They had two sons, Jim Junior and Bobby, ages nine and six, baseball and football players. Powers pointed out the many pictures and trophies adorning the mantle and tables around the living room, while Parquet feigned interest.

When Mrs. Powers finally returned, she carried a couple of three-inch-thick photo albums. Parquet's heart sank. Already this had the look of a wasted trip. He could envision hours spent poring over pictures of family and friends, none with even the remotest ties to the murder.

About fifteen pages into the first album, he suddenly returned to a picture that had caught his eye, a middle-aged couple smiling at the camera, eyes glowing red in the reflected flash. The man wore a loud plaid coat over a lime green shirt. His companion, an overweight woman about fifty, had straight brown hair and crooked teeth.

"Oh, that's George and Ethel May," offered Mrs. Powers.

"Okay."

The couple stood with their backs to an open doorway that afforded an unobstructed view of the bar. There sat a man with his back to the camera, perhaps Dennis Ramsey, engaged in animated conversation with a tall brunette, his outstretched hand around her waist. The brunette had turned slightly, and her profile caught enough light for

Parquet to make out her features. He stared at the picture, knowing, despite its poor focus, that he'd seen that face before. He needed a closer examination, perhaps by a lab.

"Do you mind if I borrow this?" He felt almost embarrassed to ask.

Before Mrs. Powers could answer, her husband said, "Of course we don't mind."

Cutting her husband an angry glance, she asked. "You don't think George and Ethel had anything to do with that murder?"

Parquet smiled. "No ma'am. I just need a closer look at these folks at the bar. I promise I'll take good care of this and get it right back to you."

Mrs. Powers reluctantly agreed. Parquet thanked them and left before she had a chance to reconsider. He pulled to the side of the road twice on his way back to Clewiston, staring at the photo. The brunette looked to be about five-eleven and wore tinted glasses. Returning around dusk, he stopped at his office long enough to dial the home of Cissy Johnson.

"Hey, Cissy. Sorry to bother you. I'd like to come by if you don't mind. I've got a couple of questions."

"Sure. Mind if I ask about what?"

"Don't mind at all. I'll discuss it with you as soon as I get there," he said as he hung up.

He arrived to find her standing in her driveway, peroxided hair pulled back, smoking a cigarette. Her halter top and tight jeans displayed the same taught muscles he'd seen when she played power forward for the girls' basketball team.

In her senior year, Cissy led them to the state finals before a torn ACL ended her promising career. Her grades wouldn't get her into college, so she went to work at the diner, rehabilitating her knee with weightlifting.

Parquet recalled the night he drove to Memphis to see her compete in a women's bodybuilding contest. He barely recognized her when she strolled onstage in her carefully applied makeup and blonde wig, bright lights reflecting from her well-oiled body. Looking back now, he imagined her lifting a man's lifeless body from the trunk of a car long enough to get it on the rack of an ATV.

Cissy spoke in a voice devoid of emotion. "I didn't want to upset my mama. She's resting right now."

"That's okay. How's she doing?"

"She has good days and bad, mostly bad. She hasn't got much longer, I'm afraid."

Parquet gazed down the street at the remnants of an orange sunset. "Well, she sure is a fighter to have lasted all this time . . . What an inspiring story, how everybody pitched in and helped raise money for her treatments. She was in remission for, what, nine years?"

Cissy's stare turned cold. "You said you had some questions, Chief."

He pursed his lips. "Cissy, those treatments must've cost hundreds of thousands of dollars, and I'm fairly sure your mama didn't have any insurance back then. I've always wondered how your friends managed to raise that much money from a can full of coins sitting next to a cash register . . . kind of a *loaves and fishes* miracle, wouldn't you say?"

Cissy remained silent, glowering at him.

"There must have been at least *one* really big donation, don't you think? In fact," he said, "I'm betting I could subpoena the bank records of Dina Savage, a.k.a. Dawn Sawyer, and find some large transfers into that medical fund for your mama. Dawn did pretty well for herself after college, and, from what I heard she could clean out a casino."

Parquet reached into his pocket, pulled out the rehearsal dinner photo and handed it to Cissy without a word.

She glanced at it, started to hand it back, then stopped. Her face went pale. As she struggled to maintain her composure she asked, "What's this supposed to mean?"

"Somebody took that picture at the Colony Inn in Greenwood the night Dennis Ramsey disappeared. You can change your hair color and put on as much makeup as you want, Cissy, but our forensics folks can still ID that woman using facial structure analysis. I'll even bet they identify that man as Ramsey, with just a partial profile."

He paused before improvising. "The medical examiner found blood and skin tissue under Dennis' fingernails . . . somebody else's blood and skin tissue. What you want to bet it matches your DNA?"

Cissy glared at him without a word. Face flushed, she clenched her fists and shook her head violently, but her welling tears gave her away.

Parquet waited patiently for her to process her situation. He thought of arresting her on the spot but discarded the idea. He'd known Cissy all his life, and no way would she run off and leave her mother.

As he studied her, she took a deep breath and put her face in her hands, emitting a long, soft moan. Parquet couldn't imagine what had driven her to kill Ramsey. Perhaps Dawn *had* paid her. But why would she have done it with such fury? The medical examiner counted more than two dozen stab wounds. This had been a crime of passion.

In the end he knew she'd confess. *But would she dime out her best friend?*

"Cissy, we can work out the details later. Right now, before you lie to me again, you need to think carefully. We've got you dead to rights. We got nothing on Dawn. If you don't cooperate, you're going away for the rest of your life, but she'll walk, Scot free, assuming those folks in Atlanta don't put her away for murdering that artist. Drop by and see me in the morning and bring your lawyer. Call Hamilton's and tell 'em you'll be late coming in."

About twenty years late.

At nine a.m. the following morning Cissy showed up at his office. Parquet had invited the Banks County prosecutor, Bo Riles, and Leflore District Attorney Win Perkins, along with Sheriff Tyler Brown. Throughout the meeting Cissy said nothing, staring at the floor as though she might bore a hole through it and escape.

Instead, her attorney spoke on her behalf. Giving it his lawyerly best, under the circumstances, the public defender said, "Cissy ain't confessing to nothing, you understand. You and I both know you can't positively identify the folks in this picture, and nobody's gonna remember them from a hotel bar more than eleven years ago. Unless you have something stronger, we're gonna walk out that door and Cissy's going back to work . . .

"What we wanna know is if, for argument's sake, she did confess, what're you offering?"

The prosecutors retired to another room for a brief consultation. Given their tenuous evidence and the time elapsed, they agreed to second degree murder, *take it or leave it*. If forensics came back with evidence linking Cissy to the crime, she'd be looking at the death penalty.

Cissy's attorney took her into the next room and returned fifteen minutes later.

Parquet looked her in the eye. "Cissy, Sheriff Brown's gonna take you into custody pending a hearing. What can I do for your mama?"

"There's a neighbor who looks after her during the day while I'm at work. I have a cousin over in Tupelo who can come stay with her tonight."

Parquet chewed his lower lip, not sure what else to say. "Okay. Cissy, I'm real sorry about this . . . Did you bring your things with you . . . you know, toiletries and stuff?"

She gave him an ironic smile. "I can run home and get them, Donny, if you don't mind."

"Probably better you should have someone bring 'em."

Within an hour everybody in Clewiston knew of Cissy's arrest. But try as he may, Parquet *could not* get her to give up Dawn. She swore she'd acted alone out of anger when Ramsey tried to force himself on her. Dawn's contributions to her mother's medical fund were just that, a generous gift from an old friend.

A little time in a Mississippi women's prison, Parquet thought, might convince Cissy to change her story. Meanwhile, Dawn sat in a lockup over in Atlanta, not going anywhere for a while. In a day or so he'd call over there and ask permission to interview her.

* * *

Two days later, Cissy went before a Leflore County judge and pled guilty to a single count. Before a packed courtroom, she said she'd invited Ramsey to meet her at the Colony Inn, intending to compromise and embarrass him. She'd worn her disguise as part of a fantasy they'd agreed to.

While in the bar, Ramsey tried to get her into his room, but she asked him to drive her back to *her* motel instead. When they arrived, he wanted to go inside. She said no, and he tried to make her have oral sex with him in his parked car. When she refused, an argument ensued. Ramsey backhanded her across the face and, as she crumpled over, began punching her.

Under her skirt, for protection, she carried a hunting knife with a ten-inch blade. In her anger she pulled it out and stabbed him repeatedly in the abdomen, groin and chest. Realizing what she'd done, she panicked, got out and shoved Ramsey's limp body into the passenger seat. She then drove to a secluded spot, intending to dump it.

There she noticed a farmhouse with no one home. She searched for a pickup truck or tractor she could hot-wire, finding an ATV instead, and managed to wrestle Ramsey out of his car and onto the rack, strapping him down with a bungee cord.

An unpaved road on the back side of the farm led to a maze of trails through the woods, which she somehow navigated using the ATV's headlight. After disposing of the body and ditching the ATV, she cleaned up Ramsey's car, as best she could, and returned it to the Colony Inn. She drove back to Clewiston, burned her bloody clothes, and disposed of the knife.

Throughout the story, onlookers and reporters from nearby towns hung on every word. Neither the judge, the prosecutor nor her attorney interrupted her. Though none of them believed her, they couldn't challenge her story, given that she'd confessed, and her details fit the scant physical evidence.

At no time did Cissy say she'd acted in self-defense. She admitted she could have left the car and reported Ramsey for assault. The prosecutor had no evidence that she'd planned the murder in advance. He requested a ten-year sentence with eligibility for parole in two, which the judge granted.

What could Parquet do now? Cissy had pled guilty. For her to implicate Dawn, or anyone else, she'd have to admit she premeditated the murder. The prosecutor had closed a cold case. The public defender got his fee. For the time being, unable to arrest Dawn, Parquet returned to his routine.

Book Three

Chapter Twenty-Eight

Jeff Sax

Alpharetta, Georgia
Monday, August 25

As he awaited his morning staff meeting, Sax switched on his television and turned to Headline News. A red and gold banner proclaimed, "Breaking News." A heavyset woman in a long, gray jacket stood on the Fulton County Courthouse steps facing an array of microphones. The caption below her read, "Sophie Weinstein – Attorney for Dina Savage."

Leaning forward, she shouted as though addressing a protest rally. "I am here today not only to speak for Dina Savage, the *real* victim in this case, but for all my sisters around the world and throughout history who've been victimized by the bestiality of a male-dominated society. Dina Savage was raped, first by a sadistic sociopath, and again through a miscarriage of justice."

Weinstein struck a pose reminiscent of Benito Mussolini.

A reporter off camera began, "but the video at Sanstrom's trial clearly showed . . ."

"That video proves nothing," she bellowed. "It doesn't show the rape that followed."

Sax studied Weinstein, her unbuttoned jacket revealing a white blouse stretched so tight over her ample frame that the buttons seemed ready to pop. Her dark plaid skirt extended past her knees, and she'd topped off her ensemble with a flat-brimmed leather hat. A string of beads hung down her back atop a waist-length plait of steel gray hair.

"Sappho Whinescream . . ."

Sax startled, unaware Cheryl had come up behind him.

"What?"

"That's what we called her in law school. Every case she argued somehow related to the oppression of women and minorities by the *white, male, capitalist establishment*. It didn't matter if it were a building code violation or a jaywalking arrest."

"You know her?"

"Oh yeah, I know Sophie."

"I hope those aren't the arguments she plans to use in court."

"Don't worry. She's just playing to her radical feminist fans. Sophie may be a flake, but she's a *damned* good defense attorney. She can charm a jury into believing anything. If anybody can get Dina off, Sophie can. And the change of venue to Fulton County won't hurt. It gets her away from a potential lynch mob in Marietta."

"I understand Dina's pleading temporary insanity."

"What else can she do? Normally that's a risky defense, but she's fresh out of options. She's not likely to convince a jury that somebody else killed Sanstrom. Every TV camera in town captured it, for Christ's sake! She can still argue that Sanstrom raped her, no matter what his security footage showed. She can say she changed her mind, and he forced himself on her. If that's what really happened, then it's easy to see how the thought of his going free could set her off. The next thing she knew, she was standing over him on the courthouse steps with a warm gun in her hand, unaware of how she got there. To some that might seem plausible enough."

Sax smirked and shook his head. "Don't forget, I saw the whole thing. She didn't just stand over Sanstrom looking bewildered. She even tried to shoot his attorney."

"Whatever."

"Do you think this temporary insanity argument will work?" he asked.

"Who knows? It might. Sophie doesn't have to convince *all* the jurors. They don't even have to believe her. If they sympathize with her, they'll vote to acquit. Temporary insanity will give them a convenient cover."

CNN cut to a closeup of Cobb District Attorney Butch Lowry.

Cheryl perched on the corner of Sax's desk. "This must be a high profile case for the DA to get involved. He has about as delicate a job as Sophie does. His office prosecuted Sanstrom for rape. He can't come back now and try to make Sanstrom look like an innocent victim. Instead, he'll say Savage took the law into her own hands. I'm just not sure the jury will care."

"The judge brought this case to trial in a hurry. It took them a year and a half to put together the rape case."

"This is different," said Cheryl. "There's no question of what happened. Dina shot Liam on television. The only question is her state of mind. Butch Lowry has as good a case as he'll ever have, and Sophie's just as confident in her defense. She wants to try this case now, before somebody else grabs the headlines. With Sophie it's all about the exposure."

CNN replayed a brief shot of Dina's arrest.

"You know, I wouldn't mind going downtown to watch that trial," said Sax.

"Why don't you? It should prove interesting, and you could use a break."

"Would you like to come with me?"

"Sure."

"Let me ask you. Do you really think Dina tried to break into our servers?"

"You found her picture on Lance's computer under an assumed name."

"Yeah, but it doesn't make sense. Why would she do that? What could she gain for all that risk? It's like somebody wanted to frame her and derail the trial."

"I guess we'll never know."

* * *

Parquet straightened his forest green dress uniform, just back from the cleaners, in honor of the occasion, before stepping out into a hot, sticky, overcast morning. As he strolled across the Full Gospel Baptist Church's neatly mowed lawn, an errant raindrop struck the back of his neck. He paused, opened his umbrella, and gazed across the crowd gathered around a fresh mound of black earth.

A week earlier, Parquet, joined by Banks County emergency units, responded to a call from the residence of Cissy's mother, Martha Johnson. Martha's caregiver arrived that morning and found her unresponsive. Following Cissy's conviction, Martha's health had declined rapidly, and in the previous week she'd stopped eating altogether. The hospital pronounced her dead on arrival.

On returning to his office, Parquet called several long-time friends and acquaintances, including a former governor. He asked Martha's family if they could delay the funeral for a couple of days.

His efforts proved successful. There, on the front row, among the mourners, clad in her prison uniform, sat a much thinner Cissy Johnson. A paper fan covered her handcuffs, but her shackles remained clearly visible across her ankles. In the folding chair beside her sat a thickly built prison matron who'd accompanied her from Rankin County.

To Parquet it seemed Cissy had aged ten years in the past few months. Her eyes had withdrawn into the dark hollows of her face and lines had formed across her brow. As he'd feared, she had not done her time well. If only he could find a way to tie in Dawn Sawyer, perhaps he could get Cissy an early release.

The preacher gave a brief homily on the great rewards Martha enjoyed now that her long night of suffering had passed. On behalf of *the family,* he thanked everyone for coming, never mentioning Cissy.

Cissy gazed at Parquet, who stood at a respectful distance behind the friends, neighbors and relatives, most of them members of the church that sat only a dozen yards away. She smiled as tears gathered in the corners of her eyes, and he smiled back.

A clear soprano voice rang out the opening lines of the gospel classic *I'll Fly Away*, and, one by one, the mourners joined in. The sky, pregnant with clouds, suddenly erupted as black umbrellas popped open like so many mushrooms.

Walking back to his car, Parquet's thoughts returned to the reporter from Atlanta, Tom Williams, and the conversation that had reopened Dennis Ramsey's murder investigation. At the time, Williams mentioned researching the archives of the *Clewiston Gazette*, starting from the week of the tractor pull. The local Chamber of Commerce held a parade that Saturday, the same day Shorty Watkins saw Dawn downtown.

Could the Gazette still have old photos of the event, perhaps some crowd scenes? Parquet dropped by to visit Delia Crabtree. In the end, his search took less time than expected.

* * *

Colleen Gentry Williams made a promise to God the day she received her diagnosis. Determined to keep that promise and make amends for a life she now regarded as largely wasted, she placed the last white bread and bologna sandwich in its baggie and stacked it with the other fifty she'd prepared.

She leaned against the counter, closed her eyes, took a deep breath and waited for a wave of nausea to pass. She'd just completed another round of chemo, and it seemed each treatment only made her worse. She filled a cup of water in the sink and downed two pills her oncologist had prescribed. These days she wondered why she bothered. They no longer did any good.

Marie had called the night before saying she'd be down for a visit that weekend. The mere thought made Colleen feel better. Tom carried the cooler of sandwiches out to his aging Mercedes and helped Colleen into the front seat.

On any given night, the Atlanta Union Mission's five locations might serve as many as a thousand people. When Tom and Colleen arrived, she felt too weak to get out of the car, so Tom parked at the curb, leaving the window down and air conditioner running while he ran inside. As Colleen entertained herself watching passersby, she tore open an old saltine she'd found in the console, crushed it, and tossed the crumbs to a sparrow on the sidewalk.

Moments later, as Tom re-emerged, a young Black man approached the car. He wore a stained and frayed wife-beater and filthy jeans with holes in the knees. Tom sprinted the short distance to where the man stood, then pulled up short as he heard him speak.

"Miz Williams?" the man asked.

Colleen studied him, and a glow of recognition spread across her face. "Tashawn . . . Tashawn Darcy?"

"Yes ma'am, Miz Williams. I thought I recognized you."

Colleen gazed past Darcy at her husband, not three feet behind him. "Tom, this is Tashawn Darcy, a former client."

"That's right. And I want you to know I ain't forgot how you helped me out of that little jam I was in."

"Well, I hope you've stayed out of trouble since then, Tashawn," Colleen said.

"Yes ma'am. I'm trying to. And how about you? How you been?"

Colleen started to reply and then caught herself. "Well, Tashawn, I'm afraid I've been a bit under the weather." She forced a smile. "But I'll mend."

The look on Darcy's face told her he knew better. "Well, Miz Williams, you helped me out, and I'd like to help you out too, if I can. If there's anything I can do, anything at all, you let me know." With that he reached into his pocket, pulled out a pen and an old scrap of paper, wrote out his number in a neat hand, and handed it to Tom.

"This is my cell phone number. You can reach me any time."

Colleen found the young man's generosity touching. "Thank you, Tashawn."

On the way home, Colleen again felt ill. Tom cranked the air conditioning as far as he could and slowed so as not to jostle her any more than necessary.

When she'd begun to recover he asked casually, "Exactly what sort of jam did you get that young man out of?"

"Possession and distribution." Colleen winced.

They arrived home without further incident and Tom gave her a moment's rest in an old chair on the patio. He carried her inside and, with the help of a newly installed chair lift, up the stairs to their bedroom. He watched in anguish as she struggled to undress and climbed into bed. He offered help, but she refused.

* * *

As she drifted to sleep, Tom excused himself. "Get some rest, honey. I have some work to do in the yard."

Out of earshot, he pulled his phone from his pocket, along with the scrap of paper he'd taken from Darcy.

"Mr. Darcy, this is Tom Williams, Colleen's husband. I thought about what you said just now, and I believe there *is* something you can do for us."

That evening Colleen felt well enough to watch television from the living room couch. Tom found her old Harvard blanket, wrapped it around her and folded it under her feet. Returning to the kitchen, he laid out the ingredients for a salad. Colleen had recovered some of her appetite thanks to the green gunpowder and chamomile tea Tom made for her every night.

Sprinkling the loose leaves into an old-fashioned strainer, he added a generous dose of heavily manicured marijuana. Darcy had met him earlier that evening on the corner of Ponce and Argonne during Tom's nightly walk with Bogey.

It angered Tom to think he'd broken the law, endangering himself *and* Darcy, just because a few sanctimonious assholes thought it better that Colleen and others like her should suffer rather than take a medicine the government hadn't approved. Pot, they reasoned, had harmful long-term side effects. Tom leaned against the kitchen counter and closed his eyes, slowly coming to terms with the fact that Colleen had no long term.

He brought her the tea and returned to the kitchen to make the salad, hoping she hadn't noticed anything different about its smell or taste.

"Dina's trial starts next week. If I'm up to it, I'd like to go watch," she said as Tom returned with the salad.

"We'll see. It depends on how you feel."

"I'm actually feeling much better right now. It must be this tea. It has a familiar taste, but I can't quite place it. What did you say it was again?"

"Green gunpowder and chamomile."

"That's what I thought." She gave him her best enigmatic smile and turned her attention to the news.

* * *

Dina leaned across the passenger seat and opened the opposite window of her Cessna. Closing her eyes, she let the warm sunlight and fresh salt breeze caress her face. She'd had her pilot's license for several years, and on weekends she'd fly down to Savannah or to the Florida coast.

To either side, white sand beaches stretched as far as she could see, broken by rivers and deep, blue inlets. Straight ahead lay the open ocean, a bright splotch of yellow sunshine reflecting from its rolling aquamarine surface.

Panicked, she realized she hadn't filed a flight plan. She'd come all this way without bothering to check her instruments and had no idea whether the Gulf or the Atlantic lay below her. She searched for familiar landmarks.

From far below came the crash of waves and the cries of gulls. Suddenly, the plane disappeared, and she now flew on her own. Overcoming the shock, she smiled, stretching her arms and legs, luxuriating in a sensation better than any sex she'd ever had. Suddenly a cold darkness overcame her, as the sea reached for her with malevolent arms.

She awoke drenched in sweat, recognizing now the cell where she awaited trial. It all came back to her, the vague memories of her date with Liam, the rape trial, the sudden rush of anger, the vindication she felt as his head snapped back under the bullet's impact. She thought back to her Mississippi childhood and wondered how she'd come so far only to descend so fast.

Since leaving Clewiston as an eighteen-year-old, Dina had prided herself in her control of every situation. The one exception, it seemed, had been her date with Liam. How could she have let him take advantage of her?

Nearly two years had passed, and that night had diminished now to little more than a faded memory. She'd been so certain that Liam *carried* her down the stairs, tied her to a bed, ripped off her clothes and raped her. *Where in the world did that security footage come from?* It didn't make sense. Harkening back, she could almost hear Liam's voice whispering, "Let's play a game."

She closed her eyes and watched him transform into Dennis Ramsey. She again smelled the stale bourbon and felt the sharp pain between her legs. Ramsey warned her not to tell anyone. Nobody, he assured her, would believe a little white trash cunt.

She'd promised herself that, if she accomplished nothing else in life, she'd rid the world of Dennis Ramsey. She planned it so carefully. Through four years at Case Western and two at Harvard, that thought never left her mind.

She'd rent a car under an assumed name and drive to Clewiston. No one would recognize her. She'd lure Ramsey to some secluded spot. Her every fantasy bore a clear image of his face, the register of surprise as she rammed a knife into his testicles and identified herself.

When the day finally came, she lost her nerve. Parked outside the tractor dealership, she realized someone still might recognize her. She needed an alibi. How might she arrange for him to die, while far away in the presence of numerous witnesses?

Returning to her hotel room, she hacked Ramsey's email account and discovered his upcoming trip to Greenwood to visit a customer. Once he got there, even a moderately attractive woman could lure him into a compromising position and . . . But who could pull it off?

Then she remembered Cissy. Dina had called her many times and knew of the fundraiser for Martha's cancer treatments. An idea germinated, one that would eliminate Ramsey and still protect everything Dina had worked so hard to build.

That had been ten years ago. Following the discovery of Ramsey's body, no one questioned her. The lone newspaper account she found never mentioned Ramsey meeting a beautiful brunette in Greenwood.

Dina shook her head and wondered how she could have pulled off one murder, only to shoot another man in a fit of rage at a crowded courthouse, surrounded by police and television cameras. To escape conviction now she'd have to let her attorney bring up the prior rape, in front of the press. She could only hope no one made the connection between that rape and Dennis Ramsey.

Chapter Twenty-Nine

Atlanta, Georgia
Monday, September 16

As Tom and Colleen made the short walk from the Underground Atlanta parking deck to the Fulton County Courthouse, they passed a homeless man curled up asleep in a doorway. Pigeons ignored him as they pecked at the remnants of last night's restaurant traffic. At eight a.m. much of the street remained in shadow. An empty paper bag skipped down the sidewalk in the stiff breeze, the kind of bag that usually carries a tall can of malt liquor or a bottle of cheap wine. Relieved of its burden, it seemed eager to discover what lay around the next corner.

Tom turned to Colleen, thinking how cute she looked in the pale blue scarf hiding her thinning hair. Despite her illness and the lingering effects of chemotherapy, she'd insisted on seeing the trial. Never had he met anyone so courageous or so headstrong. The tea seemed to help.

As they rounded a corner, they encountered a CNN crew setting up across from the courthouse entrance. A street vendor hawked sausage and egg biscuits on the corner. A man in a powder blue suit with a slicked back pompadour held up a sign reading, "God Hates Queers" as he harangued passersby with misquoted Bible verses.

Across from him, three members of an obscure feminist group walked a silent picket line with white poster board signs reading, "Uppity Women Unite" and "Self-defense is NOT a Crime." Occasionally they'd stop long enough to hurl insults at the itinerant preacher. If he heard them he gave no indication. The scene, Tom thought, had the festive atmosphere of a medieval witch burning.

As they passed through the security scanner, Tom saw Jeff Sax ahead of them in line. He caught Sax's eye and waved. They arrived to find most of the seats in Judge Quentin Alexander's courtroom filled. A Fulton County sheriff's deputy at the door turned away late arrivals.

As Tom and Colleen took the last adjacent spots on the back bench, two men near the front gave up their seats to an elderly couple. Tom stared at them for a moment before recognizing Bjorn and Brigid Sanstrom.

When the jurors arrived, Judge Alexander explained that, while the State had filed its case in Cobb County, it had moved the trial to Atlanta in response to a motion for change of venue. "Our objective," he said, "is to assure that Ms. Savage has every opportunity to receive a fair hearing, untainted by local publicity and rumors." He admonished on-lookers against any disruption.

As oral arguments began, Tom scanned the jurors, men and women, young and old, of every ethnic background. One of them, in heavy makeup and big hair, appeared to be a transvestite.

Butch Lowry stood about five-eleven, perhaps a shade over forty, and appeared to have spent a good deal of time in the gym. Pacing back and forth in front of the jury, he promised that the State would prove Dina brought her gun to the Cobb County Courthouse for the express purpose of murdering Liam Sanstrom in the event the prosecution failed to obtain a guilty verdict.

His office, Lowry said, did everything in its power to prove Sanstrom's guilt, based on representations made by Ms. Savage. But, in the end, the misconduct of a single juror led to a mistrial.

When the prosecutor in that case, Mr. Rainey, told Ms. Savage he could not retry it given her inconsistent testimony, Savage left the courtroom, calmly strode to her car, took a pistol from her glove compartment and returned.

There, with callous disregard for the safety of innocent bystanders, she just as calmly shot Sanstrom through the head and tried to gun down his attorney. As he spoke, Lowry acted out the shooting with hand gestures to dispel any doubt the jurors might have. Ms. Savage's temporary insanity plea, Lowry asserted, constituted nothing more than her desperate attempt to escape punishment for her crime.

"Despite the months of investigation preceding Mr. Sanstrom's trial, we have no way of knowing what happened at his home on that September night two years ago. The Cobb County District Attorney's Office relied, in good faith, on Ms. Savage's representation. Mr. Sanstrom's attorney, however, proved that Ms. Savage had, at the very least, *embellished* her story.

"What we do know, with absolute conviction, ladies and gentle-men, is that no one has the right to take the law into her own hands. In the interest of justice, we ask that you examine the facts as presented, setting aside any emotions regarding the parties involved. When you do, you will see that this defendant is, and *always* will be, a threat to this community and that you must return a guilty verdict."

As Lowry returned to his seat Sophie Weinstein rose quietly, look-ing each juror in the eye as she slowly strode the length of the rail. Starting in a low, calm voice, she said, "With every ounce of my being, I hope none of you will ever suffer the pain and humiliation of rape, as Dina Savage did. It is, for those who've never experienced it, unimag-inable. Make no mistake, ladies and gentlemen." Her cadence and vol-ume grew like an oncoming train. "This was *not* a sex crime. It was a crime of violence." She shouted as she turned and glared at Lowry, "And the honorable district attorney, of all people, knows that very well."

Recomposing herself, she continued. "Mr. Lowry is not a psycholo-gist, nor is he a therapist, and he has no basis whatsoever for his statements about temporary insanity. Neither do any of his witnesses. Not one of them can evaluate Dina's state of mind that afternoon, because none of them were there. None of them experienced this egregious, and deeply personal, injustice. Contrary to Mr. Lowry's claims, Dina's victimization and the mistrial were more than enough to make anyone snap. Contrary to Mr. Lowry's claim, his prosecutor's decision not to retry Liam Sanstrom had nothing to do with doubts about his guilt. Mr. Rainey had simply reached a point where he no longer cared about Dina or prosecuting her assailant."

The judge frowned at this last remark but said nothing.

Sophie now spoke in a stage whisper every ear in the hushed courtroom could hear. "What made this experience even more traumatic for Dina, was the fact that, at age thirteen, a man raped her in her own bed while her mother slept in the next room. He *also* went unpunished. To suffer that horror again was simply more than Dina could bear."

An eerie quiet hung over the courtroom as all eyes followed the defense attorney. *She has them,* Tom thought, *an artist at work.*

"Now, as the district attorney has stated," Weinstein continued, "Dina is an avid shooter. But he failed to mention she has never used a weapon against anyone or threatened anyone before the day she saw that *monster* walk out of that courtroom a free man. Never in her life has she committed a violent crime. For Dina, marksmanship is little more than a healthy outlet for a bright and conscientious woman in a *very* stressful profession. She has a permit to carry that weapon, issued by the State of Georgia. Sadly, that small pistol happened to be in her glove compartment on the day Cobb County set her attacker free. She'd planned to go to the range after the trial adjourned."

Tom whispered into Colleen's ear, "Maybe Sophie should put the gun manufacturer on trial."

Colleen elbowed him in the ribs.

"Ladies and gentlemen," said Weinstein, "there is no one in this courtroom who would rather go back and undo that event than Dina. As it is, she has no memory of it. We will produce expert witnesses who will testify to that fact. They will also state, in their professional opinions, that Dina suffered post-traumatic stress disorder not unlike that of a wounded war veteran. You cannot hold her accountable for actions of which she is unaware. To find her anything other than *not guilty* would only pile on further injustice. I trust that, at the end of this trial, you will search your hearts and souls and make the right decision. In doing so, you will, without doubt, release Dina so she can begin rebuilding her shattered life."

Sophie returned quietly to her seat.

The state's first witness, Cobb Police Sergeant Henry Hollingsworth, testified that he'd been on the courthouse steps the day of the shooting and happened to be standing at Sanstrom's right. With the judge's permission, he left the stand and indicated on a chart his position and that of Sanstrom. Sanstrom, he said, had turned to answer a reporter's question when a look of alarm came over his face.

"I followed his gaze and saw the defendant standing not five feet away with a raised pistol." Hollingsworth paused again and pointed to a mark on the chart indicating the position where Dina stood.

"The defendant fired once, striking Mr. Sanstrom on the right side of his head, then turned the gun toward his attorney, Ms. Radford. Before she could shoot again, I blocked her shot, forcing her arm up into the air. She fired another round. Officer Kim Kelly grabbed her from behind. We pulled her to the ground and subdued her with the help of two bystanders."

Tom whispered into Colleen's ear, "Do you think Lowry will call Radford to testify?"

"I don't know. I'm not sure what she'd add."

"Sergeant Hollingsworth," asked Lowry, "did you get a good look at the defendant's face as she shot Mr. Sanstrom?"

"Yes."

"How would you describe her appearance?"

"She appeared perfectly calm, like she knew exactly what she was doing."

Weinstein objected that the police officer had no professional qualifications for evaluating behavior and emotions.

Lowry said he'd merely asked Hollingsworth to describe what he'd seen.

The judge allowed the testimony provided the officer stuck to his visual observations.

On cross-examination, Weinstein asked Hollingsworth if he had a psychology degree.

"No ma'am."

She turned to the jury with an ironic smile. "Would you consider yourself a mind reader, Sergeant Hollingsworth?"

"No ma'am. I am not."

"Then are you, in any way, capable of rendering a professional evaluation as to a person's mental state based on that person's appearance or behavior?"

"What I saw . . ."

"Answer my question, Sergeant."

"No ma'am. I don't suppose I am."

"I don't suppose so either."

Lowry started to rise, but Weinstein, with a dismissive wave, announced she had no further questions.

Lowry's next witness, a VA psychologist, specialized in post-traumatic stress disorder. He testified that he'd interviewed Dina following the shooting and did not believe she'd suffered PTSD.

Weinstein, on cross-examination, asked if he'd ever worked with rape victims. He had not. He also admitted that his interview with Savage occurred several weeks after the courthouse shooting. On redirect, the witness reiterated his conclusion.

Lowry went through an array of witnesses, including the proprietor of Sharpe's Firearms and Munitions, Burton Davies, who described Dina as a regular customer and one of his most accomplished shooters. On cross-examination Davies also called her one of his politest and most safety-conscious clients.

Tom recalled something called "Locard's Exchange Principle," the notion that criminals always leave traces of themselves at crime scenes and carry away evidence as well. He wondered if Dina had the slightest awareness of the wreckage she'd transferred in her wake, the shattered lives of Liam, his family, Ron Dalrymple, David Curry, Oleg Simonov, and countless others. If so, her expression gave no indication.

Lowry's last witness, a local news cameraman named Delaney, described in detail how he'd maneuvered for a close-up of Sanstrom answering reporters' questions before hearing someone shout, "Oh my God! She has a gun!" As he swung his camera around, he captured a tight shot, not of the gun, but of Dina's face.

The prosecutor turned on a large television monitor and pressed the *Play* button on a video recorder. "Mr. Delaney, is this the footage you took of Mr. Sanstrom's murder?"

"Yes sir."

On the screen, Liam appeared relieved but exhausted, a hint of a smile playing at the corner of his lips. Then a startled look came over him. Someone shouted in the background. The camera swung to a tight shot of Dina and froze. The audio continued . . . one shot, followed by people screaming, and then another. The image closed in tighter on

Dina's implacable face; no hint of emotion, no remorse, no hesitation . . . a portrait in serenity.

Weinstein declined cross-examination, instead requesting a thirty-minute recess. Pulling a phone from her pocket, she stepped out of the courtroom, as the district attorney and his co-counsel conferred.

When everyone returned, Lowry unexpectedly announced that the prosecution would rest. The judge pulled back his sleeve, studying his watch. "Ms. Weinstein, would you like to call your first witness?"

"It's rather late, Your Honor, and I think everyone would prefer to go home and get a good night's sleep, so we can return refreshed in the morning."

"Okay, then. Court is recessed for the day. I expect all parties here tomorrow at eight-thirty sharp." He banged his gavel and retired to chambers.

As they walked out, Tom commented to Colleen about the speed with which the State had presented its case.

Colleen replied, "He only needed to prove that Dina shot Liam intentionally and knew what she was doing. He proved the first point. The second? Who knows? I don't think anybody on that jury believes Dina's insanity claim. Sophie's task tomorrow is to convince them that Dina's the real victim, and that no one gains, at this point, by sending her to prison. *Temporary insanity* will simply provide an excuse for an acquittal."

* * *

Parquet examined the digitally enhanced copy of the eleven-year-old photo before sliding it to Cissy. "I got this from the *Clewiston Gazette*. One of their guys took it the Saturday before Dennis Ramsey disappeared. You want to tell me about it?"

The glossy black-and-white showed the last ranks of a high school band marching down Main Street followed by what appeared to be the front end of a float. The ten-foot gap revealed two women standing on the opposite sidewalk in front of Hamilton's.

Cissy's face registered no recognition.

"Cissy, that's you standing there in your waitress uniform holding a white envelope. You want to tell me what's in it?"

No response.

"The woman on the left, in the sun hat and dark glasses, is Dawn, Cissy. I wouldn't have recognized her myself, nor would anyone else in Clewiston . . . besides Shorty."

Ignoring her stony silence, Parquet continued. "You'd be surprised what the crime lab folks can do these days. Dawn can change her name, clear up her complexion, dye her hair, whatever she wants, but she can't change the shape of her head or her jawline."

Leaning toward her, he said softly, "Dawn is going to stand trial for paying you to kill Dennis. It's just a matter of time, Cissy, whether you help us out or not. Your assistance, however, could help shorten your sentence, maybe get you into another facility. I know you want to get out of here as fast as you can."

Cissy fidgeted as he spoke, studying her hands as though they belonged to someone else.

Parquet sat patiently for what seemed an eternity, then let out a long sigh as he retrieved the photo. "Cissy, when the court convicts Dawn, she'll probably wind up right here in the CMCF." He paused to let the ramifications sink in. "No matter how many times I tell her you didn't rat her out, I can't promise she'll believe me. She'll think whatever she damned well chooses, and you and I both know this is not the Little Dawn we grew up with. This woman carries grudges, and she gets revenge, no matter how long it takes. She's already murdered two people. She won't think twice about killing another."

He paused again, but Cissy gave no sign she understood. He shook his head, rose from his chair, and donned his jacket. "When you change your mind, let me know. The day you leave here, Cissy . . . I'll come back to get you."

Halfway home, his phone chirped, the warden calling. Cissy wanted to talk.

Chapter Thirty

Sophie Weinstein

Atlanta, Georgia
Tuesday, September 17

Sophie began her defense with a series of character witnesses, including the senior partner of Moore and Frye. Each testified to Dina's integrity, reliability and compassion. Tom glanced at Colleen in time to catch the smirk on her face.

On cross-examination, Lowry asked each witness the same questions. "During the days leading up to her shooting of Liam Sanstrom, did you witness any indication the defendant had lost her ability to reason, to distinguish right from wrong? Did you notice any changes in her behavior?"

In each case the witness answered, "No."

Sophie's next witness, the gynecologist who examined Dina the day after the alleged rape, gave graphic descriptions of the resulting vaginal damage. Lowry, not anxious to impeach his witness from the previous trial or create further sympathy for the defendant, declined cross-examination.

For her final witness, Sophie called Elizabeth Strong, the psychiatrist who testified against Liam. Sophie began by establishing the woman's credentials, much as Horace Rainey had done. Strong described her numerous interviews with Dina over the days and weeks following the rape and subsequent interviews following her shooting of Liam. This time she repeatedly used the term "post-traumatic stress disorder."

Sophie asked, "In your experience, Dr. Strong, is it uncommon for PTSD victims to show little or no outward emotion?"

"I'd say it's quite common. Under such circumstances the victim is usually suffering a sense of detachment, what we refer to as dissociative fugue."

Tom noticed that both attorney and witness used the word *victim* in referring to Dina.

Sophie continued. "Doctor, you've seen the close-up video of Dina at the time of the courthouse shooting. How would you characterize her apparent detachment?"

"I'd say Ms. Savage's demeanor indicates a complete incomprehension of what she's doing."

On cross-examination Lowry asked Strong if she'd ever worked with war veterans suffering from PTSD.

"No. I have not."

"Then on what basis can you compare a woman with no combat experience to someone who has seen *up close* the horrific, violent deaths of close friends and innocent noncombatants?"

"Over the years I've conducted extensive study of rape victims and compared my results to the literature on combat-related trauma."

"The literature . . ." Lowry gave the jurors a skeptical look. "Your Honor, I have no more questions for this witness."

Following a brief discussion with Dina, Sophie announced, with dramatic flourish, that the defense would rest. After lunch, both sides presented their closing arguments in what had been an unexpectedly short trial. Lowry, once again, reminded the jury of the cold-blooded way Dina gunned down an innocent man, her reckless disregard for the lives of others and her tacit admission of guilt.

Sophie, in reply, played on their sympathy for the monumental injustice of a brutal rapist walking out of a courtroom a free man. She pointed out, again, that no jury had acquitted Sanstrom, his mistrial having nothing to do with the merits of his prosecution.

Tom and Colleen rose and exited, Colleen having, once again, succumbed to nausea and fatigue. As they departed, a Cobb policeman entered, followed by another officer in a dark green uniform.

* * *

Returning to her table, Sophie glanced at the man. Heavy-set, he wore a buzz cut so tight she could see the pink of his scalp. Looking uncomfortable and out of place, he sat directly behind the prosecution table. The Cobb officer leaned forward, whispering to Lowry. The officer in green stared intently at the back of Dina's head.

Sophie turned to Dina, who faced the officer and froze, her expression morphing from surprise to distress. Fidgeting with the yellow note pad in front of her, she pretended to write. Turning back to him, Sophie could now read the patch on his shoulder, *Clewiston, Mississippi - Chief of Police.*

The jurors returned in less than an hour. Dina remained rooted to her chair, never looking in the officer's direction. Puzzled by her behavior, Sophie shifted her focus in anticipation of the verdict.

"Ladies and gentlemen of the jury, have you reached a decision?" asked the judge.

The tall, masculine-looking woman with the prominent Adam's apple replied, "We have, Your Honor." Turning to Dina, she smiled. "We find the defendant, Dina Vaughn Savage, not guilty by reason of temporary insanity."

The ensuing mayhem drowned the judge's reply. Sophie screamed in joy, nearly smothering her stunned client in the depths of a bear-like hug.

* * *

Parquet made his way to the defense table, assisted by the Cobb officer and a Fulton sheriff's deputy. With some difficulty, he squirmed through reporters mobbing the newly acquitted Savage. In his extended hand he proffered, not to Dina but to her attorney, an arrest warrant bearing the seal of the State of Mississippi.

"Dawn Sawyer," he said in his slow drawl, "you are under arrest as an accomplice to the murder of Dennis Ramsey."

Weinstein's expression went from joy, to incredulity, to rage.

"How dare you?" she screamed. "Where did this man come from?" The question seemed addressed not to Parquet, but to onlooking reporters.

The Fulton deputy managed to insert himself between Weinstein and her client as Parquet Mirandized Dina and the Cobb policeman handcuffed her. As the drama unfolded, cameras clicked and hummed like swarms of locusts.

Shocked and speechless, Dina offered no resistance. She seemed incapable of comprehending what had happened. Assisted by a female officer, Parquet ushered her through a rear door to his waiting police car.

* * *

Sax and Cheryl stood on the courthouse steps in the crush of reporters and onlookers as Sophie emerged, minus her client, and addressed the crowd. Cameras flashed and microphones jockeyed for position. Sophie assumed her signature stance, right fist planted firmly on her hip as she gesticulated with her left, her face a mask of righteous indignation.

"Once again, the forces of male oppression have conspired to prevent the administration of justice. Knowing that a jury of Dina's peers would find her not guilty, they have again arrested her on specious charges and whisked her away to rural Mississippi, where they believe they'll find a more gullible and insensitive court. I can assure you that Dina's fight goes on. *We will not abandon her.*"

"Do you think she'll go to Mississippi to represent Dina?" Sax asked Cheryl above the din.

"Not in a million years. Sophie's already booked her next client, some celebrity no doubt. She's off to Los Angeles or New York, where she'll continue to build her cachet as a defender of the female underclass. The last thing she'll do is travel to some God-forsaken Mississippi hamlet to convince the unwashed masses that her client shouldn't go to jail for murder. She'd much rather perform on a large media stage like Atlanta. The next time you see Sophie she'll be on CNN, MSNBC or Fox News."

* * *

Neither Parquet nor Dina spoke a word on the trip to Clewiston. He'd had little difficulty convincing Banks County Criminal Court Judge Potter Wilkins to issue an arrest warrant, despite the eighty-one-year old jurist's inability to read the paperwork.

Nor did he doubt he'd get a conviction. The photo of Dina, standing beside Cissy as the parade passed, and Cissy's signed statement were all the prosecutor and jury needed. The envelope Dina handed Cissy contained a cashier's check for $75,000, obtained from a bank in Boston using a fake ID and made out to the medical fund for Cissy's mother.

Chapter Thirty-One

Atlanta, GA
Friday, November 8

Colleen's sallow skin hung on her frame now like a faded house dress. A few wisps of white were all that remained of her once luxuriant blonde curls. For eight long months Tom had watched helplessly as she wasted away, alternating between anger and denial, at last settling into a profound sense of resignation.

Afternoon sunlight cast dancing shadows across the bedroom ceiling and its ornate cornice work. Tom followed their movement, imagining vague images in the play of dark and light, like sepia-toned photographs stuffed into an old album; faces of parents, grandparents and friends, now gone. Mostly he saw pictures of happier times with Kathy and Marie, children again, perhaps seven and five years old.

From somewhere down the street came the sounds of a leaf blower and the hammering of a new roof. Out in the yard Bogie barked, no doubt chasing squirrels. Tom and Colleen had purchased this home in 1975 during the great revival of Midtown and surrounding neighborhoods.

He'd done most of the renovation himself, contracting out the roofing, plumbing, heating and wiring. What he didn't know he soon learned. Over the years they'd turned the place into a showcase, on two occasions opening it to the Midtown Tour of Homes. As Colleen closed her eyes, he imagined her taking her own photograph, one she'd carry with her and treasure for eternity.

Beside the bed hung an IV bottle connected by a long tube to a needle into her arm. With little effort, she could press a button and send another rush of morphine into her system, something Tom knew she resisted whenever possible, determined not to waste a minute, separated from her family by a drug-induced fog.

Colleen found words difficult now, speaking slowly, if at all. Kathy sat on the other side of her, caressing her hand and speaking in low tones. From time to time, she'd moisten Colleen's lips with a cold, wet washcloth.

Marie would arrive soon from her home outside D.C. No one had to say it. Tom could see it in Colleen's eyes. They were gathering to say goodbye.

He gazed at his older daughter in wonder as the forty-two-year-old physician brought a plastic cup of water to her mother's lips. Tall and thin, her long black hair bore streaks of gray. She'd been Tom's rock throughout the ordeal. Together they took turns retelling Colleen stories of their past.

Tom's thoughts returned to a sultry night more than forty years ago now, when he'd taken a long stroll to the end of a dock overlooking Tampa's Hillsborough Bay, drawn by the sight of a beautiful young blonde standing alone, drink in hand, staring out at the lights across the water.

Later today, on the advice of Colleen's doctors, he'd arranged for her to move to a hospice. Her bags, already packed, waited by the door. Tom had chosen photos to go beside her bed when she got there and had purchased dozens of flower arrangements.

From downstairs Marie's voice rang out. Tom met her at the bottom of the stairs, embracing her for a long time. Neither of them said a word as they climbed the stairs.

An hour later, he heard a soft knock at the front door. Father John O'Malley from the Shrine of the Immaculate Conception joined them at Colleen's bedside. At the sight of the elderly priest's kind and beneficent face, a tear came to Colleen's eyes. She and Tom had been at the bedsides of both her parents for the Anointing of the Sick, still frequently referred to as "Last Rites." At the end, Colleen mustered enough strength to mouth with her family a final *Amen*.

As Tom walked Father O'Malley back to the front door, the priest turned and handed him a business card. "Sometime soon," he said, "I want you to give me a call. We can meet somewhere for coffee, perhaps the Starbucks over on Monroe." One corner of his lip turned up in a smile. "I promise you won't need to confess anything . . . unless you choose to."

Returning to her bedside, Tom held Colleen's hand. "I love you so much," he rasped. "I know I haven't always been the best husband. You deserved so much better."

She gave him the best smile she could manage and, summoning her remaining strength, said in a hoarse whisper, "I know, baby. I reconciled myself to that a long time ago."

When the private ambulance arrived, Kathy helped the attendants transfer her mother to the gurney. Tom slept the next three nights, as best he could, in a chair beside Colleen's bed at the hospice. He refused to leave her side despite the pleas of nurses and his daughters. On Saturday evening Kathy and Marie joined the vigil. A nurse awakened them at sunrise to say Colleen had gone.

* * *

Parquet had promised Cissy that when the day came for her to leave prison, he'd be there to take her home. He kept that promise.

On a cold, sunlit November afternoon he sat alone in his patrol car outside the women's prison waiting for the guards to bring her out. To his left sat a long, black hearse.

He'd received a call that morning from the warden. Cissy's cell-mate awoke in the wee hours to find that Cissy had hanged herself from the top bunk. In the span of three short months, Cissy had lost her freedom and the only two people in the world she truly loved. Trying to imagine what her future must have looked like, Parquet leaned against his steering wheel and wept. As the casket emerged, he backed out, took up a position in front of the hearse, and hit his light bar for the long drive home.

Chapter Thirty-Two

Atlanta, GA
Monday, November 11

Tom woke from a deep sleep and a dream he'd already forgotten. Extending his right arm across the bed, he felt the empty space before remembering he now lived alone. Taking a deep breath, he stared at the ceiling.

Then, as he'd done most mornings since his sophomore year in high school, he rolled out of bed, stretched his legs and donned his shorts, t-shirt and running shoes. These days it took him longer to loosen the stiff and sore spots, especially on cold mornings. In the bathroom he splashed water on his face and stared at himself in the mirror, wondering why he still bothered.

Donning sweatpants and a hoodie against the November chill, he trotted down to the kitchen where a wide-awake Bogie greeted him. He fed the dog, placed a leash around his neck and walked out to the front porch.

Bogie sniffed at the breeze, then, heedless of the leash's limited reach, lunged after the neighbors' cat. Tom smiled at the thought that the guys had named it Hercules after the old Elton John song. He gave the retractable leash a light jerk, bringing Bogie to his side as they set out at a light pace. For the first time in months, he made the five-mile course without a stop.

Kathy had returned to her oncology practice and Marie to her family. Likewise, Tom needed to get back to work. At seventy-one he still couldn't reconcile himself to the idea of retirement. A week ago, he'd received an invitation to a trade show for conspiracy buffs, scheduled for the spring, just the kind of offbeat story he might enjoy. *It'll do me good to get out of town for a few days. But what do I do in the meantime?*

It came to him in a flash. He Googled the Central Mississippi Correctional Facility and jotted down its phone number.

* * *

Four hundred miles away a Greyhound bus made an unscheduled stop on Highway 468 outside a prison gate. A single passenger stepped down. At six-foot-four he had to duck and bend his aching knees to keep from bumping his head. He turned to thank the driver, who nodded and drove away.

Shorty Watkins shielded his eyes against the harsh sunlight of the cold, clear morning and gathered in his tattered second-hand coat. Gazing down the long rows of trees, their branches clicking and clattering in the arctic breeze, he smiled, knowing exactly how they felt. He'd ridden that stinking bus for more than sixteen hours, coming all this way to visit an old friend, and soon he'd catch another one back to Clewiston.

At her sentencing, Shorty sat directly behind the young woman he'd known all her life as "Little Dawn," reaching out and caressing her shoulders as if she were his own daughter, come home after all these years. He'd prayed to God every night to spare her life. In the end He answered those prayers. Now, on tired and aching feet, Shorty began the long walk to the visitation center.

In the six months following the shooting of Liam Sanstrom, Dina had been out of work, spending all her savings in legal fees to Sophie Weinstein. Sophie left for greener pastures, a wrongful discharge suit against a toney Manhattan ad agency. Without her, Dina found herself with neither a competent attorney nor the money to hire one.

A Clewiston real estate lawyer with no trial experience took her case pro bono. Seeing the state's evidence stacked against her and faced with the inevitability of conviction, she accepted a plea bargain, life with eligibility for parole in ten years.

Chapter Thirty-Three

Atlanta, Georgia
Saturday, November 16

Heather Lindsey greeted late arrivals, dazzling in her white sequined halter top and matching slacks. In honor of the occasion, she'd streaked her short-cropped hair in highlights of red and gold.

In the main hall, decked in a matching outfit, Bonnie adjusted the sound system and gave last minute instructions to her caterers. In the main room flecks of light danced across the ceiling and walls.

Guests stopped near the entrance to admire a collection of Heather's drawings, in charcoal and ink, prominent among them a wash portrait of Bonnie. When the last had arrived, Heather joined Bonnie beside a champagne fountain. Bonnie tapped a wine glass with a silver spoon.

"First, I want to thank you all for coming. It's been far too long since we've had you here. We invited you tonight to help us celebrate our special event." Bonnie placed her right arm around Heather's narrow waist. "This afternoon, Heather and I were married in a ceremony at the Metropolitan Church."

Heather blushed and extended her left hand, revealing a diamond that rivaled the disco ball overhead. Onlookers erupted in thunderous applause, hugging and kissing the two women.

As the eruption subsided, Bonnie again signaled for everyone's attention. "We have another announcement." In a corner of the room, seemingly unnoticed, stood a large object under a white shroud. More cheers arose as Bonnie unveiled a new sandblasted sign in white letters on a silver background reading, "The Art Agency of Baron-Lindsey."

Someone made the mistake of opening an office door Bonnie thought she had locked. Out bounded a three-month-old Irish wolfhound puppy. The guests squealed as he jumped up and licked their faces. Excited by all the attention, he stopped, spread his hind legs, and wet all over the floor.

"Liam!" cried Bonnie, as Heather ran to gather a roll of paper towels. The guests dissolved in laughter.

* * *

Tom had politely declined his invitation. Bonnie assured him she understood and that her thoughts were with him in his time of loss.

Settling in on the couch with a spinach salad topped by black beans, roast chicken strips, black currants and balsamic vinaigrette, he poured a glass of chardonnay. Colleen's Harvard blanket still lay folded at the far end.

Reaching for the remote, he channel-surfed until he came upon a PBS presentation of the works of Jean Sibelius by the London Symphony Orchestra. As the camera panned slowly across the string section, he glimpsed a familiar face.

Brigid Sanstrom sat, eyes closed, drawing her bow over the strings of her cello in the mournful chords of the composer's best-known work, *Finlandia*. Tom felt a deep chill despite the fire crackling in the hearth.

* * *

On the following Monday, he finally succumbed to his daughters' pleas and kept his appointment with a therapist. Stopping outside the office, he hesitated, surrounded by absolute quiet, as though he were the only person in the building.

A discrete copper plaque beside the frosted glass door read "Brandon Markham, PhD – Consulting Psychologist." Tom took a deep breath, tried the knob and found it locked. He noticed a small white button, which he pressed. From somewhere inside came the low tone of chimes.

Moments later a middle-aged man, trim and athletic looking, introduced himself as Markham. In his navy blue polo shirt, white sail cloth slacks and dock siders, he resembled a charter captain more than a psychologist.

"Come on back and make yourself comfortable," he said. "Can I get you a soda or a glass of water?"

"No thanks."

Rather than sitting at his desk, Markham settled into a heavily padded armchair and motioned Tom to take the other. Markham pulled out a small wire bound notebook like the ones Tom used as a reporter.

"So, what brings you in today?"

"Well," he shrugged, "I promised my daughter I'd come see you. Her name's Kathleen O'Meara. She said she knew you from her work and recommended you highly."

"Oh yeah, Kathy," he said. "She and I go way back. I've counseled several of her patients and their families."

Markham studied Tom for a few moments, a look of professional concern creasing his brow. "So, how do you feel about coming here? Do you think this is something you might have done on your own, or are you just doing it because Kathy wanted you to?"

"Well, I suppose I could use somebody to talk to," said Tom. "You see, my wife passed a week ago. Now I really don't know what to do with myself."

Markham nodded. "I'm sorry for your loss."

"Thanks. The truth is I've probably needed to talk with a professional for a long time. I've never done anything like this, and . . . I really don't know where to start."

"I understand." Markham made a couple of notes as he spoke. "What, besides grief over the loss of your wife and being at loose ends, would you like to discuss?"

Tom took a deep breath and studied the tassels on his loafers. "I'm not even sure. My wife tells . . . used to tell me I had anger issues, whatever that means."

"Do you think you have anger issues?"

"Well . . . I get pissed off sometimes, not as often as I used to."

"What changed for you, that you no longer feel so angry?"

"Well . . . Colleen helped with that."

"How long were you married?"

"Forty-five years."

"Wow! That's a long time . . . So, when you get angry, how does it show up for you?"

"What do you mean?"

"Do you feel like attacking someone, destroying something, hurting yourself?"

Tom began to feel that he'd wasted his time and money. "Something like that."

"When was the last time you had a fight?"

"It's been years."

"Do you see all the stress you've been through, with the loss of your wife and all, possibly reviving your anger?"

Tom shook his head. "I don't know. When I was younger, I got in fights all the time. Colleen had a calming influence on me. If I started to overreact, she always knew what to say."

"What's your earliest memory of getting truly violent?"

"I lost my parents in a car wreck when I was eleven. It wasn't until years later that I discovered someone had murdered them. My dad's parents raised me. Right after I turned sixteen my grandfather died suddenly, and a few months later I lost two close friends on the same day, both murdered."

Tom paused and studied his folded hands before continuing. "One of those two people was a thirty-two-year-old, married woman with whom I had what people today would call um . . . an inappropriate relationship." He made air quotes with his fingers and gave the doctor a rueful smile. "The other was a young Black man falsely accused of her murder."

Markham continued making notes.

"There were other traumatic events. I had a couple of severe concussions, and I suffered a leg wound in Vietnam."

Markham gaped at him. "And this is the first time you've sought professional counseling?"

"Yeah . . ." Tom let out deep sigh. "I come from a small rural community. My family was strict Southern Baptist. We didn't visit shrinks."

"So, you see this, perhaps, as a sign of weakness?" he asked.

"I guess so."

"That's not uncommon. You'd be surprised at the people who've sat in that chair, police officers, firefighters, EMTs, and more combat veterans than you can imagine. Most come here only when forced to. They usually come back, not necessarily for treatment, but to have someone they can talk to."

Tom stared at his hands and nodded. "Yeah."

"If you don't mind my asking, given all you've been through, how is it you've managed to cope for . . ." he consulted his notes. ". . . sixty years or more?"

Tom fought back the tears. "I spent forty-five years married to the most beautiful and loving woman in the world. We talked about every-thing."

"What happened when you found out who murdered your parents?"

Tom closed his eyes, massaging them with his fingertips. "I killed all three of them."

Markham again gave no visible reaction. "Did that give you satis-faction, knowing they'd paid for their crimes?"

"Well . . . yes."

"What do you think that says about you as a person?"

"I'm not sure."

"Sounds like you've been asking yourself that question for the past . . ."

"Forty-five years."

"Forty-five years . . . That's a long time, don't you think?"

"I suppose so."

"Maybe you're thinking about it too hard. I tell you what, why don't we talk about something else for a while, and then, when we come back to this, perhaps it'll become clearer."

For the next thirty minutes they spoke of everything from Tom's family and religious convictions to the Falcons' prospects of making the playoffs, something Tom cared nothing about.

When they'd finished, Tom felt relieved, but no closer to answering his nagging questions. Whether relieved of his emotional burdens or simply relieved of two hundred and fifty dollars, he couldn't tell.

"Before you leave," said Markham, "I have a suggestion for you."

"What's that?"

"You're a writer, correct?"

"Yes."

"Sometime tonight, when you have a moment, I want you to sit down and put into writing the story you related to me. Make it as

298

detailed, objective, and unemotional as you can. Nobody else has to read it. When you finish I want you to reread it as if it were the opening chapter of a novel you're writing. Then ask yourself what comes next. If you get stuck," he smiled, "you can always come back here for ideas."

Tom nodded. It sounded like a silly idea, but it couldn't hurt.

Driving home, he noticed a young man, perhaps in his thirties, gesticulating wildly as he spoke with someone on his cell phone, apparently unaware the other person couldn't see his gestures. The man seemed angry.

Tom studied the drivers around him, all intent on their destinations, oblivious to the bright sunshine and the unseasonably mild weather. He wondered what quiet desperations they carried, what unexpressed rage lay pent up inside them, waiting for a weak moment when their resolve vanished, giving way to God knows what tragic events.

This brought him back to Dina and the mess she'd made of her life and those of others. He tried to picture her now, sitting in a cell. What would it take, he thought, for him to snap, as she had done? Were they really that different, or had he been more fortunate, thanks to Colleen?

Further down the street he passed a small karate studio offering special pricing and financing for new members, perhaps the only psychotherapy he needed. Another idea came to him as he pulled into his driveway. He parked, went straight to his office, and looked up the number for the Central Mississippi Correctional Facility.

* * *

Jeff Sax leaned back in the salon of his newly purchased sixty-five-foot Sea Ray L-Class as the Dewees Island Ferry passed nearby, casting waves that gently rocked the boat in its moorings. Following the sale of his company to Simonton Duval, Sax acquired the yacht at auction, along with a home backing up to Morgan Creek on South Carolina's Isle of Palms, a steal at $3.5 million.

In celebration of the clear, unseasonably mild weather, he wore a light windbreaker and sunglasses against the glare from the surrounding water. Folding his copy of the *Wall Street Journal*, he set it on the captain's chair.

From across the creek came the sounds of music and laughter from a local bar and grill. A flotilla of brown pelicans glided past, while on the dock a pair of sparrows pecked at crumbs left by a vacationer. Sax took a deep breath, amazed at how far he'd come in the past year.

Down the walkway echoed a high-pitched squeal and the sound of running feet. Sax looked up as his daughter, Misty, jumped aboard and threw her arms around his neck.

"Daddy," she screamed, "I love it." She gave him a quick kiss on the cheek and went below to explore.

At the top of the ladder stood Barbara, wearing a white, terry cloth wrap over an aqua and teal bathing suit, complimented by wraparound sunglasses and a broad-brimmed straw hat. Straight black hair, with touches of silver, hung past her narrow shoulders. She carried a picnic basket and a cloth bag filled with beach towels and suntan lotion.

Sax smiled.

She smiled back.

How long had it been, he wondered, since he'd noticed her incredible beauty?

"Well," she said, "I guess this was worth the six-hour drive from Atlanta after all. Are you really serious about moving here?"

Tears came to his eyes and his voice caught. "Can you think of a better place for starting over?"

She tossed her straw hat onto the floor and leaned across to kiss him. She pulled him to his feet and led him into one of the staterooms where they closed the door.

From the forward deck Misty called out, "Okay, you guys, keep it PG down there. Remember you have a minor on board."

The wind picked up, and the boat again began to rock. A neighbor took a break from cutting his grass to admire the new arrival. The freshly painted name on its starboard bow read "*DataScape II.*"

Epilogue

On entering the brightly lit visiting room, Tom underwent a cursory search by a guard with arms as big as his thighs. He showed the man his palm recorder, notebook and pen. Taking a seat on the visitor side of the glass divider, he came face-to-face with a woman he didn't recognize. Thinking he'd made a mistake, he turned to the guard.

"Hey, Mr. Williams," the woman said.

The voice had more of a Southern drawl than Tom remembered. Gone were the makeup and at least ten pounds. Her hair, hanging limp and cut just below her ears, accented the contours of her cheeks and eyes.

"Hey, Dina."

"You can call me Dawn." The corner of her mouth twitched in what might have been a brief smile. "Dina was somebody I made up a long time ago to get away from who I really was."

He nodded. "Call me 'Tom.' You don't mind if I record this, do you?"

She gave a light shrug. "What do I have to lose?"

"How are you holding up?"

"I reckon I'll survive . . ." She studied her clasped hands. "It's a lot better than when I first got here."

"Are they treating you okay?"

"Yeah . . . Most of the girls are much nicer than I expected. There are a few I have to stay away from."

"Tell me what it's been like."

She pursed her lips. "That first night I couldn't sleep. I sat up and cried all night, which pissed off my cellmate, but then she climbed up, sat beside me and held me close. I don't know what I'd have done without her."

"What's her name?"

"Jacanda."

Dawn's eyes bore in on Tom's. She gave him a disarming smile. "You know, you haven't asked what most reporters want to know."

"What's that?"

"Did Liam actually rape me, or did I make it all up?"

Tom shrugged. "Okay," he said, "Shoot." The word left his mouth before he could reconsider.

She smirked. "The truth is, I don't remember. I was in a drugged-out fog, which I guess means he raped me. The main thing is it really wasn't about Liam. I came to realize much later that it was all about Dennis Ramsey. His murder never put to rest the fact that he raped me and got away with it."

Tom considered this for a moment. It made sense. "What would you say has been your biggest surprise since you got here?" He had no idea where this question came from, but he liked it.

"I guess . . . the things I've found out about myself."

"Like what?"

"Well, about a week after I got here a woman asked me to join a Bible study group she'd started. I laughed at first, but then I figured, 'What the hell?' It wasn't like I had other plans."

"Has the Bible study helped?"

"I guess. The idea that I'm not alone, that there's somebody up there who can help me, gives me strength. It also helps me better understand how I got here in the first place.

"I've learned to take responsibility for my choices. When I was a child, other people controlled and abused me. It made me mad as hell. I told myself that, if I ever escaped Clewiston, *I'd* take control of my life, and things would get better. You can see how that worked out." She shook her head. "To think what I could have done with all that talent. Instead, I used it to get rich and take revenge on people who'd done me wrong. I never even thought about all the people *I'd* wronged."

She examined the faded tattoo on her shoulder and chuckled. "When I was little, I believed if I tried hard enough, I could fly. I'd just flap my wings and soar out of that town to someplace far away. The problem was, I couldn't fly far enough to get away from my past. It kept clawing me back. I thought all I had to do was get rid of the people who'd harmed me, and my past would go away."

She gave him a look of resignation. "I guess that's how I wound up here. Now, I've decided to put God in control. I don't see how He could screw up any worse than I did. All I ask Him to do is get me through one more day. Get me through today, Lord. I'll pray about tomorrow when it comes."

"Have you thought about what you'll do when you get out?"

"That's a long time off. If I start thinking about that now, I'll go crazy."

Tom couldn't believe the transformation she'd undergone. He'd expected to interview Dina Savage. But now he saw someone else, the scared, hurt little girl in the photo he'd borrowed from Sheila Mitchell.

"Do you think you'll ever forgive your mom?" he asked.

Her face hardened. "I'll have to work on that."

She looked down again. "You know, I think about Cissy a lot these days. Of all the people I've hurt, she's the one I blame myself for the most. As far as I know, she loved only two people in this whole world, her mama and me . . . And I exploited that love to get rid of Dennis

Ramsey. I didn't even have the guts to kill him myself. I had a new life and a career to protect. It didn't matter to me if Cissy took the fall. And now she's dead. I'll have to live with that for the rest of my life."

Tom waited to see if she had anything else. When she didn't, he continued. "So, tell me, what do you do to pass the time?"

Her face brightened for the first time since she'd entered the room. "You won't believe this. I've volunteered as a GED instructor. A lot of the women here never graduated from high school. Some can't even read and write. I'm hoping the prison might let me start teaching computer classes. That way maybe I could put what I've learned to good use." She laughed at the thought, "But with my history, I'm not sure they'll let me near another keyboard."

"But one day you *will* walk out of here, Dawn. And when you do, if I'm still around, I hope you'll give me a call." He smiled and handed her a worn business card.

She returned his smile. The visitation had ended. "I just might do that," she said, as she stood to go.

Perhaps, Tom thought, Dawn had begun writing the remaining chapters of *her* life, just as he had. Outside the prison, he fished out his phone and dialed Father O'Malley.

The End

About the Author

A writer, lecturer and consultant, Ray Dan Parker lives in suburban Atlanta with his wife of more than forty years. When not writing, he spends his time working outdoors, teaching and serving in his community.

As a student at the University of Georgia, Mr. Parker studied literature and history and wrote for several campus publications. It was there he developed his love of writing.

Mr. Parker's first novel, *Unfinished Business*, is the story of Tom Williams, a young newspaper writer who returns to his hometown in 1968 to investigate the deaths of his parents and the lynching of a friend for a murder he didn't commit.

Coming Soon!

RAY DAN PARKER'S

PRONOUNCED PONCE:
THE MIDTOWN MURDERS
A Tom Williams Saga
Book Three

Ray Dan Parker's third novel takes us on a high-speed chase through some of Atlanta's most colorful neighborhoods.

Suburban homemaker Allison Embry believes she has gotten away with killing her young boyfriend... until she gets a call from his drug supplier with a proposition that threatens to destroy her family and the comfortable life she has built.

Atlanta police lieutenant Paxton Davis, nearing retirement, must find the Midtown Murderer before he strikes again. For Davis, this case is all too reminiscent of the 1979-1980 child murders that marked the beginning of his career.

Widowed newspaper writer Tom Williams plans to pursue his lifelong dream, to travel the US and chronicle his experiences. Then Tom receives word that an unknown assailant has killed a third lawyer nearby...

For Parker, storytelling is all about the characters. Here we meet an assortment of eccentric people, from the affluent to the destitute, the good, the bad, the unforgettable.

For more information
visit: www.SpeakingVolumes.us

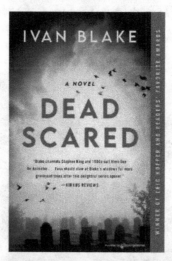

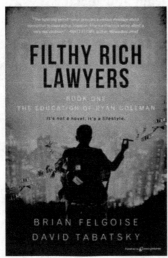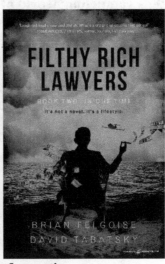

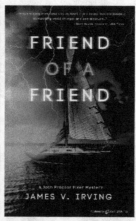
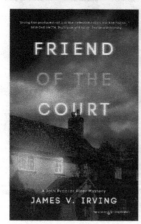

Printed in the USA
CPSIA information can be obtained
at www.ICGtesting.com
LVHW041450311023
762636LV00001B/118